Silver Threads of Hope

SILVER THREADS OF
HOPE

Short Stories
In Aid of Console

Editor Sinéad Gleeson

NEW ISLAND

Copyright *Samuel, Oh Samuel* © Declan Burke 2012
Copyright *The Fir Tree* © John Butler 2012
Copyright *I've Hardly Slept At All* © Trevor Byrne 2012
Copyright *The Hitchhiker* © Mary Costello 2012
Copyright *Urban Myths* © Emma Donoghue 2012
Copyright *Karaoke* © Roddy Doyle 2012
Copyright *Along the Lines* © Dermot Healy 2012
Copyright *Windows of Eyes* © Christine Dwyer Hickey 2012
Copyright *Gloria* © Declan Hughes 2012
Copyright *The Doorbell* © Arlene Hunt 2012
Copyright *Yes* © Colm Keegan 2012
Copyright *Prisoner* © John Kelly 2012
Copyright *First Anniversary* © Claire Kilroy 2012
Copyright *Perfidia* © Pat McCabe 2012
Copyright *As If There Were Trees* © Colum McCann 2012
Copyright *Sacred Heart* © John MacKenna 2012
Copyright *Something To Say To You* © Belinda McKeon 2012
Copyright *Mass for Four Voices* © Mike McCormack 2012
Copyright *Looking For The Heart of Saturday Night* © Siobhán Mannion 2012
Copyright *The Gloamen Man* © Peter Murphy 2012
Copyright *Squidinky* © Nuala Ní Chonchúir 2012
Copyright *Creation* © Phillip Ó Ceallaigh 2012
Copyright *Kissing* © Keith Ridgway 2012
Copyright *I Follow a Character From One of My Novels* © William Wall 2012
Lyrics to *Bless our Tiny Hearts* by Adrian Crowley are used by kind permission of Domino Publishing Limited

The authors have asserted their moral rights.

PRINT ISBN : 978-18-4840-181-5
EPUB ISBN : 978-1-84840-182-2
MOBI ISBN : 978-1-84840-183-9

British Library Cataloguing Data. A CIP catalogue record for this book is
available from the British Library

Typeset by JM InfoTech INDIA
Cover design by Martin Gleeson.
Printed by TJ International Ltd, Padstow, Cornwall

New Island received financial assistance from
The Arts Council (An Comhairle Ealaíon), Dublin, Ireland

10 9 8 7 6 5 4 3 2 1

Bless Our Tiny Hearts
Written by Adrian Crowley

Bless our tiny hearts

We braved it to the sea

On the restless determination

We're bound together

By the silver threads of hope

Bless our tiny hearts

Bless our tiny hearts

If it goes down

And faith in our trusty helmsman

Guides us with a steady hand

Headlong into the breakers

With a hull of gossamer bark

Just one fickle heart

Just one fickle heart

And it goes down

Bless our tiny hearts

Bless our tiny hearts

If it goes down

We wade in the wetlands

Searching for a fog light

Searching for a beacon

Searching for a flare

Just one fickle heart

Just one fickle heart

And it goes down

Bless our tiny hearts

Bless our tiny hearts

If it goes down

Contents

Editor's Foreword

The seeds of this anthology sprouted from one out-of-the-blue email in May 2011. Paul Kelly, who runs Console – a suicide counselling and bereavement service – had discussed the idea of an anthology of Irish writers with Anne Enright. There was no publisher on board and just one story – from the legendary Roddy Doyle – in the literary coffers. New Island came on board with heartening haste, supporting the project from the start. And so began the task of cadging email addresses and approaching writers – some I had met, many I hadn't – to ask if they'd consider handing over a pristine, unpublished story for free in aid of Console. Nearly everyone I asked said yes without hesitation, and it's these 28 wonderful writers whose work makes up this wide-ranging collection. There are writers who live here, some who don't, many who are not known for short stories, and others who revel in its brevity. These pages host many writers with a multitude of styles, but there is nothing unifying about the collection, other than its commitment to the short story, and an articulacy within it.

The stories vary hugely thematically. There are tales of lost love, family favouritism, of wanting to be an artist, missed opportunities, snooty Dublin dinner parties, a dead child, failing to be a Premiership footballer, kissing, a ghost story, a mature student's odd relationship with a lecturer, weddings, affairs, the effects of poverty on youth, hitchhiking, Spanish holidays, runaways and an artist who creates work out of clouds. The book features stalwarts like Colum McCann, Emma Donoghue, Pat McCabe and Claire Kilroy and is proud to provide a platform to a new generation of writers like Kevin Barry, Siobhán Mannion, Colm Keegan and Mary Costello.

Two of the stories centre on suicide, one about a suicide attempt. Their inclusion is happenstance, but seems fitting given the connection to Console. Paul Kelly and his organisation work tirelessly to raise awareness of suicide. They provide counselling, outreach services and support groups and funding is crucial to their survival. "Depression" said Susan Sontag, "is melancholy minus its charms – the animation, the fits." Many writers and artists have been sunk by its effects; others have battled through it. Anne Enright, who was very much the instigator of this book, has written a powerful opening essay. It explores her own experiences with depression and suicidal feelings in her 20s and is unflinching and honest. In it she concludes: "I believe in the power of fiction, because it examines the way that people are uncoupled or connected, in a safe, imagined place. Sad stories are, sometimes, the most consoling. And I know that we must continue to write, and talk, and chase away the silence. We must test the connections, and make them right."

Silver Threads of Hope is a book that would not have happened without Anne Enright and Paul Kelly, or Eoin Purcell and Edwin Higel at New Island. Thanks also to Adrian Crowley for permission to use 'Silver Threads of Hope', a line from his song Bless Our Tiny Hearts, and to Martin Gleeson for designing the cover. Mostly, thank you to the writers who donated their work for Console.

Sinéad Gleeson
Dublin, September 2012

Introduction

Anne Enright

I spent an amount of time in my twenties feeling suicidal. I have written about it since. And regretted writing about it – public life is a bit of a bear pit. 'Cue the nervous breakdown,' as one journalist put it, as though my falling apart was the most boring and predictable thing in the world. But, you know, the whole business of dying or staying alive was too important to me not to mention, sometime in my writing life; it was the elephant in my personal living room. The response to my talking about it, privately or in print, has been interesting. We all know something about the experience of depression, but we don't talk enough, perhaps, about how it makes other people feel; the helplessness and anger and, sometimes, bizarre malice that people in mental distress elicit from those around them.

An admission of weakness unsettles people, especially when, as with a suicidal impulse, it feels like a declaration of great strength.

'Selfish' is one word we use about people who are depressed, especially in Ireland, especially about women. When I was growing up, a woman was called 'selfish' if she chose not to have children – as though just living an independent life was a luxury no woman deserved. And if women were obliged to suffer, they were also expected to do it in silence. This still applies, even to fictional women who only speak

11

within the pages of a book. 'Is she not a bit selfish?' I get asked by Irishwomen about Veronica Hegarty, the narrator of *The Gathering*, a woman who does nothing bad except experience grief, and talk about it.

Levels of depression are higher among women, but the suicide rate is higher among men. We can talk about attitudes to pain or attitudes to violence, but one thing Irish men and woman suffer in common is the pressure to remain silent. And though we are getting better at this, though we have a neutral and useful language in which to discuss these things, the word 'suicide' still sends us diving for cover. What can an ordinary person do in the face of such a word? It is too large, too final.

I wrote about feeling suicidal because I wanted to look at this terrible, absolute idea, and break it down a bit. I thought it might help someone in difficulty to see that you can survive these feelings; that though they carry a great weight of inevitability, this is a false weight – there is nothing inevitable about your life or about the way you will leave it. I wanted to show that you can overcome, or just live with, depression with good enough grace and with your conscience intact.

'Conscience' might seem like a strange word to use, but to be depressed is to hold on to something that feels truthful and right. And, yes, I have to confess, I felt a tiny sense of betrayal as I left my anguish behind, as though it was an essential part of me, and still, in my head, I have the sense of a closed room where that particular emotion went to die. What would be in there if I opened the door now? Ashes. Sunlight.

I wanted to say you can change and still be yourself.

Change was not an elegant process for me. My depression was not coaxed, cajoled, or quieted by family and friends. I didn't talk it out with therapists or counsellors. And though I altered the course of my life, by leaving a stressful job and fol-lowing my own star, there was no Hollywood cure of love or a standing ovation. Love helped, I have to say: love really does help, but what kept me alive, back in the day – what kept me functioning and breathing – was a really basic six months of high-dose antidepressants; a major chemical cosh that made me feel I had lost access to a part of my brain – a very important part which, as the years went by, became less important.

I want to say that I don't miss it, but I am not sure I can say that. No. Of course I can. I do not miss the feeling of being suicidal. But I can also still hear – very faintly – its false promise.

I also remember how much and how often I wanted to die – many times a day, and all night. I wanted to die more often than I wanted a cigarette, and with violent intensity. I wanted it with a yearning that imitated romance, and with the longing of the traveller for home. I don't know how it is for other people, but my thoughts had many of the qualities of addiction.I don't mess around with them, now, or think about them for too long. The only way deal with them, for me, was to go cold turkey.

I haven't taken antidepressants since, though I would not hesitate to do so if things got bad again. I still muddle along with various strategies: fresh air, sunlight, giving myself a break. I like the cognitive behavioural techniques of testing your worst thoughts against reality, I like the mindfulness of yoga. And though I know this doesn't work for everybody, I have great kids, and they make me very happy. I am so grateful to be here, when I remember where I was. Which I do remember, now and then.

Twenty years ago, I spent some weeks in a hospital and told no one. The people who had to know; my partner and family, were incredibly open and careful in how they dealt with the situation. When I started to talk about it, then write about it, years later, strangers (at least, those who were not journalists) managed the information in a neutral and sympathetic way. It was the reactions of the people I knew that were interesting. These people, colleagues and friends, reacted in character and some of them – to my great surprise – didn't quite believe me. I don't know what there was to disbelieve, but nevertheless, belief of a kind was withheld. You may say I was hanging out

13

with the wrong people, but I think they were fine, it was just what I had to say was too confusing, or threatening. I was the wrong 'kind' of person to suffer from depression, perhaps. Or a competing sadness of their own made them feel suddenly 'selfish'. Or they thought I was trying to make them feel guilty. Or.

We are connected.

We are not connected.

It is sometimes tempting to say to a depressive 'it's not all about you, you know'. It is doubly important to say to those who care for, work with, or love someone in mental distress that they do not have to give more than they are able, because it isn't – in the best sense – 'about' them. It is not their fault.

I am not trained in dealing with mental health issues, so I am a kind of amateur in all this. I deal in words that stir, not settle, and I don't know if anything I have written ever helped anyone. But I believe in the power of fiction, because it examines the way that people are uncoupled or connected, in a safe, imagined place. Sad stories are, sometimes, the most consoling. And I know that we must continue to write, and talk, and chase away the silence. We must test the connections, and make them right.

Kevin Barry

Kevin Barry is the author of the story collections *Dark Lies The Island* and *There Are Little Kingdoms* and the novel *City Of Bohane*. He has been awarded the Rooney Prize for Irish Literature and was short-listed for the Costa First Novel Prize. His stories have appeared in Best European Fiction, the Granta Book of the Irish Short Story, the New Yorker, and many other journals and anthologies. His story *Beer Trip to Llandudno* won The Sunday Times EFG Private Bank Short Story Award 2012. His plays have been performed in Ireland and the US. He also writes screenplays, essays, and graphic stories. He lives in County Sligo.

Supper Club

It was not yet light at the Botanical Gardens and the Achenko tree was before me: a miniature, like an African bonsai, and somehow radiant in the pre-dawn dim. I worked its bark carefully with my knife. I took it off in strips eight inches long and lay them carefully in my backpack. I put the pack on top of the wall and shinned up after it. I may have been seen by some people on a bus turning down Glasnevin Road but I would have been no more than a moment's curiosity: a pale, fashionable man of forty, in corduroys and a duffle coat, climbing a wall.

I walked quickly across town. It was a relief to get to the old terraces that lead up to our small artisan home. I turned onto Carnmore Road and I got to No 9, at last. Ciara rushed the hall:

'Oh thank God, Riob!'

'I'm sorry it took so long.'

'I thought you'd been caught! I was thinking the worst!'

'Relax. It's going to be fine. We're on track. How's the kitchen?'

'You're set. The kitchen is go.'

We kissed.

'Can I… see them?'

'Go, Ciara! You'll be late.'

She threw me her filthiest leer as she made gleefully for the door. I hurried through to the kitchen. She had laid everything out to the letter. I lifted out the Achenko shavings, cooing as though over a newborn child, and unwrapped them carefully.

They needed to take the fuggy kitchen air for a few minutes to breathe. Meantime, I could get on with the marinade.

The city rumbled outside and was oblivious to my magic. The low groans of the traffic; the nasal mewling of the aborigines. I zipped about in an ecstasy of precise labour: I ground, I pestled, I sliced, I stirred. Silently I gave thanks for my skills, and I gave thanks too for the worktop space, which was generous as these terrace kitchens go. I had some suitable music on: M'gubu Bota Jnr., one of the earlier throat-singing things. I gurgled along with it happily and, by mid-morning, an unearthly aroma had started to flavour the air. I was sweaty and tired and elated all at once. I was a man in the prime of his achievement.

We had discussed the thing at length. October nights between the cool sheets, plotting and debating. Flambé or flash-fry? Marinade or a just a quick, rough rub? I admit that I favour elaboration. It should be complex, it should be involved, it should be difficult. Ciara always maintains that the higher calling is to reduce, to clarify, to give an essence. Three ingredients, she says, bang bang bang, and your spell is cast.

Our circle had become one of the most accomplished in the city that year. Since we had fallen into the regular series of Supper Club invites, each couple had continuously upped the ante.

I chopped shallots, my eyes streaming. I pounded chillies and garlic. I made a mash of pistachios and blanched almonds. I conjured a fish stock from prawn heads. I allowed the Achenko shavings to marinade for the full seven hours. I sealed and I scored. I was rancid with alliums, bloodied with berry juice. I worked myself into a bit of a lather getting together an extraordinarily complex rub for the piglet starters. I put on some Sun Ra and shook out my limbs.

Come teatime, I was still hard at it, but starting to gain control. Ciara came back from work. She had that high, excited colour: event-colour.

'Oh babe?' she said. 'I think I smell a good one?'

'They are going to want to die,' I said, thoughtfully. 'They are going to want to go home and fucking well die.'

She put the finishing touches to the dining room. We had decided on a system of muted golds and tans. I wasn't over-confident – that way lies disaster – but I felt there was every possibility we were about to set a new standard.

Muiris and Lenore's was the first of these affairs. And strange, but what seemed the height of edge that night at the Nic Choinneacha's seems bland in memory. They mained with a gingered kelp thing. One of these 'found' dishes – the kelp from Wexford, allegedly. Rico and Jill did better, they pushed it out a bit – they did the rotten shark and the pan-fried hawk-meat. Quickly, the stakes were being raised.

I beheaded six piglets; Ciara hovered.

'What?'

'It's just … nothing.'

'What?'

'It's just … I'm thinking out loud here, Riob? Okay? I'm thinking are we maybe going a bit ethnic-y again?'

'What do you mean?'

'Just … are we maybe going a bit West of Ireland-y again?'

'We're not.'

'Okay, fine! It's just I'm remembering the night of the pigs' feet?'

'The crubeens were a hit.'

'I don't know that we can say that, actually? And all I'm saying is it's pigs again and I'm just getting the ethnic-y worry now? I'm worried we've *done* the West of Ireland thing?'

'It's a bit late in the day, Ciar, to be honest?'

I knew we'd overplayed the ethnic thing. Who did she think she was talking to? She was putting together some amuse-gueules of an Isle of Skye fennel licked with a San Tremino chilli oil.

'What did you honestly think of Rico's hare the other week?' she said.

'Actually, I thought he let himself down.'

'Thank you! About time somebody said it! It was so bloody dry and so bloody bland and the way he tries to pass it off as this gamey thing that's *supposed* to be dry? When frankly we all know that ...'

'It's not just the dryness. With Rico, it's the entire package. His sides? The seasonal thing? I mean, seasonal is fine, but Rico is *aggressively* seasonal.'

It was in July that Jarlath and Mona had pulled out a big one. It was just when we all thought the outré stuff had been done to death, just when everybody was thinking about going ironic; thinking Spag Bols and fish 'n' chips. But then came that hot night in Ringsend, and the wok-load of stir-fried dog.

'And what did you do to the dog, Jarlath?'

Later, in the cab home, as Ciara and I sat through the night traffic, the air was stifling and rich, the city smelled of open sewers, and we were light-headed with Chablis and envy.

'It's not just that they served dog,' she said. 'It's that they served it so *simply*.'

'Chillies and fucking coriander.'

'Straight off *Ready Steady Cook*, Riob! Chillies and coriander! But *dog*.'

'Where do you go after dog? The meat thing is dead in the water now.'

'Meat thing's done. Meat thing's history. We've got to be talking vegetables now?'

'Muiris and Lenore are next,' I said. 'I wouldn't worry about them. But we're up in October.'

'Muiris and Lenore aren't an issue. He'll be stuffing his little vine leaves, won't he?'

So who would have thought it? Who would have predicted that Muiris would rip up the rulebook and annihilate us all? He did beef cheeks for a main but his starter had already secured the triumph. He had battered and deep-fried little Reuben's placenta, and served it with a tangy mayo. Not just tasty but meaningful. Everybody wept that night in Rathgar. Rico and Jill stormed off to a three-week intensive refresher with some kitchen Nazi in the hills outside Marseilles. Ciara was depressed for weeks. She took to going to bed at half past eight. I worry when she gets depressed like this because usually, after the depression, comes the hardness. The tide goes out and the rocks are exposed.

The bell rang.

'We're on,' I said, a quake of fear in my voice. 'Positive thoughts, yes? Belief!'

As always, Rico and Jill were first on the doorstep. What it was, basically, was they hated their children.

'Hi.'

'Hi?'

'Hiya.'

'How you getting on in there, boss?'

'Don't even think about sticking your nose in here. Off limits!'

'Well, something smells weird.'

'There's nothing weird in here, thanks.'

'Do I smell de leeeekle pigs?'

Yeah, and fuck you too, Rico. And what did he mean, weird?

Ciara took them to the room. I could hear polite *hmmms* about the colour scheme. I took in some bottles of Nigerian Guinness from the icer. N'gutha Baal gargled his jungly wisdom on the system.

'Hey,' said Rico, as I poured, 'nice decision.'

'This is just right, now?' said Jill. 'I've a throat on me.'

'So we're doing the African thing again, yeah?' said Rico.

'What are you talking about?'

'Pay no attention, Riob,' said Ciara, 'he's winding you up.'

'What do you mean, the African thing?'

'Don't even humour him, Riobaird,' said Jill. 'He's a wind-up merchant.'

Rico smiled that horrible, orthodontic smile: 'What are we listening to, Riob?'

'Some N'gutha? One of the earlier things.'

'Okay,' said Rico. 'So the 2008 revival has started already, yes?'

'I, ah … better get back to it.'

The bell, in its mercy. It was Muiris and Lenore. They looked tired but happy. They had lately been attempting to reintroduce the wolf to Connemara.

'Hi!'

'Hiya!'

'How're we fixed?'

Now, I cannot handle Muiris. At all. I mean, sure, I myself have been accused of playing up the West of Ireland thing, but this fucker? He even does the 'sh' business – the Wesht, how're we fikshed, I'd be losht without ye. The disgusting thing is the women love him. He's six foot five and built like one of the Cliffs of Moher. I sent in some more of the Guinness, and took a couple of deep, connected breaths. It was time to taste the main.

'Ciara,' I called, 'I want you!'

'Don't we all, hah?' said Muiris.

'Did you just think that, Muiris,' said Rico, 'or did you actually say it?'

Ciara, flushed, came through to the kitchen.

'What's up?'

'I want to try this thing, okay?'

I ladled from the pungent, greyish stew; we tasted.

'Hmmm,' said Ciara.

'Yeah.'

'Interesting.'

'Kind of …'

'Yeah. I know what you mean.'

'Kind of …'

'Yeah, yeah. Kind of … *woody*?'

'What do you mean, woody?'

'Well, not woody, but …'

'I mean, sure,' I said, 'there are wood *notes*.'

'Exactly.'

'But it's not …'

'It's fantastic.'

'Isn't it?'

'Honestly. It rocks.'

We brought in the *amuse-gueules*, and a couple of bottles of a merlot-cabernet blend made by an anarchist vineyard in New Zealand.

'Ah,' said Rico, 'the old Blood River yoke, is it? Good man, Riob, that's a nice drop.'

'It is.'

'And you can't turn around lately without falling over a bottle of the stuff.'

'You wouldn't see it *that* much,' said Lenore.

'No attention, Lenore,' said Jill. 'He's on a wind-up.'

'I mean, you'd see it,' said Lenore. 'I mean, they do it in Tesco and that.'

'Actually, they don't do it in Tesco,' I said.

'Oh? I was sure I'd seen it there.'

'You didn't.'

'Are Fiachra and Bubby running late?'

'So what's new?'

'D'ye have any joy at all,' said Muiris, 'with the auld spot of damp ye were having in the landing?'

'Sorted.'

'Go 'way?'

'Done and dusted, we reckon. Don't we, Riob?'

'Absolutely.'

'Don't worry,' said Rico, 'it'll be back.'

'You reckon, Reek? Why so?'

'These old terraces? Come on, Riob, fucksake. The damp is all part of the charm.'

'There's an underground river goes right by here,' said Ciara.

'Still waters run deep,' said Lenore.

'Excuse me?' said Rico.

'Still waters run deep,' said Lenore. 'The old saying …'

'Yes, I know the saying. Apropos of?'

'I just … she was saying there's a river, like, and …'

'And are rivers still, usually, Lenore?'

'I …'

'Hello, good evening and welcome to non sequiturs tonight,' said Rico.

'Did you know, Rico,' I said, 'that sarcasm is disguised anger at the self?'

'Jesus,' said Rico. 'Are the Weetabix boxes doing Freud now?'

'How'd ye sort the damp, peteen?'

'What we did, Muir,' said Ciara, 'was …'

The bell rang. It was Fiachra and Bubby.

'Hi!'

'Hiya!'

'Ye're pushing the auld clock?'

'Bubby, you're looking fantastic!'

'Thanks, Ciara,' said Bubby, bravely. 'I've had no more problems since, thank God.'

'I hear you actually went cold turkey?'

'Don't mention the war,' said Fiachra.

'You were the first I'd met?' whispered Lenore. 'I mean, I'd read about gym rage but you were the first I knew who'd … suffered?'

'The amazing thing is there's an actual rash involved.'

'Cleared up easy enough.' said Bubby. 'The rash wasn't the worst of it, by any means? Was it, Fiach?'

'Jesus, no,' said Fiachra.

'So that's it with the gym, Bub, fineeto?

'Fin,' said Bubby, '*eeee*to.'

'No Hugo and Bob?' said Fiachra.

'Riob can be a little rough-edged for some tastes,' said Rico. 'We're going to have to find a new token gay couple.'

'We could think about starters, Riob?'

The kitchen fumed. The piglets were as good as they were going to be. I arranged them on the rough earthenware plates we'd bought from the lepers in Niger. Even if there was failure, I knew the integrity of the effort would be applauded, and I wept quietly for a moment. Anyway, we'd all had our disasters. Jarlath and Mona ... oh the famous night of the penguin shanks! And Bob and Hugo's soul food fiasco ... Bob and Hugo with the R&B, and the baseball caps, and Bob a fucking guard. I spooned jus. I drizzled blossom-water. Ciara came for me.

'Deep breath, wren,' I said. 'We're going in.'

Some junkie-period Miles squittered from the system. Lamplight only, with the golds and tans of the night's colour scheme muted and subtle.

'Okay,' I said. 'Nosebag.'

'Oh ...'

'It's the leeeetle pigs alright,' said Rico.

'Lovely arrangement, Riobaird.'

'Thanks. And listen, can I announce a moratorium on the Old Macdonald jokes?'

'Durn,' said Rico.

'Sorry, Reek.'

'Actually, no?' he said. 'I wasn't going to go with Old Macdonald. I was trying to work something up about, like, reductions in the EU piglet mountain?'

'The pig mountain.'

'Pig mountain, yes. And actually, Riob, "pig mountain" sounds like it could come from one of your poems.'

'Fuck off.'

'I take it you're still working the old West of Ireland seam, yes?'

'Thank you, Rico.'

'And how long since you actually *lived* in the West of Ireland?'

'He's on a wind-up, Riob.'

'Riob, this is sensational.'

'It's like ... it's like it's ... like, melting?'

'Incredible.'

'Quare bit o' pigeen altogether.'

'Phen,' said Bubby, '*ommm*menal.'

'No, actually, Riob, I've got to hand it to you. This *is* good.'

'Thanks, Rico.'

'Seriously. It's a bloody nicely cooked bit of meat.'

'Cheers, Reek,' I raised a glass, and I felt a glow within, like grace.

'You're putting it up to yourself, Riob! How do you main after this?'

'How *do* you main after this?'

'Anyway how is the poetry, Riobiard? Busyish?'

'*Fuck* off.'

'The poetry is treating Riob very well. Sure hasn't he got tenure now?'

'Oh, wow, actually, congrats on that,' said Lenore, 'or have we seen you since?'

'No, I …'

The siren of a squad car screamed past outside. It came within feet of the dining room window, which rattled. We paused, forks frozen in midair, and all wryly smiled.

'I thought,' said Rico, 'that this place had been gentrified. No?'

'Much done,' smiled Ciara. 'Much remains to do.'

'There's always going to be the odd scumbag,' I said.

'Edgy!' said Ciara.

'What can you do?' I said. 'There'll always be aborigines.'

'Could we nearly think about mains, Riob?'

'Peasants,' said Rico, 'is essentially what we're talking about. The northside is the northside and a terrace is a terrace, you know? Terraces are peasant housing and you're not going to change that overnight.'

'You have to let 'em die off, basically, I suppose?'

'I'm not saying anything against terraces,' said Rico. 'We were on a terrace ourselves long enough.'

'The North Circular!' cried Jill.

'The horror,' said Rico. 'The horror.'

'Most people around here I'm sure are professionals now,' said Lenore.

'Professional whats?' said Rico.

'Actually,' I said, 'I think an area is most interesting when it's in a kind of transitory phase? When it's neither one thing nor the other? You have *edge* but also you have *facilities*. Kind of like the journey is more interesting than the destination?'

'Whatever it is you're on,' said Rico, 'I want the prescription.'

The area *was* a disaster. It had been on the cusp forever, but it had never turned. You couldn't get the smell of butter vouchers out of the place. It was still full of faceless youths beneath baseball caps. Ringtones, belly-tops, and bastard adolescents everywhere. The death drone of Piaggios and yellowy living-dead junkie skin.

'Food, Riob?'

I went to the kitchen, with Ciara directly behind. We smiled. The starter was a triumph. Now we would present the Achenko tree bark main. Now we would stun the table to silence. Now we would rip these motherfuckers to shreds! I felt a slight wobble of nerves during the plating. The lead note was distinctly … woody. There was no denying it. But innovation demands courage, and I piled the slathered shavings into a delicate tower structure atop each of eight plates, and I arranged the barley risonterelle for a side, and I dressed with dill, fennel feathers, a squeeze of lime.

'Done deal,' said Ciara.

'You think?'

'You've *closed*, Riob.'

'These two have breathed long enough,' I indicated a couple of burly Armenians. 'Bring them and I'll throw on some of the mellower N'Gutha. Then we roll.'

We began the procession, and conversation subsided to a chorus of *oohs* and low whistles.

'Wow.'

'Riob? This looks absolutely … Christ!'

'Now what in the name of Bosco,' said Rico, sniffing, 'have we got here?'

I took my place at the table's head. I allowed a moment for everyone to examine the plates before them. I laced my elegant fingers beneath my chin.

'In the back streets of Mombassa,' I began, 'I came across one morning this book cart with just like a little toothless old dude working it? And I found there a text? In the French? And it explained how the natives of the far interior would sometimes harvest …'

They listened, awestruck, and tasted.

'Mother of God!'

'Riob? I'm tellin' ya …'

'Interesting.'

'Very interesting.'

'It's like …'

'Yeah, it's …'

'Now!' cried Lenore. 'Now we have *Africa* on our plates!'

Were these the herald notes of a triumph? I allowed a humble smile.

'The risonterelle,' said Jill, 'is top class.'

I drew back, stunned. This was outrageous. Ciara's eyes darted to mine. In praising the accompaniment, Jill was placing a question mark over the focus of the dish – the Achenko bark. She was opening a debate. This was the initial salvo. There was no way that it was accidental. She knew what she was doing! And I still believe – to this day – that the room was ready to go with it, the room was ready to place the garlands, but Jill's remark (may the blubber-nosed whore die roaring) created pause. Who might come forward to fill it?

'Okay,' said Rico, and I sucked down a breath. 'Now tell me again, Riob? What we're eating here, essentially, is the kind of … outer sheath, is that how you put it? The outer sheath of this whatchamacallit plant?'

'Pretty much.'

'Now. When you say outer sheath, Riob, do you mean like an epidermal layer or a, you know …'

'Yes. The outer layer of the arm, of the plant's *stem?*'

'Plant?' said Rico.

'Yes.'

'And I mean it's definitely a *plant* we're talking about? As in a vegetable?'

'How'd you mean?' I said.

'No need to be defensive. I'm just tasting the thing and … the texture, you know? I'm just thinking, it couldn't like be a … I dunno. A kind of a … tree, maybe?'

My breathing went shallow.

'I … suppose, you know, six of one, half dozen the other, you could probably call it a kind of a miniature tree.'

'We could probably call it,' said Rico, 'a kind of a miniature tree.'

'Yes.'

'So if I'm hearing this correctly, Riobaird? What you're telling us is we're sat here eating the bark off a tree. Like some kind of …'

He paused. He looked all around. He smiled.

'Pygmy rats?' he said.

'It's so … interesting,' said loyal Lenore.

'I think it's unbelievable,' said Ciara, huskily.

'Definitely it's unbelievable,' said Rico.

'It is interesting,' said dear Fiachra.

'Mighty altogether,' said Muiris.

Maybe, just maybe, if everybody else came onside … But Rico put down his knife and fork. Rico pushed back his plate. Rico eyeballed me. And Rico spoke.

'No,' he said.

Everybody looked to the floor.

'This isn't interesting,' he said.

There were sharp intakes of breath.

'And it isn't edgy,' he said. 'What it is, Riobaird, is it's the bark off a fucking tree.'

Never before had there been anything like this. There had been a curled lip over an amuse-gueule. There had been a sniffy comment about a vine leaf. But this?

'I think you're being harsh, Rico,' said Ciara, dabbing her eyes with a napkin.

'I'm not,' he said. 'I just think it's important this is said. I'm not just being a bollocks here. I think the time has come to ask ourselves. What are we at?'

'Maybe,' I conceded, 'I've been a little adventurous.'

'It's not that it's adventurous, Riob,' he said. 'It's that it's not *food*.'

'Great starter,' said Fiachra.

'The starter was fabulous …'

And we were in the kitchen then, numbed, and Ciara wordlessly sliced the pear tart, and with dead eyes I doled out the crème fraîche – she wouldn't even look at me.

'So I walked up to the motherfucker,' said Rico, 'and I said, "Friend, listen up." I said, "Did you hear what I actually said about the spritzed effect? What is it you think we're designing here, a sitcom garden?" I said, "Do I look like Felicity fucking Kendal?"'

'Rico!'

'And your man is stood there, slackjaw. With his little roto-vator. I nearly had to be dug out of the fucking savage.'

'Nice tart, Riob.'

'Sensational tart.'

An amped-up Honda Civic flashed by outside, took a speed ramp at pace and all four of its wheels left the tarmac, as though it had been hoisted by angels.

'Lupine,' said Muiris, 'is to wolf as canine is to dog. And I would think, what? Arra … 1780s? That'd have been about the lasht of the wolves. County Carlow, I believe, was the …'

'Yeah, right, get you,' said Rico. 'Anyway, Bubby, this latest regime. Please don't tell me it's got to the stage where you're drinking your own piss?'

'Is it Angeline Jolie does that?'

'Apparently she was in Cork the other week. Something about Buddhists?'

'All Cork has is the English Market. If you take away the English Market, it's a dreary little town.'

'Thank you! It's about time somebody said it! I mean they were going on like it was Barcelona!'

'Sure Barcelona is gone to God itself?'

'It is, actually. All stags and hens. Death by easyJet.'

I closed my eyes. I came outside myself. I rose up. I went to the night sky and I looked down on Carnmore Road. I saw how the walls that bounded us were so flimsy from up there but the castle holds if the castle can, and why fret for its fall until all the dust has blown and rubble fills the moat?

Greg Baxter

Greg Baxter is the author of two books, *A Preparation for Death* (2010) and *The Apartment* (2012). Born in Texas in 1974, he moved to Ireland in 2003. He is the founder of Some Blind Alleys, a literary organisation that supports new writing in Ireland through events, publication and workshops. He now lives in Berlin, where he translates and writes.

The Bendy Wood Experiment

for Adrian Duncan

I went to see Schlomo at his studio because I needed some tools and supplies to repair a cement wall I'd nearly destroyed while trying to hang an Egon Schiele print that my wife, Jasia, bought for me at the museum. He was in an excited and distracted humour because an experiment that might lead to a larger project was coming to an end. Schlomo is a small man, in his late twenties, with black hair and thick black eyebrows, and he is very thin.

I arrived in the afternoon. It was a sunny day, very warm and blue-white. The studio is gray and large, with dirty windows and there were two girls lying around in t-shirts. From time to time one of them would make some orange juice or smoke a cigarette. They were listening to Tchaikovsky, Symphony No 6. I had that awful paroxysm you get when in the presence of art – of artists at the work of art – that you've interrupted something sacred, and you ought to leave. This feeling is a sign of the artist's mystique.

Here is a brief description (I should not say explanation) of his experiment, and how he had arrived at it. He became interested in the idea of bendy wood. He sat me down on the couch – the girls were sitting on another couch, so that we faced each other in an L shape – and made an invisible piece of wood in his hands.

He began to bend it and speak: I am fascinated by the bendiness of wood right now, he said. I asked a tree surgeon what was the bendiest wood he knew. This tree surgeon was tall, brutal, and artless. When he said *the willow*, as though he had been waiting all his life for someone to ask him his preferred bendy wood, I knew this was an important experiment.

Here is how Schlomo's experiment worked. He admitted there was no purpose. It was a sketch, and if he liked how it turned out, he hoped it would inspire him. The first thing he needed to do was take a piece of bendy wood – a willow branch – and remove its bendiness – or rather to accelerate its drying out. This was simple – remove the bark. The next step was to maintain the wood's bendiness artificially once the bark was gone. For whatever reason, Schlomo decided to insert a small string into the wood, through a tiny hole he bored, needled the string up inside, and placed the other end of the string in a glass jar filled with water.

And if it works, what next?

Art, perhaps, he said.

What does that entail?

Schlomo said nothing for a moment. One of the girls yawned and lit a cigarette. The breath that she drew in seemed to draw the whole world in, as though she were tasting it, and the exhale seemed to say it disgusted her. The sunlight poured over the two of them in a syrup-like gunk of heat that gave their skin a fishy shininess.

How should I know, said Schlomo at last.

The experiment did not work. We all walked to the storage closet in which he had hung the branch, and in which, every day, he monitored the level of water. He took the wood down from its fixture and tried to bend it. It was brittle. It snapped. The girls said nothing. They eyed the branch in his hands without heat or rancour or any disappointment, like starfish – no, more distant, more implacable: like two rhinoceros, standing in a dusty wood, watching an old jeep, miles and miles and miles and miles away, speed incrementally across the horizon. Schlomo held the string between his fingertips. Dry, he said, and yanked it out.

Well, what now? I asked.

It's possibly the thread. I may need something else.

One of the girls – the one in the yellow t-shirt – said: Perhaps butcher's string would conduct the water better.

Maybe, said Schlomo, maybe …

But one could see the annoyance he felt at having a non-artist suggest a collaboration. One could see immediately that he would pick any number of things to conduct water, but never butcher's string.

Thankfully, a neighbour called, a woman named S. I'd never met her, but Schlomo had said a lot about her. S was a photographer and had, upon moving to the city, dropped the other letters from her name. I feel that there is art, and there is a struggle to create the illusion of art. There is nothing in between, and the two have nothing to do with each other. And all the artists are dead. And all the people who can tell the difference are dead. And everything is irrelevant. But I look at Schlomo and think, good! The alternative is great suffering, or money, or an idiocy that is greater than derivation.

S said: Do you have any mounted heads of large cats?

I'm sure I do, said Schlomo.

I need a lion, but something else will do.

It turned out, after Schlomo left S alone for ten minutes to be glared at silently by me and indifferently by the two girls – S had very frizzy red hair and soft white shoulders, and the way she dressed made you think that she had crawled like some lady who lives in a lake out of a dumpster – that there were no heads of cats, just whole stuffed birds, but dozens of them.

Why don't we have some drinks? proposed Schlomo.

And by then I had forgotten what I'd come for. I followed everyone onto a small, rectangular terrace that stood on stilts over a small garden and overlooked a network of cramped but lush and flowering gardens. Descending toward the city, rusted rooftops of old warehouses. Birds. Birds everywhere – white, fat, and circling, or loitering, or fighting. The two girls sat together on a chair and rolled a joint. Schlomo took off his shirt, and I saw that his chest was covered in tattoos. The Tchaikovsky – it must have been repeating – was now going very loudly in the background. I could not help thinking of the degradation of genius that this terrace represented. And I could not help but think of the very cruel predicament of being men, women, now – that art has vanished, but the desire to make it remains. Which is not to say that I am entirely uninterested in the idea of bendy wood, either. I am rather intrigued by it. And it is true that I am the alternative – the grief, the greed, the idiocy of participation.

S began to take photographs. I wasn't paying much attention to her. I presumed she was taking pictures of the girls. I too was fascinated by them. They looked so different; they were different in every possible way – for instance one was tall and one was short, and the short one was beautiful and the tall one was not – yet together on that chair they seemed exactly similar. I mean you really could not tell the two of them apart. Then I realized S was taking photographs of me.

I noticed this, she said to Schlomo. Had you?

Schlomo leaned in. I hadn't, he said, but I see it now, clearly.

What? I said, though it bothered me to say something so predictable.

S did not answer. It's strange, she said to Schlomo: I've never quite seen such a case of it. Then she took many more pictures.

Finally I put my hand in front of my face. She frowned and put the camera down.

What are you talking about? I demanded. What do you see?

I looked at the girls for a moment. One was looking directly at the very centre of the sky. The other was blowing smoke out of her mouth.

This will be a funny thing to tell Jasia, I thought. She hates artists.

Would you let me take a few more? asked S.

Take a picture of his cock, said Schlomo.

Huh? I said. I looked at the girls. Nothing. Except that the one smoking was now looking up, and the second was smoking.

I am thinking of my bendy wood experiment, he said, without irony.

S stood quietly and waited for me to speak. When I did not, she sat down next to Schlomo and sighed. I don't think I can use the birds, she said, trying to change the subject.

It became very uncomfortable after that. A few times I considered taking my cock out. Had it not been for the girls, I might have, but I couldn't bear their indifference to my cock – anything but my cock. A man feels that, even if he is unnoticeable in every way, when he pulls his cock out, a woman should notice. So I drank another Italian beer – it was in one of those short, fat bottles – warm. Then I left. I left with nothing in my hands. When I got out on the street, I remembered the tools and supplies, but I felt too embarrassed to return.

I found a café, grabbed a newspaper, and ordered a double espresso and a pastry. What would Jasia say if I came home empty-handed and drunk after destroying a wall in our house? The front page of the paper was about the flu pandemic. Yesterday it was revealed that two men – two men my age – were in critical condition in hospital because of it: this was the newspaper story. The pandemic had killed a lot of people in other places, and though no one had died here, it was inevitable that someone would. Perhaps dozens would die. Perhaps the virus would mutate, and tens of thousands would die. When I looked up from my paper, everyone was reading the same story.

Death is the force behind all human personality. When a child first recognizes his parents – that is the moment he witnesses his death: what he actually witnesses is self, and the self is death. Of course, a child does not know this, and it is only a small thing – so much smaller than the wonderful and joyous recognition of life. Also, it does no good to go around talking about death to children. Give them toys and tell them they can achieve anything.

When I was a child, I foresaw my own death from a plague. At a museum I saw a photograph of Egon Schiele dying from Spanish flu. I went home and, for many months, saw myself die in the same way. My father was an artist, and I was very angry that he had not died of Spanish flu. I asked him why he had not, and he said, because I am not a good enough artist.

Then he added, and I would rather be alive than be a great artist.

My father is still alive, and he spends his retirement drinking sparkling water in his boat, which is docked at the marina, and never moves.

Dostoyevsky witnessed his own death, and he became Christ. Kafka died at childbirth but became a writer anyway. Those are just two examples of something that is vague in my brain, yet expresses itself constantly through a specific kind of agony.

I want to conduct death, not mirror it.

Dermot Bolger

Born in Finglas in North Dublin, Ireland, the poet, playwright and novelist Dermot Bolger has also worked as a factory hand, library assistant and publisher. He is the author of nine novels for adults, including *The Journey Home, Night Shift, The Valparaiso Voyage, The Family on Paradise Pier* and most recently, his radical reworking of a twenty-year-old book in *A Second Life: A Renewed Novel*. His first young adult novel, *New Town Soul*, in 2010, reached back to the rich tradition of 19th century Gothic Dublin writing. His thirteen plays include, *The Lament for Arthur Cleary*, which received The Samuel Beckett Award for best Debut Play performed in Britain, *Blinded by the Light, The Holy Ground, April Bright* and *The Passion of Jerome*. In recent years he has worked extensively with the Axis Theatre in Ballymun, who have staged his plays on tours across Ireland and abroad. These include his *Ballymun Trilogy* (published by New Island), *The Parting Glass* which toured extensively in 2011 and was a direct sequel to his 1990 Gate Theatre play, *In High Germany,* and his latest play *Tea Chests and Dreams*. Bolger has been The Writer Fellow in Trinity College, Dublin, Playwright in Association with the Abbey Theatre, the author of nine poetry collections, including *The Venice Suite* (to be published in autumn 2012) and writes for most of Ireland's national newspapers.

www.dermotbolger.com

Coming Home

His cousin Anto saw him first on his return, just after dawn, though Shane knew that nothing would prise Anto away from leaning against the open doorway of the corrugated workman's hut as he looked out at the light drizzle that had halted work. Anto was only in his second year as a Corporation workman, but already he had acquired the ingrained mannerisms of the older men among the squad of road workers he worked with. Shane thought that 'work' was a big word for what Anto was now securely employed for life to do: to tentatively poke at potholes as if they were unexploded landmines and scurry back to wherever their hut was parked to drink tea and play cards at the first drop of rain.

During his first few months working for the Corpo, Anto used to laugh about the farce of officially starting work at the hut at eight o'clock and then lounging around inside it until a truck driver arrived at nine to transport them a few hundred yards to wherever the roadworks were currently located. But now, he got annoyed if anyone in the family slagged his job. Shane had teased him more than most, but at least Anto had a job, unlike Shane, and was not suddenly having to play catch up with his own life.

Anto had never got on with Shane. Not since the time Shane nutmegged him twice on the green in front of all Anto's mates when Shane was twelve and he was nineteen. Anto had fancied himself as a footballer once, but Shane could now tell that, at twenty-four, Anto was past it and beyond caring. The flab on his stomach said it; the fag always on his lips, the slouch that came from perpetually leaning on a shovel or a bar counter.

Anto shouted something, but Shane could not tell if it was directed at him or at one of Anto's workmates who was filling a kettle for tea at a fire hydrant opened up farther along the pavement. Shane kept his head down and cut across the huge green where horses were always tethered. The horses shied away from him, like he was a stranger, when he – of all the lads who lived on the Crescent – had always possessed a gift with animals.

Maybe there had been a time when horses didn't graze on this sodden green, ridden in and out of Finglas to the Smithfield horse fair to be bought and sold by boys.

But Shane's earliest memories were of waking to the noise of whinnying, and knowing that, at any time of night, he could pad across the lino to stare from his bedroom window at these patient animals standing like sentinels on the moonlit grass.

The horses were what he missed most during the past three years of living in digs in England. He had missed his family, of course, and the pals he grew up with, but everybody else who signed schoolboy forms at the football club missed their family and friends too. The horses were different, and he had never been able to properly talk about them – not even to the other Irish boys training at the club – until Ray O'Farrell was signed. He had known instinctively that the British lads would not have been able to understand and would have simply cracked jokes about the Wild West.

But often, in the hours that the club allowed him to himself between training and studies, he had taken a bus into the city centre. Not to buy anything in the shops – this wasn't likely on the £15 a week pocket money that the club supplied – but simply on the off chance of seeing a mounted policeman on horseback. Sometimes he would follow the horse through the crowds until the policeman got suspicious and noticed him. Homesickness was a symptom the club understood.

They even had pep talks about it from the Under-17s coach, a former Scottish international who had broken his leg playing for the reserves while trying to come back from a series of cartilage operations. But wanting to wrap your arms around a horse's neck – especially a police horse – would have been a step too far.

Not that he had even been likely to approach a policeman on horseback in his first year in Manchester when local shop-owners were still clearing up the city centre after an IRA bomb attack and the youth coach had advised the Irish lads to avoid betraying their accents when using public transport.

Shane put his bag down on the wet grass now and tried to approach an old black horse, whom he recognised, tethered to a rope. The horse shied away at first, then let Shane run his fingers through its tangled mane. But Shane couldn't be sure if this was because the horse remembered him or if it was just so broken down in health as to be beyond caring who touched him.

The green sloped slightly towards the church before falling away down a steep incline. On a thousand occasions he had chased a football down that slope, deftly taking it under control with a flick or a back heel to prevent the ball bouncing off into the path of oncoming traffic. He had always been the youngest player on any team back then, dismissively sent to do fetching jobs like that and yet still always the first to be picked. By the age of nine he had been sick of playing with kids his own size. Three years, four years, five years older, he didn't care: the larger they came the easier they were to nutmeg. Older lads used to shy away from kicking him at first because of his size, but then, ten minutes into any game, they would forget about his age or become fixated by it and lash out angrily.

The disorganised, never-ending games played on this waterlogged green had prepared him for any rough treatment received when he later togged out for Tolka Rovers. At least in League games there was a referee. By the age of eleven, he was aware of arguments at the club about what age group he should play for. The Under-12s would win the League that year without him. The Under-14s had desperately needed a striker. But Eddie, the Under-12s manager, was never going to give way. Shane was his star and Eddie was his protector. Shane trusted him with implicit devotion, even though Eddie had never been slow to give Shane as much of a bollixing as any other player who stepped out of line.

All the scouts came out to watch Eddie's team that year when the Under-12s went unbeaten in the League and two cups: scouts from Arsenal, Liverpool, Spurs and Celtic and from clubs like Brighton and Tranmere, whom you would not suspect of having scouts in Ireland. 'You can look but you cannot touch,' Eddie would mutter to them, and they certainly did look. Not just at him, but at Derek Brown in midfield who was convinced he would get a call that never actually came.

If Eddie made sure that no scout could tap him up on the football pitch or the dressing room, Eddie was not around in the evenings. The polite knocks on the front door always came at the same time – two minutes past eight approximately. Maybe the clubs presumed that all players' mothers watched Coronation Street and there were strict rules about scouts making a poor impression by interrupting their favourite soap opera. After three years at the club, no detail would surprise him about the tricks and strategies that they went in for.

The scouts always arrived quietly: friendly, middle-aged men with weather-worn faces who wanted nothing stronger than a cup of tea and a quiet word. He didn't want them to be quiet. Back then he had wanted to open his bedroom window and shout out to the whole of the Crescent that a representative from some Premiership team was sitting in his kitchen. There were certain parts of the conversations that he was allowed sit in on, but for other parts he was sent upstairs. His age was the big stumbling block at first; he was too young to sign for anyone. But with his fifteenth birthday coming up everything would change, if his parents would stop listening to Eddie's cautions and simply give him his chance to go.

Not that he had always been sure that he did want to go. Eddie had gone to Liverpool for two years back in the 1970s – though Eddie didn't talk of it much. It was hard for Shane to imagine that this man who sold cylinders of gas door to door from an open-backed truck had once been photographed by the *Evening Herald* about to get on an aeroplane, with newspaper headlines hailing him as the future of Irish football.

Shane's dad never wanted Shane to go, but Shane had known that he would not stand in his way. All through his life, until the age of fifteen, his Da had had been like a shadow on the touchline, never interfering or shouting advice but always a quiet, supportive presence: never allowing him to get too excited about scoring a hat-trick or too downhearted if he played poorly.

Back then, his Ma had been the stumbling block. The closer his fifteenth birthday came, the more the pressure had got to her. Was she standing in his way and holding him back because he was her first born? But why did the clubs want him so young, she would ask, why couldn't he finish his education and have something to fall back on? Once or twice when Da was at work and the younger kids, Marie and Sam, were playing upstairs, his Ma would look at him and start crying and he would cry too, both of them at the kitchen table not knowing what to do.

But then THE CLUB came knocking; a summons that nobody could ignore. His dream had never been to play for THE CLUB – because he had never dared to believe that he was good enough – but just to simply travel to see a match in their ground one day. His bedroom wall was covered in posters of that team. When their scout came, he had sat in the kitchen and known that this was it. When he looked across at his mother he saw that she knew it too. Her resistance was broken. Not even Eddie's arguments about starting out at a smaller club, where he might have more chance of a breakthrough, had worked.

Shane had grown furious with him on the evening when he called over. Shane was one step away from paradise and this raggle taggle gas cylinder salesman was trying to keep him a little boy forever. 'Just because you were a total failure doesn't mean that I will be one too,' he'd shouted at the man. There had been no way to take those words back. Eddie had left the house soon afterwards. Shane always planned to make it up to Eddie, by stating in press interviews how much Eddie had done for him. But those press interviews never came.

Shane knew now that he should not have boarded a cheap coach by himself last night to get the boat back to Ireland. He should at least have told his family that he was coming home, but this would have made the moment worse. They would have insisted that he fly and would have been waiting for him at the airport, not knowing what to say. He remembered his Ma talking about how her sister went off to a convent in the 1950s to become a nun and arrived home, with her tail between her legs, after just eighteen months. It had taken weeks for their mother to address her and all she finally said was that 'you would have brought less shame on this family if you'd only had the decency to come home in a wooden box.'

No one became nuns or priests anymore, and nobody in his family would say a word against him, but Shane knew that he had failed himself and failed them. It would come out in whispers, and Sam would be taunted at school. If Shane ever bothered to play on this green again, the tackles would rain in from people who had still been in awe of him this time last year, when he came home with Ray O'Farrell, still a success story to be reckoned him.

He remembered that weekend of his sixteenth birthday: Ray and himself sitting on the garden wall like kings with girls gathered around and Sam shyly sitting between them, basking in his big brother's fame. Ray wasn't somebody he would have palled around with in Ireland. They would probably never have met, except as rival fans at Shelbourne and Cork City matches. Ray was built like a hardman and acted like one too, whereas

Shane was slight and swift and always being told to stay behind in the gym and work on the weights. But because they were both Irish, the club had paired them off when Ray arrived from Cork, switching their digs so they shared a room where they could sink or swim together.

No one over in England knew the difference between Cork and Dublin anyway. Ray and he had needed to endure the same jibes and sly digs. Yet generally people liked the fact that they were Irish. It made them seem novel, expected to be the life and soul of parties, to sing and tell jokes at the drop of a hat. And Ray could do that. Not just pop songs, but ancient come-all-yeah songs from Cork about cider and poitín and women that nobody had ever heard of. Even the driver on the team bus would stop talking to listen and to laugh along.

Indeed, even the pros tolerated Ray, especially the continental ones who loved it when he stood on the sideline of the training ground to give a loud running commentary, mispronouncing their names in a mock BBC accent, before one of the coaching staff chased him away. Nobody else would dare to do it, but nobody else could have got away with it. It was the Cork charm, laid on in thick doses whenever necessary. Ray could have talked his way out of any situation except the sliding tackle that came, two minutes into injury time, during a meaningless match in a deserted stadium in France.

That pre-season tour was just a perk to kick-start their final season together as a youth side, before apprentice contracts were offered to a chosen few at the year's end. The tour consisted of a succession of soft games against soft French kids who might as well have been playing in snowshoes for all the talent they possessed. When Ray got the ball that afternoon he didn't even look around. The team were seven goals up. God knows why the referee was bothering to play injury time. Ray should have laid the ball off first time but delayed for too long, drawing out the moment for effect like he sometimes stretched out the punch-line of a comic song. He never even saw the tackle come from behind: not that it was really a tackle, though – it was more of an assault.

There had been no cameras, no photographers, but Shane didn't need reminders. Every night for the following month he had relived it slowly in his head, the studs thudding in against Ray's knee bone, the leg contorting out of shape and then that snap – a sound like no other – before the blood came and the bone protruded. Ray had started screaming but Shane hadn't really heard him. It was as if that snap had silenced everything else and had kept reverberating inside his skull. The fight that followed had become a free-for all, with even the coaches involved. The kid who had crippled Ray was a puny nobody who had just been told by his club that he was being let go. The French players had defended him with the mob mentality of all footballers, even though Shane could see that they wanted to kill him too. Then suddenly the pitch was cleared, the players bustled back onto the bus and told their clothes would be brought by car to the hotel, while Ray still lay, screaming on the grass, being attended to by medics.

The doctors had needed to operate twice. 'Shag it,' Ray joked when Shane visited him in hospital. 'I went to France hoping for a screw: I didn't expect to come back with three of them permanently in my leg.'

Nobody could say that the club didn't do enough for Ray. He had the best of doctors and physiotherapists: then they flew him back to Cork first class. Anyone can break their leg at any time, but Shane always imagined it happening at Anfield or Highbury, with the crowd rising to you in a blaze of cameras and lights. But a career-ending tackle could come at any moment, even during a meaningless training session of a wet Tuesday afternoon. It affected all the youth players so much in the first few weeks that the coach kept screaming at them 'Are you men or Nancy-boys!' 'Nancy-boys' was his favourite expression, making him seem like a brylcreemed fossil from another era. He had obviously been proving that he was no 'Nancy-boy' when he broke his own leg and subsequently lost his house and his model wife. Gradually, the other lads forgot their fear. But they weren't going back to digs with an empty bed across the room and to Mrs Allen, who broke down in tears on the night Ray left.

'He was the loveliest lad,' she said, 'but I knew he was wasting his time. I've almost stopped taking in your type.'

'What type?' Shane had asked.

Mrs Allen looked at him and stopped speaking, as if realising what she had just said.

'You Irish boys,' Mr Allen answered quietly for her. 'I know the club has a long history of Irish pros playing for it, but they've always been seasoned pros who cut their teeth elsewhere before being bought in. I've seen dozens of young Irish lads go up and down the stairs here or hanging around at the club, but it has been forty years since any Irish lad has made it from bring an apprentice to playing for the first team. Sure, with all the money at stake now, who is going to take a chance on you at that club anyway, unless you are God almighty? The stakes are too high. If a gap appears in the first team they just go across to Europe with a cheque book and buy experience.'

Shane remembered Mr Allen's words as he stepped off the grass now and crossed the road to reach the first terrace of houses on the Crescent. Nobody was up and about yet, but a kid in his pyjamas appeared in the window of McCormack's house to stare down at him. It must be Joey's brother, who had only been a baby when Shane left. Since the age of four Shane had called for Joey McCormack to walk to school together. They were inseparable once, kicking football for hours against the wall in his garden. Every time that Shane came home during his first year with the club, Joey would run over to his house, wanting to know about the dressing rooms, the grounds and training schedules. But in more recent times Joey had become distant, often looking slightly puzzled as to why Shane was calling in to see him. Shane put it down to jealousy at first, but now he realised that it was simple indifference. Life had moved on: Joey had new friends, new interests, a new life. All his old pals were the same. Eddie's famous team had broken up, the better ones playing for Cherry Orchard and Home Farm. Eddie had started from scratch again and was now coaching a bunch of snot-nosed eight-year-olds, giving them his heart and soul.

With Eddie, Shane had always known where he stood. In England, you learned to mull over every remark. Anything of importance was always said out of earshot, behind your back. During these last months, when people from senior management started coming to look at him again, it was utterly different from being twelve and thirteen years old and under Eddie's wing. Now faces from higher up in the club's hierarchy would stop by unannounced to watch the second half of youth games. All the lads on the youth team knew that this was for real – they weren't making a selection, they were plotting a cull. There was nowhere to hide from those merciless, calculating eyes. The mood among the lads was different now, with everyone watching everyone else, aware that not even a handful would survive the cut.

Before the pre-season trip to France, Shane never doubted that he would be offered a contract. Maybe one or two other youth players had more skill, but they were headless chickens, not so much without discipline as without brains. He had overcome homesickness so bad that on many nights he had packed his bags for a cheap coach to Ireland. He had put on enough weight and shown enough strength of character and leadership to be allowed to wear the captain's armband. But now, when it really mattered, he found himself chickening out of challenges. Not so blatantly that an ordinary spectator might notice, but holding back just enough for the experienced eyes on the touchline to notice and for other players to sense his fear and exploit it.

Nobody had questioned his courage before. He had stitches above his eye and had broken three ribs in his first year. But every night he woke in a sweat, after hearing the snap of bone and the sickening silence before Ray's scream. No Irish player had made it in the club in forty years, so why the hell did the scouts keep calling to parents with their promises? He could be sitting his leaving certificate exams in Dublin now, walking to school still with Joey, eyeing up the girls, maybe playing for the B side of a League of Ireland club, with his Da quietly watching the matches from the empty stand.

Instead, he was out of sight and out of mind. On one occasion he had made it onto the panel for the Irish Under-16 team. His mother phoned to say that a neighbour had just seen it on the Teletext. The FAI put in a call to the club, but then some kid on the books of Huddersfield Town had recovered from injury and regained his place. Huddersfield Town? That Irish team had gone on to win the Under-16 European Championship: the final shown live on Irish television. They came home as heroes, like Jack Charlton's teams, a big crowd at the airport, an open-topped bus and everything. Half of them were on the books of Mickey Mouse teams, down in the lower divisions or back in Ireland. For some reason his mother had sent him the press cuttings about their homecoming. Da would have known never to do that.

This was his homecoming and he knew that he would never go back to that stadium, even as a spectator. He would never return to the meat factory of that famous football club, which worked like a mincing machine. You were officially a player: you had your swipecard. You walked along the plush carpets, ate the best of food in the canteen, had doctors attend to your every ailment and bruise and yet, in reality, you were nobody. A face in the corridor leading to the dressing-rooms whose absence would go unnoticed when you got the call to the manager's office. Shane had seen it too often already: lads of seventeen and eighteen sitting alone in the empty stand, crying their eyes out. The way that people passing by averted their eyes until a groundsman was sent up into the stands to quietly tell them it was time to go, because some starry-eyed fourteen-year-old was due to be shown around the stadium with his parents.

During the last four games of the season Shane had bottled it altogether. It felt as if his body was filled with lead. He had worn himself out during the opening ten minutes, so frantic to make up for lost time that he didn't properly pace himself. During each match he was substituted, sitting apart from the others on the bench, noticing how the coach had stopped offering him encouragement or advice. The other lads on the bench said nothing to him either: with Shane dropping out of the frame there might be an unexpected chance of a contract for some other one of them.

Shane wasn't just coming home this morning, he was running away. He told himself that at least he was doing so in his own way, saving himself from the indignity of being called into the manager's office. Almost the entire youth team would endure this fate over the coming days, with only two of them at most remaining on for another season. His ex-teammates still all wanted to believe that it was going to be them, because they were afraid of the emptiness that would face them once they walked out of that office, with their swipe cards cancelled, their names already forgotten.

He didn't know if he would bother ever playing football again. Because even if one day he got signed by Shelbourne in the League of Ireland, as Eddie had suggested years ago, he would never be known as the kid who was good enough to play for Shelbourne. Instead, he would always be the kid who came home from England, the kid who was only good enough to play for Shelbourne: the boy with the golden touch and a glistening future already behind him.

Shane stopped at the gate to his family house. There seemed to be nobody up yet or at least no light on in the hall. His Da's old Sunny was parked in the narrow driveway he had built in the front garden. A burst football lay there that Sam must have been kicking around. A wooden gate blocked off the side passageway, but Shane knew that if you reached your hand over it you could open the bolt on the far side.

The dog came down by the side passageway to greet him, not bounding but moving slowly, his leg stiffened by arthritis. At least he didn't bark as if at an intruder. Shane dropped his bag and knelt to put his arms around the dog. The old dog panted after the effort of just taking those few steps, but his eyes had the same look as always, as if slightly puzzled by life.

Once Shane stood up from embracing the dog he knew that he would have to face them all: Da, Ma, Sam and Marie. To face the cramped kitchen that seemed to get smaller with every visit home; the small bedroom that he would now share with the younger brother who didn't really know him, after three years away. He patted the dog one last time and rose. There was a light on in the kitchen. He knew that his Da would be up before any of the family, starting the breakfast, ready to call up the stairs.

His Da turned as Shane pushed open the kitchen door. He had a fish-slice in his hand and was frying rashers. He eyed his son's travel bag.

'It's yourself,' was all he said. 'Would you go a rasher?'

Only twice in his life had Shane ever seen his Da lose his temper. That unflappable quality, the way you never quite knew what he was thinking, used to annoy Shane. Even when Shane signed youth forms for the club his Da had refused to get over excited. But now Shane was thankful for the lack of questioning, for the way his Da was buying him time.

'I wouldn't mind a rasher,' he said, 'and a few sausages. I'm starving.'

Shane sat down at the table. Not even the mugs had changed in three years. He had missed this house so much. Yet now it didn't seem like his home. How would he ever fit back here? His father was cooking away, making as little noise as possible.

'I got sent home,' Shane explained. 'They don't think I've got the bottle. They're not going to offer me a contract.'

'The Club should have phoned,' his Da said. 'It shouldn't be you having to tell us like this.'

'It's not official till Friday. I just didn't want to wait around and have everybody looking at me with pity. It's hard enough without the whole world knowing that you've failed.'

'Failed?' Shane saw that his Da's hand was shaking as he put the rasher and some black pudding on a plate. The man turned. His eyes were clear and blue, staring directly at him.

'Son, you're eighteen years old, so stop talking bollix. Is Eddie a failure, the way folk around here respect him? Am I a failure, the way I have raised the lot of you? You're no failure, son. You haven't even started living your life yet.'

John Boyne

John Boyne was born in Dublin in 1971. He is the author of 7 novels, including *The House of Special Purpose* and *The Absolutist*. He has also published 3 novels for younger readers, including *The Terrible Thing That Happened To Barnaby Brocket* and *The Boy In The Striped Pyjamas*, which won two Irish Book Awards, the Bisto Book of the Year Award, topped the New York Times Bestseller List and was made into an award-winning Miramax feature film. He has published over 70 short stories. His novels are published in 44 languages.

Like Charlie

He loved his father and he loved his mother but was afraid of them both. He didn't care for numbers but treasured words. He felt awkward when he was surrounded by people, preferring to be left alone whenever possible. Instinctively, he ran from moments of violence and towards the possibility of an embrace. He never cared for sports, had no abilities with bat or ball, but kept his books in pristine condition and could find the one he needed at a moment's notice. He hated the tall, beech-surrounded brownstone on Manhattan's Upper West Side that his family called home, was terrified by the crowds that pushed past him when he made his way towards the open spaces of Central Park, but felt safe in the quiet Essex Green cottage on Nantucket Island where they spent their vacations. He was happy when his parents left him alone for the day with only the housekeeper for company; he felt sick whenever they announced that they were hosting a party.

He was ten years old – he; Nick Dartie, that is – when his father, Lewis Dartie, took him on board his yacht, the *United States Constitution*, for a morning's sailing. They were at their leisure and were to cruise northwards from Great Point towards Monomoy Island, then tack for Oak Bluffs on Martha's Vineyard, where they had an appointment for lunch with Jimmy Cox, who was running on the Democratic ticket for president. It was 1920. The election was more than three months away but the talk was that if Cox won, there would be a job in it for Lewis.

'Lose the shoes, boy,' said Lewis as they sailed out that morning, clicking his fingers and pointing in the direction of his son's feet. 'Why in God's name are you wearing them monk-straps anyway? Don't you know you only wear deck shoes on board?'

'I forgot,' said Nick, staying as close to the centre of the deck as he could so he wouldn't have to look over the sides, where the waves were crashing against the gunwales. There'd been an incident a year or two before. A boy at school who drowned at sea. It had put him off.

'Get rid of them,' barked Lewis. 'You scratch my deck with those things and I swear you won't sit for a week.'

Nick took off his shoes carefully and placed them, side by side, beneath one of the cushioned seats that lined either side of the bow. He hadn't brought any deck shoes with him so he took his socks off and decided to stay barefoot. He could do very little damage barefoot. He glanced at his toes and touched the dark bruise along his left arch where his older brother, Charlie, had stood on him the day before. He was wearing hiking boots and pressed his foot down on the boy slowly, slowly, waiting to see how much pain his brother could take before he started to cry. It didn't take long. Nick had learned a long time ago that the quicker he cried, the sooner Charlie would leave him alone. But still, his foot hurt something awful. He'd read somewhere that the human foot contained over two dozen tiny bones and he wondered how many of them Charlie had managed to snap. *An accident*, Charlie said, marching on, laughing. *Your own fault for being in the way.* When he pressed on the bruise now a dark purple circle appeared in the centre, like a twist of lava at the base of a volcano.

'Winds are good this morning,' said Lewis.

'Yes, sir,' said Nick.

'What?' he asked, looking at the boy irritably.

'I said yes, sir. The winds are good.'

Lewis considered this for a moment, nodded and looked away. He hadn't been talking to the boy, of course. Hadn't even realised that he'd said what he'd said out loud. He hadn't wanted Nick to come with him that morning. It was Charlie he'd asked. Charlie, who at thirteen years of age looked like a junior version of Lewis himself and was already shaving. Charlie, who'd scored three touchdowns to beat the Cincinnati Juniors at the inter-school play-offs only a few days before. Charlie, who was everything his younger brother wasn't. But Charlie, good ol' Charlie, had taken ill during the night and was throwing his guts up at six in the morning and when Annabel arrived up from the guesthouse – Annabel, the boys' mother, who lived down there for reasons unknown to her younger son – she had said, why don't you take Nick instead and God knows why, but in a moment of weakness Lewis had said, well alright then.

'Jesus, will you take a look at that?' he said, turning to his left and shaking his head, which made Nick glance in the same direction to where a small fishing boat was resting in the water with two people on board, an old man with a small boy, most likely his grandson, a kid only a little older than himself. Seeing the boy made Nick press backwards in his seat, afraid of being noticed, nervous of being drawn into conversation, even at this distance. The boy might shout out a greeting; a response might be required. That same sensation he felt at school, when he walked along a pathway and just knew that a ball would fall out of play and head in his direction and that he'd be the only one there to answer the cries of 'Hey – throw us our ball back, won't ya?' Awful moments. Balls picked up. Kicked with care but sent a mile wide. Thrown with caution but landing in a tree. Everything he did leading to the groans of his classmates, the expressions of contempt, a punch in the arm or a kick on the seat of his pants.

Charlie never made mistakes like that. Charlie could kick a clean thirty-yard field goal with his eyes closed.

'What a pair of jackasses,' said Lewis, talking directly to the boy now as he pointed at the vessel. 'Look, fishing rods, no less. Getting in the way, that's all they're doing.' He reached across to a large red button on the steering column and pressed it, holding his thumb there for half a minute while the horn sounded deep and aggressive. The pair in the boat jumped and turned in his direction, surprised for a moment, then offered a friendly wave. *See that yacht*, Nick could imagine the old man saying to the boy. *If my numbers had come up just once in my life, I could have had a boat like that too.*

'Pair of jackasses,' repeated Lewis, seeing how they had mistaken his irritation for friendliness. 'Serve them right if I tipped them over.'

Nick stepped away and sat down again, reaching into the satchel he'd brought with him for his copy of *A Connecticut Yankee In King Arthur's Court*. He'd been reading books since he was four. He liked the image on the jacket; the dragon-vested knight on the left, the knickerbockered Yankee on the right, the line they were crossing together. He pressed both hands to his ears to block out the sound of the waves but that was no good when he wanted to open the book. He turned to where his page-holder rested and picked up the story at the point where Hank Morgan had become The Boss. Before reading, he turned back to the title page and ran his finger along the dark black lettering where the author himself had inscribed the book.

Nick didn't know how his father had known the writer, there were fifty years between them after all, but he'd heard a rumour about a newspaper story that his father had held back, something to do with a group of girls called the Angel Club that the dead writer had squired around town. And Lewis had gone to 'Old Brick' for the funeral, taking Charlie with him, even though his older brother had never read a word of a story in his life and reserved his eyes for the funny papers and the sports column.

'Quit it,' said Lewis, plucking the book from his son's hand and tossing it across the deck where it landed, perfectly centred, on top of his own jacket. Had he aimed, he never would have made the shot.

'Sir!' said Nick, looking up, shielding his eyes. The sun glaring down already. No hat either; he'd forgotten his hat in the rush to leave.

'You're here to sail, not to read.'

'Just one chapter,' he pleaded.

'No,' said Lewis, stepping back towards the wheel, his feet barely touching the deck. For a big man, he moved as easily as Bojangles Robinson ('A *negro*?' Lewis had said when someone told him this once. 'You're comparing me to a *negro*?') He put his hat on, the one that said *Captain*, the one the boy knew better than to touch.

Nick sighed and looked ahead. He touched his stomach. Hungry now. No breakfast. He narrowed his eyes and stared down the horizon but Monomoy wasn't visible yet. Later, he knew, they would make full circle in return, passing the stubby isles of Muskeget, where only rats and seals resided, and Tuckernuck, that loaf of bread in the heart of Nantucket Sound. There wasn't a cloud in the sky.

The boy looked around and thought of a way that he could make his father like him just a little bit.

'Sir,' he said.

'Whadya want?'

'Let me take the wheel?'

Lewis frowned and stared at the boy, as if he was only now realising how frustrating it was to have brought the kid along with him. He'd said before that the boy needed to learn how to handle the boat, that he was old enough to know, and why didn't he show any interest, Goddamit. But he'd said that indoors. When they were on the boat he didn't like anyone to touch his precious mechanisms. Except maybe Charlie. Charlie could do what he wanted.

'No,' said Lewis.

'But sir, you said you were going to teach me.'

'You're not ready,' said Lewis, harsher now. 'And listen, you better keep that big trap of yours zipped when we meet Mr Cox, you hear me? Don't keep asking stupid questions. You can read your book then if you want.'

Nick stood up and walked forward carefully on the balls of his bare feet. He couldn't sail, he couldn't read, he couldn't walk with his shoes on. What was he supposed to do then? His eyes focussed on the bowsprit that tapered into a white-nosed needle before him. Someone had once taken a great deal of care to carve and buff a stretch of Douglas Fir into this spike, he thought, and despite how much he hated being out here, he knew that it was deserving of his admiration. A piece of craftsmanship as beautiful and eternal as a poem. He thought he might be able to put some words together about it, something he could write in his journal.

If he showed a little passion for the boat, then maybe his father would show a little tenderness towards him. It might please the old man, after all, to hear his son taking an interest in such masculine pursuits as carpentry and nautical engineering. The kind of things that Charlie knew everything about. Impossible, of course. To describe the confidence of the shipbuilding would take sentences, and every noun would be complemented by a suitable adjective, and there was nothing his father despised more than suitable adjectives. He hated when his son dressed things up in colourful language, even more so when he described anything as beautiful. Only women are beautiful, Lewis had told him once. Boats are fine.

Still, it was worth a try.

'What are you staring at?'

Lewis had come up behind him now and was looking at the bowsprit too. Nick turned around for a moment, glanced at the wheel, wondered whether it was safe to leave it to its own devices.

'That,' he said, pointing.

'What?'

'That,' he repeated. 'The bowsprit.'

'Well what about it?' asked Lewis, impressed, despite himself, that the boy knew what to call it.

'It's beautiful,' he said, forgetting for a moment that he wasn't supposed to use that word. In an instant, Lewis struck him, sending his small body crashing across the boat in surprise. The slap had come out of nowhere; he could feel a narrow line of blood opening above his eye as he lay on the cold, water-spattered deck. In sympathy, the bruise on his foot began to throb.

He was close to the side now, almost hanging over it. A dolphin was passing by, alone, separated from his school. His skin was like oil. Nick wanted to touch it. He thought it would be a fine idea to dive into the ocean and befriend a dolphin. He could find a place between fin and blowhole to serve as transport, press his thighs into the oleaginous flesh and swim away to an island someplace. A deserted island. A place no one else could ever reach.

'That dolphin is beautiful too,' he said, turning to look up at his father, not knowing what possessed him to make such a provocative remark.

'This is your mother's fault,' muttered Lewis, walking away as if from a stinking tramp on the street and taking up his position behind the wheel once again, turning the boat a little towards port, a touch back starboard, raising her, dropping her, settling her, guiding her straight ahead. He ignored the boy on the deck, who didn't seem like much of a boy at all. Least not as he understood the term. He tried to pretend he wasn't there. That Charlie was, instead.

Nick rolled over and lay on his back, wondering how long it would be before his father roared at him to get up and stop laying round like an indolent. He might let him read his book then. His eyes turned away from the sea and he looked directly up into the heavens. Not even a bird in sight, despite how close they were to land.

He wondered how much provocation it would take to make his father kill him. If he murdered him out here, where no one could see, he'd probably toss the boy overboard, leave him to the fish, then sail back to land and tell them about the terrible accident that had taken place out at sea. And no one would doubt him.

He reached down and unbuckled his belt, letting the two ends fall to either side of his waist before opening the top button on his trousers, then the second, then the third, and placed his hand inside, letting it rest there, closing his eyes, counting slowly in his head, wondering what number he might get to before Lewis noticed.

Seventeen.

'What's the matter with you?' shouted Lewis, dragging him to his feet and pushing him against the railing. He leaned close in and the boy could smell nicotine and whiskey on his breath, despite the hour. His teeth were yellow. A stalagmite of saliva stretched taut between his two lips.

'What's the matter with you anyway?' he roared, shaking the boy violently, shaking him with so much force that Nick allowed a strange sound, something like *huuuurgh* to escape his lips in a voice that sounded barely human and when he did, Lewis let go and stepped back as if he was in danger of contamination. The boy fell to the deck and giggled.

'You're like a … you're like an animal,' said Lewis. 'What's the matter with you anyway?' he repeated. 'Why can't you be more like Charlie?'

Nick stood up now, buttoned his pants, tied his belt. He smiled at his father and walked over to him, the old man staring at the boy as if he was almost afraid of what might happen next, and when he was standing next to him, he pulled his right foot up, balanced himself on his bruised left, then let his heel descend as hard as he could on his father's, a sound of something snapping making itself heard over the sound of the waves as his father cried out and fell over.

'An accident,' said Nick quietly, walking away. 'I didn't see you there.'

Declan Burke

Declan Burke is the author of *Eightball Boogie* (2003), *The Big O* (2007), and *Absolute Zero Cool* (2011). He is the editor of *Down These Green Streets: Irish Crime Writing in the 21ˢᵗ Century* (Liberties Press, 2011), and hosts a website dedicated to Irish crime fiction called *Crime Always Pays*. His latest novel is *Slaughter's Hound* (2012). He lives in Wicklow with his wife and daughter, where he is not allowed to own a cat, or be owned by one.

Samuel, Oh Samuel

For such a big man Andy had comically small hands. Women would lay their palms against his to compare, and giggle. As a young man he had been embarrassed and occasionally ashamed, but that had been before he discovered that small hands were to be preferred to large ones, especially when a job required dextrous precision in confined spaces, as his jobs usually did. And even though he was now married to Angela, with two daughters old enough to go to school, Andy still didn't know too much about how women thought, or the real reasons behind the things they said and did. But he had a fair idea the giggling had little to do with the smallness of his hands and quite a lot to do with the primitive delight women take in sharing an intimate space with a man of impressive stature. When they pressed their palms to his, Andy thought, they were seeking a connection through the very pores of his skin, a current that resonated back up through the sinew and muscle of his genetic swirl to a time when size was all and the female gravitated towards the biggest, the hairiest, the most likely to lead on and reach for the moon. When they pressed their soft palms to his callused pads, Andy thought, they sought to equalise his vast bulk with their petite civilisation.

The men, of course, had been less gentle. On the building sites where Andy had apprenticed his trade, the men had been coarse in their ridicule, vulgar in their comparisons between the size of hands and that of his manhood. But building site banter is as cheap as talk gets, and Andy had quietly proved the worth of small hands. The baiting had ended long before he graduated. Even the hoddies came to appreciate the excellence of his craft, a craft in which the art must be invisible to succeed. But Andy knew there was more to it than small hands, as deft and meticulous as they were. He had his secrets, as all artists do, one of which was working with Angela at his shoulder, her half-sensed presence urging him on to higher standards, more subtle methods of deceiving and pleasing her critical eye.

He knew too that the real secret lay in his love of the material, the way the sculptor must love marble or the painter his oils. He heard in his soul the scream of grain ripping, and it was only in the agony of tearing it apart that he found the inspiration to repay the wood's sacrifice, to reshape its form into more than it had been. He was personable, too, in the way of all gentle giants, those rare lucky men who have nothing to prove. His clients found him easy-going and professionally eager to please, and he was as busy as all good carpenters have been ever since Adam felled the first tree.

But if Andy was a big man, Frank was a bear. Huge and bearded, he had no choice but to swagger, and when they shook hands on the price Andy's dissolved in Frank's paw. Frank being Frank, he passed no comment on Andy's hands. He had a deep rumbling laugh and found many things funny, and his size was such that he had no need to ridicule others. Smaller men took advantage, knowing that Frank would not retaliate, but Andy came to realise that these distractions were but drops of sweat upon the shoulders of Atlas as Frank strained beneath the half-grasped burden of his impossible world.

It was a big job, although it had started small, as most of Andy's jobs began – a relatively simple job of refitting the ensuite of the master bedroom. Two or three days in, impressed by Andy's attention to detail, Frank had begun talking up the kitchen, and he mentioned that she had often suggested a hardwood floor for the hall.

'How long, d'ye think, would that take?' Frank said. They were drinking coffee in the kitchen, Andy smoking.

'Depends on how well you want it done,' Andy said.

'Fair enough,' Frank said. 'How well done would two weeks get me?'

'Good as I can get it,' Andy said.

'Good enough for me,' Frank said. They discussed a new price, how much Frank wanted to pay for materials.

'Money's no object,' Frank said. 'Do it right or don't do it at all.' He looked down into his mug, swirled his coffee. 'It'll be nice for her to come home to a new kitchen,' he said. 'Every woman likes a nice kitchen.'

Andy stubbed his cigarette, drank off the last of his coffee. 'That's good coffee,' he said.

'Don't be waiting for me to offer,' Frank said. 'And you know where the fridge is.'

What Frank was saying, Andy knew, was that Frank had more important things to worry about than Andy's coffee. Andy went back to work and wondered about how it might feel to be anticipating Angela's release in two weeks time, until the problem of the awkward corner coving finally claimed his attention.

Every day, Frank found another little something that could be improved, or updated, or refurbished entirely. Andy, anxious that the work be completed before she got home, found himself working longer and longer hours, arriving home tired and hungry long after the girls had gone to bed. But it was only on the afternoon that Frank went to pick her up that Andy realised Frank wanted Andy to be there when they returned. It was as if, Andy thought, the surprise wouldn't be enough in itself; Frank wanted the magician to explain his illusions.

Andy had planned to retire to the kitchen when he heard the car returning, to put on the kettle and be out of sight when they came through the front door. But the new banister was proving tricky and Andy was staring up into the difficult corner, absorbed, when he heard the key turn in the door. Frank stood back to allow her through first and she stepped into the new hallway, smiling. Frank picked up the other suitcase, stepped inside, and closed the door gently with his heel.

'You must be Andy,' she murmured. She seemed to glide forward, right hand outstretched to shake, the left arm across her chest, its hand resting on her right bicep. 'Frank has told me so much about you.'

'All lies,' Andy said, taking her hand. It had the feathery lightness of a sparrow's wing. She was small, dwarfed by the awkward loom of Frank behind her. Andy imagined them leaving the hospital, Frank carrying the suitcases with his wife tucked under one oxter.

'Well,' she said, looking up and around, 'he was telling the truth about your work anyway.'

Praise had always embarrassed Andy. 'I'll get the kettle on,' he said. 'Anyone for a coffee?'

'That'd be lovely,' she said.

'I'll just drop these upstairs,' Frank said, hefting the suit-cases as if they were a pair of packed lunches. 'Then we'll take the grand tour.'

He took the stairs two at a time. Andy steeled himself to look into her eyes but her gaze had wandered away. She was smoothing the banister with her right hand, her left arm still held protectively across her body.

'You've done a beautiful job,' she murmured. 'It's almost like a whole new home.' She smiled up at him then, sadly. 'A fresh start,' she said.

'It's just a few bits and pieces,' he said. 'It's amazing what a little varnish will do.'

'Isn't it just?'

Frank lumbered back downstairs again, rubbing his vast paws together. 'So where will we start?' he boomed.

'The kitchen,' she murmured, drifting past Andy. 'It's two months since I've had a proper coffee.'

It was warm in the kitchen. They sat around the table and sipped coffee while she admired the gleaming new fittings.

'Is that counter real granite?' she murmured.

'Certainly is,' Frank said. 'Money no object. Isn't that what I said, Andy?'

Andy nodded. 'I got a good deal on it,' he said.

'It looks beautiful,' she said.

'That's granite for you,' Frank boomed. 'Engineered by nature to outlast us all.'

Andy watched her over the rim of his mug, trying to spot the signs, but she wore her sleeves long and her eyes were heavily made up. Frank drained his coffee noisily and stood.

'Will we have a look at upstairs so?' he said.

She nodded, scraped her chair back, and rose still clutching the mug of coffee. Frank led on, Andy trailing behind like Pharaoh's architect.

She tired quickly and decided to take a nap. Andy told Frank that he thought he should leave, rather than work on and perhaps disturb her sleep. Frank disagreed, and finally convinced him that it would be more appropriate, more normal, if Andy were still around when she emerged again.

'Just don't do anything heavy,' he said. 'Nothing noisy. Is there anything like that you could be doing?'

'Well,' Andy said, reluctant, 'there's the banister. I need to work out how to get it flush at the return with …'

'That'll do,' Frank said. 'Good man yourself.'

She caught him unawares, only a few minutes later, hunkered on the stair's turn as he frowned into the corner. He stood and squeezed back to the wall to allow her to pass. She stopped at the bottom of the stairs and looked back up at him.

'You know,' she said, 'that really is a beautiful job you've done on the en-suite. I hope you're charging him enough.'

'Oh, he's looking after me,' Andy said.

She smiled, wan as a crescent moon. 'That's what he does best,' she murmured. 'Would you like another coffee?'

'No, I'm fine, thanks all the same.'

She didn't speak on the way back up again, eyes on her feet and each careful step, clutching the mug of coffee in both hands. From the return Andy watched her glide away down the hallway towards her room.

When Andy encountered a problem, a tricky little opportunity to stretch himself, he could be obsessive. So he wasn't sure, when he first heard her call, how long it had been since her door had closed. Nor was he sure that it was the first time she had called, and though her voice sounded clearly, it was too weak to allow the words carry very far. So he stepped up into the upstairs hallway and cocked his head towards her door.

He heard her again, faint but clear, like Samuel hearing the voice of God.

'Frank? Oh, Frank.'

There was no mistaking the resignation in her tone. Andy took the stairs in three bounds and charged down the hallway towards the kitchen and the study beyond.

'Frank? FRANK!'

Frank bolted out of the study, eyes frantic, and crashed into Andy's shoulder as he barged past. The force of the blow knocked Andy sprawling across the kitchen table, and he was still righting himself when he heard Frank rattle the bedroom doorknob. He rushed out into the hallway and again took the stairs three at a time. When he turned into the upstairs hallway he found Frank crouched at the keyhole.

'Just open the door,' he was crooning. 'Roisin, love? Can you open the door?'

Andy hung back, sharply aware that his presence was an insult to their intimacy, but anxious that he would not be found wanting if required. And tense as he was, hulked in the hallway with his hands bunched into fists, he could not prevent himself from wondering at how she had called out to Frank only after ensuring that he could not reach her to help.

'Roisin? Love? Can you come to the door?'

An image of he and Frank hunkering down before the door to build a wooden horse flashed through Andy's mind, but he had the composure to identify this as a wayward thought designed by the mind to distract him from his helplessness.

Then Frank stood, backed up a step, took a deep breath and shoulder-charged the door. And it was only in the scream of splintering wood that Andy heard how bad it would be.

But it was not only bad, this new infidelity to the promise of they, it was bloody. Frank staunched the wounds with practiced ease, all the while crooning meaningless comforts. He wrapped her in a white cotton bathrobe and hustled her downstairs, and the sleeves were stained before they made the hall. Andy opened the front door. She was barefoot, so Frank swept her up into his arms.

'The kids'll be home from school soon,' he said. Her head lolled against his chest, the lips alabaster. She was quietly weeping, berating herself and the hurt she was causing Frank, but he only shushed her without looking away from Andy. 'Would you mind hanging on until they get in?'

'No, of course not. You go on. I'll stay.'

'I'll ring and get my mother around. She'll take over from there.'

'Go on ahead, Frank,' Andy urged. 'Don't worry about here. We'll be sound.'

He watched until the car turned out of the quiet cul-de-sac and then he closed the front door. He stood in the hall for a while, shaking, and then went back upstairs to examine the damage. He thought that he could effect some temporary repairs, plane down the worst of the splintering, and it was while he was planing that he found himself wondering at the splinters that must jag at the inside of Roisin's brittle frame. He felt Angela's invisible presence, her critical eye directed not at his work but at his ability, or otherwise, to help. Because this is what a man does, Andy thought, as he nailed a makeshift brace across two shattered panels. He helps, or tries to.

He heard the car draw up outside and for a split-second's surging thought they had quickly returned. But it was only the kids being dropped off. They clattered down the hallway past Andy, swinging their schoolbags. The babble tailed off, and when they emerged from the kitchen again they wore apprehensive expressions.

'Where's Mum?' the oldest asked, and his high voice quavered. 'Is she in bed? Should we be quiet?'

Andy only shook his head. He stood at the front door that he had yet to close, looking down the hallway towards their sorry, instinctive bunching. The polished hardwood gleamed, blinding. He closed his eyes and realised what the children already knew, that the harshest lessons are easiest learned.

'Do you know your granny's phone number?' he said.

John Butler

John Butler's debut novel *The Tenderloin* was published by Picador in 2011 and was short-listed at the Irish Book Awards. He directed and co-wrote the IFTA award winning sketch show *Your Bad Self* for RTE, and his short story *First & First* was short-listed for the 2011 Francis McManus Award.

The Fir Tree

Which would you prefer; not to know the way out of a maze, or not to know that you're lost inside one? To be honest, Bun couldn't see the difference. By now he was pretty sure he hated Danny, and Danny derived an almost equal amount of joy from the weekly meeting with his life-long friend Bun. Whichever of the two made it first to the pub up by the park on Sunday would order a pint and, watching it settle, offer a silent prayer that tonight, for once, the lounge doors would not swing open and the other one would not materialise. And each, if they were the late one, would say the prayer from outside. An exquisite bind. Danny was barred from the only other pub around, this place was right across the park from Bun, and neither would concede Sunday scoops to the other, so instead, both chose to have them ruined. The Fir Tree became disputed territory. In fairness, what could they have done – talked about it?

First in tonight? Bun; one slender leg draped across the other, hunched defensively into himself at the bar. He was thinking about Hansel and Gretel. Earlier, after plenty of wine over at his sister's, he read the story to his niece as she dozed in bed, for the first time ignoring the plight of the children at the heart of it and thinking instead of the woodcutter and his wife – we've all got to eat. Creeping back downstairs after putting out the light, he had to wonder if he wanted to be a parent – not if he would be a parent, but if he wanted it – and he had to wonder that because he genuinely couldn't tell. Not unusual for him, that.

The night before, on a hopeless monthly foray into town, his friend Ciara had asked him if he was okay while he was dancing at a gig. Was he okay? He had no idea. Had he been dancing sadly?

Bun spun the cold blackness slowly, wiping condensation off the rim. Not talking was what he wanted from a Sunday night – not talking about the things that matter. At the core of him lay the business with Jenny, and he wouldn't tell anyone because people would never believe him, because really, there was nothing to it. Four-odd years ago during the maelstrom of late 20s life, Bun had gone out with Jenny King, a friend of Danny's, for under three months. She dumped him on Easter Sunday, her only explanation being that 'he didn't know how to love'. Okay, he was a slow starter, but he thought he had been getting better. Clearly not. That was that, or that should have been that, but wasn't, in fact, that at all. Thereafter, internet evidence of Jenny's continuing beauty gave light to the dark flower of an obsession. Bun never slept with another girl, and within months he was hopelessly addicted to her absence from his life. The previous Tuesday afternoon wasn't the first time he had spent the afternoon watching her at the pharmacy, from behind a wheelie bin outside.

The lounge doors swung open, Bun saw Danny beetle over and was reminded by his stocky, frank approach to stop this line of Jenny-thought immediately and never to think about telling him, because Danny just wasn't that kind of guy. Danny hopped up onto the stool and motioned to the barman for one just like Bun's. He would think Bun was mad because he was mad, probably. He rubbed his hands, looking behind him.

Tonight he seemed excited about something new, but protocol was all and Bun would never ask him. Bun remembered how, as a boy, Danny used to walk four miles to Church every morning over in Templeogue, before walking back to school, which was another three miles in another direction. Every morning, on his own, unprompted. Danny was a good boy then. Very probably he still was, with the exception of a few moments Bun had only heard about. What did Bun know?

The barman returned with his pint and Danny drained the first third in a mouthful. Bun watched him lick his lips and sit for a minute savouring; then, from his pocket, he produced a thick, beige envelope with his own name and address calligraphed across the front in a medieval font. He smiled at Bun, then slid it under his nose, patting it with his thick mitt.

– Any plans for July? Thought we could take Sunday Scoops on the road …

Bun looked down his nose at the envelope. Danny rubbed his hands in glee.

– What's that?

– Remember Jenny from the chemist? She's only getting married. Spain.

The permanent thickness of the paper, the indelible ink; Bun could feel his hands beginning to shake. He gripped the pint glass harder. Frozen, he stared at the taps in front of him. He needed to say something to keep the thing going.

– Who?

Danny looked at him, an eyebrow raised in mirth.

– 'Who'?! Your Jenny, from years ago. Have you not got yours yet? You are getting one.

Danny leaned across, feigning weariness. He opened the envelope, clearing his voice.

– Okeydoke. Jeremy & Angela Keaveney request the presence of … Daniel (here, Danny pointed at himself) at the marriage of their daughter Jenny, to Gavin Little, in the San Roque golf club, Marbella, on the 19th June, 2004. Then, Rsvp etc.

– Does it actually say 'etc'? After 'rsvp'?

Danny looked at Bun, only briefly wondering if his question was serious, then set the invite down and just sat there, as if scolded. You see, Bun was pale now, his head dropped right down between his knees, his hand still gripping the pint high above him on the counter. Danny thought he looked like a statue, kind of. He took a long drink of his pint, confused, and said nothing, waiting for whatever was going on with Bun to pass. When he heard heavy breathing from below he began to hope this was asthma, then heard sobs. He put out a hand to pat his friend on the back, but left it suspended. There they remained, Bun heaving, Danny with a hand poised above him, until finally, from beneath, a tiny voice buried beneath sobs.

– She's killed me, Dan.

He's had a few earlier, Danny thought. He's way ahead, the sneaky pre-gaming bastard.

Outside at kicking-out time and Monday's rain whipped across the car park in sheets, reminding patrons about what lay beyond and was inevitable.

Under the canopy of the smoking section Danny swayed and tried to focus, then flung a broken lighter into the night. After Bun had returned from the toilet with red-eyed apologies, they really went to town. Not much in the way of talk, just shorts with pints, a round of tequila, a caution for singing 'A pair of brown eyes', and for Danny, a heavy backwards fall off the stool at around the 10.30 mark. Bun didn't really mention the whole online stalking thing at all, and Danny did most of the talking, developing this big theory about moral compasses – what was right and what was wrong. Jenny's compass was broken, he said. Jenny was a bad person. Jenny was a cow. Danny was very moral. He grew drunker and angrier, starting to denounce her in such strong terms that Bun found himself laying a hand on his friend's shoulder and telling him to relax and that he was worried about him – which was true, but which Bun would never have said if it didn't make him feel much better.

Now, Bun watched Danny stand precariously on a seat holding his cigarette up to the heat-lamp, scorching the hair off his fingers then taking it back and coaxing the burnt end into life with a frowning suck.

– Here, I've a light if you wait two seconds.

– She's lit …

Danny jumped down with a sideways crash into a chair, and when he righted himself, the two men smoked and watched people run across the car park in two's, pointing clickers, flashing alarm lights, slamming doors, crunch of gravel.

– I'm … taxi.

Danny dug his hands in his pockets, eyes scrunched against the cigarette smoke, swaying still. He pulled out four euro. Bun felt in his pockets for show but he knew he was broke; for accounting purposes he always spent every penny in the pub. Seeing this, Danny lurched over towards the driver who must have been fifty-five, sheltering under the awning of a shop across the road, smoking a cigarette of his own. He and Danny lived in opposite directions, but Bun followed him over.

– Filthy night.

Danny had started brightly, but Bun could hear the booze. The driver wore a cardigan and slippers, and pushed off the wall with a sigh, as if it wasn't his job to drive people around.

– Where to?

– In … Lakelands. How much is … Lakelands … to go?

– How much have you got, son?

– … Four euro? But the night that's in it … swing me home?

– You joking?! Sit into the car and you're on four euro, sure. Good luck.

The driver raised a brow, leaning against the doorframe protectively, smirking. Typical Dublin taxi driver, Bun thought. Chippy cunt.

– Okay pal … grand. Relax? Deliberately asked … before, yeah?

Standing in the rain, Danny showed the driver his palms.

– And that's why I told you before you got in, bud.

– Yeah I know that, but I asked … before running me over … I could have done that first … I didn't? So just …

Had it been twenty years ago, Bun thought, Danny would have jumped in your cab without a thought, and would have done a legger at the other end, and even twenty years ago, you wouldn't have caught him. That's what he's trying to say. Can't you hear that? Can't you tell he's trying to be good?

– You alright, bud?

– I'm fine 'bud'. Just … fucking prick … asking … be so rude, yeah?

– Listen, you're not sounding too clever. Walk it off, yeah?

– Yeah … will do …

Danny muttered it, looking down, and Bun knew he was gone long before Danny made a tight fist and drove it upwards, the hook landing right on the driver's face as if in slow motion. He's far too old to be punched, Bun thought, as the driver's glasses shot up off his head, landed on the roof of the car, then slid across and off the far side. From the forward motion, Danny fell onto the driver, his weight pushing him down into the car. Danny held himself against the door frame, then pushed back and saw the driver remove his hands from his face, blind eyes wide in shock, blood pumping down into his hands and lap, sprawled across the seat and blinking blindly at the night. Wide-eyed, Danny gave Bun a sudden hug. Bun didn't get to worry about returning the embrace before his friend took off running, downhill towards the main road. When Bun saw that, he began to run too, but not in the direction of Lakelands – uphill instead, and into the park.

He didn't stop running until he was in the darkest part of the park, the most densely wooded area near the top of the hill. There he sat on a log, under the rough shelter of a bough, leaf-gathered rain pelting in fat drops above and around. His heart pounded and he lit a cigarette; rising steam from his shoulders mingling with the smoke. He vomited copiously between his legs and felt much, much better. Bun fished out his phone but didn't call his friend, instead listening to Jenny's voicemail a couple of times, out of habit, really. As a child he was terrified of this place; what was in the black core of nothing? But it was grand in here. He was fine. If anything, it was Danny people needed to worry about.

Trevor Byrne

Trevor Byrne was born in Dublin in 1981. He attended the University of Glamorgan, where he earned a degree in English and an M.Phil. in Writing. His debut novel, *Ghosts & Lightning*, was published by Canongate in 2009, and featured as a book of the year selection in the *Guardian* and *The Irish Times*. Byrne is currently nearing completion of his second novel and a collection of short stories, for which he has been awarded a bursary from the Irish Arts Council.

I've Hardly Slept At All

It had snowed heavily during the night, covering Offaly, all of Ireland, and Helen could hear Martin, her husband, dressing in the dark. It was five in the morning, and by nine Martin would be back in London, having travelled on the small bus from their house in the countryside to Edenderry, and on the coach from Edenderry to Dublin, and on the eight o' clock Aer Lingus flight from Dublin to Heathrow, and finally to the office of O'Neill Associates, where he'd speak to the senior partners, possibly even to Harry O'Neill himself, and by ten o' clock they'd know if all of this travelling to and from London could end.

– Helen, said Martin, and she turned away from him, pretending she was asleep.

She felt the bed shift and the warmth of Martin's breath as he leaned over her and kissed her shoulder, and Helen thought she would say something then, or reach out for him, but didn't. She heard him move about the house; heard him switch the bathroom light on, and the brief hissing of the taps before the light was switched off again; heard him whisper to their daughter, and Lizzie mumbling in a small, angry, sleepy voice; heard his footfalls on the stairs, a chair scrape in the kitchen.

It was too much to hope for that the meeting might go well: that there might be new investors, or the economy would rally, and these distant, unfathomable things would bring Martin home for good. If the Dublin office reopened there'd be no more long weeks apart, with Helen and Lizzie in the big, isolated house in Offaly, and Martin in the little bed and breakfast in London. There'd be no more brief weekends together, rushed and anxious like the last days of a holiday; no more lying awake in the dead hours of Monday, waiting for Martin to leave, worrying in the dark about the mortgage, if he could handle the way things were; if it meant anything that he didn't shave unless she told him to, that he didn't read any more.

Helen heard Martin cough and clear his throat, loud in a silence she had never known before, coming from the city, from Dublin.

She saw the shadow of falling snow pass the slats of the blinds. It was too much to hope that the Dublin office would reopen, but at ten a.m. they'd know. Helen closed her eyes. She wouldn't go to him; she wouldn't go to the kitchen and talk of all her hopes for better. She'd wait for his call from London.

She might have slept for longer, slept past ten and Martin's call, if not for Lizzie. Helen opened her eyes, panicked that she'd slept at all, and saw Lizzie kneeling at the end of the bed in her pyjamas, slapping the duvet with her palms, nodding her head, humming.

– Heya, honey, said Helen.

Lizzie was five. She smiled, and hummed a little louder. They went downstairs together, Lizzie in front and Helen following in her old pink housecoat and worn out slippers. Helen made a breakfast that Lizzie, who loved the snow and was wild with excitement, wouldn't eat.

– You can't stay out too long now, okay?

Lizzie nodded and stamped the mat impatiently as Helen buttoned up her red duffel. Helen was tired; whatever sleep she'd had wasn't enough. She felt guilty, too, for having ignored Martin, for her pettiness.

– You have to come back in soon and warm up, and then you can go back out, okay?

The key in the back door wouldn't turn: it was already unlocked. Martin must have been out there, to check on the back gate or use the recycle bins.

Lizzie ran into the garden, straight to the wood, or the small part of it that was theirs: the people who owned the house before them must have sectioned off a bit of the woods for themselves, and taken a few of the trees to build the fence. Their nearest neighbours were a ten-minute walk in either direction, and because of the snow it was hard to see where the garden ended and the countryside began; everything seemed connected, even the Slieve Bloom Mountains. Usually she'd go out with Lizzie, but she hadn't the energy; she'd keep an eye on her from the window. And anyway, she knew she couldn't go far.

Helen sat on a stool by the window and took out her phone. She rang Martin's number, but her call was connected to his voicemail.

– Heya Martin. I'm sorry I didn't get up with you this morning, I was knackered. Hope the plane was okay. Lizzie's out in the snow already. Let me know how you get on.

She opened the window and lit a cigarette, watching the snow fill Lizzie's footprints. When she thought she'd smoked half the cigarette she looked at it, took a quick, final pull and flicked it into the snow.

Helen set the ring tone volume on her phone to full, and placed it on the window ledge.

– Lizzie honey, c'mon! Time to come in; it's too cold in the snow!

After a minute Lizzie stepped out from behind one of the trees. She looked in Helen's direction and Helen raised her hand. Lizzie looked up at the falling snow, and then made her way slowly to the house. There was a large, sleek crow on one of the fence posts.

When Lizzie reached the door her cheeks were red and snow had settled in her ringlets.

– Where's your bobbin? Your hair's come loose.

Lizzie shrugged.

– Were you playing with the fairies in the ring?

A snowflake landed on Lizzie's eyelash and she blinked and batted at her face.

– C'mon inside, love. You have to let your hands warm up again.

Helen ushered Lizzie past her and into the hall, then into the kitchen. She tried to catch her daughter's eye.

– I'll make you a big girl's sandwich, with chicken and crunchy lettuce, said Helen. – Take them boots off.

Lizzie sat on the kitchen floor. The kitchen was big and clean, with new units and a breakfast bar and a big, wide window that looked out on to the mountains.

– Can you get them off yourself or d'you need me to help you?

Lizzie said nothing.

Helen turned and looked out into the back garden. Lizzie's footprints were almost gone and the tops of the Slieve Blooms were blurring with the low, heavy sky.

When Helen turned round, Lizzie was standing in her orange socks next to her empty boots.

– Good girl, she said.

Lizzie nodded, and wiped her red nose with the back of her hand. She looked at Helen and blinked, then looked at her boots. It was unusual for her to be so quiet.

– Hungry?

Lizzie half nodded.

– Want to watch a video?

She nodded again.

– Say 'yes', said Helen, but she'd said it too quickly, too harshly.

Lizzie looked at her with her eyes narrowed.

– What's the matter?

Lizzie looked at the floor, and Helen took her hand and squeezed it gently, and rubbed it between her own as they walked into the living room at the front of the house. Helen put on *The Princess Bride*, Lizzie's favourite film, and then went back to the kitchen. They'd been in the house for months and there were still boxes under the window, full of Helen's books. She'd told Martin to leave the unpacking to her, that it'd give her something to do, but she kept thinking that if she opened the last box then that was it – they'd moved in and there was no going back. But of course there was no going back to Dublin now anyway, to their little rented flat near St Stephen's Green, not far from Martin's old office.

Helen started on Lizzie's sandwich. She missed having her parents nearby, and meeting Martin's sister Adele for breakfast in the café they liked. It wasn't long after they took the flat that Martin started with O'Neill Associates. They'd hired Martin and a man from Cork, Sean Downing or Dowling; he'd been to the flat a few times, a tall, good-looking man with a deep line between his eyebrows that he sometimes rubbed at with his finger when he was listening. The company wanted two young architects, two architects with new ideas, with an intuitive feel for original forms; that was what they'd said to Martin at the interview.

They lived in the flat for a little over three years. It was only when Lizzie started walking that Helen saw how small the flat was. It was tiny, really. They could've stayed a while longer, but the bigger Lizzie got … and she was so mobile, so daring. She'd make steps out of Helen's books to get at things, and they were on the fourth floor. They started to look for somewhere else, for a house, but there was nothing they could afford in the Dublin area, except a few houses in estates like the one Helen grew up in – places where drugs were creeping back in – and neither of them wanted Lizzie growing up somewhere like that. She viewed a few houses on her own, taking Lizzie with her while Martin was at work, knowing before she turned up that they could never afford them, nodding her head and saying yes, very nice, lovely, I'll have to speak to my husband – he's an architect – but yes, it's gorgeous, just what we're looking for. It was Adele who suggested looking outside of Dublin. She'd meant well, of course, but Helen rued taking her advice.

She brought the sandwich to Lizzie on a plate with a glass of milk. She leaned down and kissed Lizzie's head and walked to the doorway, then turned and looked back. Lizzie was sitting with the plate on her lap and her feet in their orange socks not touching the floor, and she was looking around the room, not paying attention to the film.

– Make sure you eat it all now, love, said Helen.

Lizzie nodded, but said nothing.

Helen sat on the stool by the window, watching the snow, ignoring the clock on the wall behind her. When she looked it was twenty past ten. She waited another five minutes before ringing, but the call went through to Martin's voicemail again.

– Heya, love. Just checking in. Hope everything's okay. I'm watching the snow here. Lizzie's watching *The Princess Bride* again. Love you.

She couldn't bring herself to mention the meeting, or the Dublin office. She could hear Lizzie's film from the front room as she made herself a cup of tea. Lizzie's footprints were gone now and the sky was low and pale.

The meeting might have run over; they often did. But she was worried that Martin hadn't texted her, even to say that the flight was okay, or that it was snowing in London, or that it wasn't snowing there at all, it was freezing but clear, bright. He'd never have done this when they lived together in the flat, but things were different now, different to how they'd been before they moved, before the trouble with Martin's job. She missed how close they'd felt when all three of them were bunched up in the flat, with her books stacked against the walls, big hardbacks at the bottom and smaller paperbacks at the top. She even missed the old couple who owned the flat, Dr Abboushi and his tiny, frail wife. Dr Abboushi spoke to Helen about Palestine; he'd sit on the armchair by the window with his smooth, dark hands on his knees, his knees and ankles touching, his feet together. Most of his relatives still lived in Gaza, he said, and though it was dangerous it wasn't all bad, there was still an olive harvest every year, and God was good. Helen never told Dr Abboushi that she didn't believe in God.

Lizzie passed in the hallway, wearing her duffel coat and hat.

– Lizzie?

Helen heard Lizzie opening the back door, and a few seconds later saw her through the window lifting her legs high like before as she marched through the snow. She was carrying the red woollen scarf Helen had bought Martin before Christmas, before the weather turned bad.

The doorbell rang. Helen sat still for a moment, forgetting what she should do next, then put her tea down and walked to the front door, glancing into the living-room as she went. The film was playing and Lizzie's sandwich was on the sofa, untouched.

The doorbell rang again. Helen could see two blurry shapes through the glass, and she took a breath and tucked her hair behind her ears, then opened the door.

There was a young man and woman standing in the porch. The woman had short ginger hair and the man was blond. Their footprints led up the long drive. Both wore heavy coats. Helen noticed that the man was holding a leather briefcase and felt a stab of panic.

– Hello, said the woman, smiling. – Are we disturbing you?

The man smiled too, and shifted his feet.

The man and woman were Jehovah's Witnesses. By the time they were in the kitchen and Helen was standing by the countertop, and the man and woman were sitting at the table, glossy leaflets arranged in front of them, Helen had forgotten their names. They were smartly, formally dressed, and Helen was still wearing her old housecoat, and the slippers with no heels. The man wore a shirt and a purple tie, and the woman wore a dark, ankle-length skirt and flat, blunt shoes. Their overcoats were hanging over the backs of the kitchen chairs and the snow was beginning to melt. They were probably in their twenties, but their clothes and their practised, unflagging smiles made them seem ageless. It was hard to picture them anywhere but in other peoples' kitchens.

– Would you like a cup of tea? asked Helen.

– Coffee would be lovely, the man said, before turning his attention to the leaflets, pushing them around the table, weighing up which leaflet would suit Helen best.

– Coffee for me too, thanks, said the woman, smiling.

Helen placed her hands on the countertop behind her and did her best to smile too. She glanced out the window and saw Lizzie's new footprints in the snow.

– It's a God-given gift, said the man. He was appraising the room, nodding. – A house like this, I mean. It's a gift.

– You mustn't be here long, said the woman, looking at the boxes stacked along the wall.

– No, not long, said Helen.

She hadn't told them that she didn't believe in God, and now it was too late, and she hadn't told them that she wasn't happy in this house and she'd rather be back in her old flat in Dublin, and that if it wasn't for the price of property she wouldn't be here and she'd never have met them and she'd be happier.

– It's grand and private out here, said the woman.

– Yeah, said Helen.

The man tapped one of the leaflets and the woman glanced at it and nodded. They were shameless because they were young and sure, and thought they had her; that they'd saved her. Helen turned away and clicked the kettle again to boil the water for tea, and then she remembered that it was coffee they wanted, and that she didn't know how to work the new coffeemaker. She didn't drink coffee and neither did Martin. The expensive coffeemaker had been a present from someone.

She felt her face heat with embarrassment and leaned on the countertop. She felt faint. She wanted to call Martin.

– Is everything okay, Helen?

It was the woman speaking. Helen wished she could remember her name. That would help things, even things up. She didn't turn round to face her, though. Instead she nodded, though she wanted to slide down against the counter and sit on the floor.

– Are you sure? said the woman.

Helen nodded again.

– I'm sorry, I've run out of coffee, she said, and it felt strange to speak to someone without looking at them. Why couldn't she turn round? It seemed impossible to tell the truth now, to face them.

– I haven't been to the shops because of the snow, she said.

She kept her hands on the countertop and tried to think of something else to say, but the only thing she could think to ask them was if they thought her husband was okay, if the plane had taken off and landed safely. Maybe if she stood for long enough with her back to these nameless, ageless people who admired her home and appraised her openly, then when she turned round they'd be gone and Martin would be there, and she'd say she was sorry for not getting out of bed, for not saying goodbye.

– Are you alright? asked the man.

Helen knew she should tell them she was fine, but though she was lonely she wanted them to leave. She closed her eyes for a few seconds, took a breath, and when she turned round smiling she saw that the man and woman were looking at her and smiling still, though now they looked quickly at each other and she knew that they'd spoken but hadn't used words. The man swiped together the leaflets he'd laid out and tapped them on his briefcase, and the woman stood. The man packed the leaflets into the briefcase, all except one, which he handed to Helen. She took it and he looked around the kitchen again, peering into the corners of the room.

They walked together down the hallway to the front door.

– You should visit our church one of these Sundays, said the man. – You'd be very welcome.

– It's near the big roundabout, said the woman. – Near the Tesco in town. It doesn't look like your typical church. We don't have a steeple.

The woman smiled and touched Helen's arm. Helen didn't want to be touched and yet she wouldn't stop her. If the woman had stayed standing in the porch, her hand on Helen's arm, her and the man smiling in their professional way as the snow fell about them, Helen would have done the same, unable to do anything else. But after a long moment they turned away, and Helen stood with the leaflet held in front of her, against her chest, and watched them make their way down the driveway, arms linked.

It was almost midday. Helen could hear Lizzie rummaging upstairs, her footsteps, the sound of drawers opening and closing. She was smoking by the window and watching the snow falling. It was wilder now.

She wondered if she should ring the office, or maybe even The Old Canaries, Martin's bed and breakfast. It wasn't far from the office and Martin sometimes had his lunch there. Helen and Lizzie had stayed with Martin for a weekend, in his small room, not long after he took the London job. The Old Canaries was owned by two brothers from Norwich who had never married. The younger of the brothers had a bad stammer. When he struggled with a word the older brother waited patiently, nodding slowly, knowing that the word would come.

Helen could hear Lizzie coming down the stairs, in her slow, deliberate way, holding on to the banisters and putting one foot down, then following with the other. She stood in the doorway wearing her duffel, and she was holding Martin's red woollen hat.

– What are you doing with Daddy's hat?

Lizzie sat and placed the hat beside her, and started pulling on her boots.

– Are the fairies helping you make a snowman?

– It's very cold, said Lizzie.

Helen nodded, glad to have heard her daughter speak.

– Yep, said Helen.

She took Lizzie's hands and slipped on her woollen mittens, fetched the bobble hat that was hanging in the hall and pulled it tight over Lizzie's ears.

– Nice and snug, said Helen, smiling. But Lizzie looked hurt, and Helen hugged her out of fear, out of sheer lack of ideas, and then stepped back and looked at her.

She led Lizzie to the hall, opened the back door and immediately felt the cold. Lizzie let go of Helen's hand and left her side, walked past her into the garden and through the snow, back to the wood.

Helen left the door open. She felt weak and deeply tired, and the cold might keep her awake. On the countertop was the leaflet the Jehovah's Witnesses had given her. It was called 'Would You Like to Know the Truth?' and there was a picture of a sunset over still water. She folded it and put in into the drawer with the takeaway menus, then took it out again and dropped it into the paper bin.

Helen took out her phone and looked at the number for Martin's desk at O'Neill Associates for a long time, then selected it, listened to the phone ring, and then to Martin, her husband, saying that he wasn't at the desk at the moment, but please leave a message or call back. She was shaking when she selected Andrea Simpson's number.

– O'Neill Associates, Andrea speaking. How can I help?

A southern English accent, placeless. They'd met when Helen and Lizzie visited. She was the office receptionist, young and clever, dark skinned.

– Hello?

– Hello, said Helen. – I'm looking for Martin Sheridan.

– Can I ask what–

– Hello, Andrea, this is Helen, Martin's wife. We've met. You met my daughter.

– Helen … Yes, I remember. We've been—

– Lizzie's five now, she asks about you sometimes. She thinks you look like Halle Berry. She asks Martin to—

– Helen, we've been trying to get in touch with Martin, he hasn't been in yet.

– Okay. Thank you.

– Helen, we'd like to—

95

Helen pulled on her boots and wrapped the housecoat tight around her, and stepped into the snow. Her breath came in frosted bursts and she could feel the blood in her ears, could hear her heart beat. She began to panic.

– Lizzie! she shouted.

She could taste the morning's tea on her breath.

– Lizzie!

The snow was coming down heavily, swirling. She walked quickly, her hands pressed to her stomach. Beyond the trees the mountains were huge, long and low like a pale wave. The crow was still sitting on a fence post, watching her. As she passed it squawked and flew, its call blunted by the weight of the weather, the huge silence.

Helen stepped over the broken branches and leafless bushes at the edge of the wood, passed between the trees in the dim light.

She saw Lizzie walking through the trees towards her, and called her name. Lizzie stopped and looked at her, twenty feet away.

– Where's Daddy's hat, honey?

Lizzie looked back the way she'd come.

– Did you leave it back there? Are you making a snowman?

Helen was shivering. It wasn't just the cold; it was all she could do not to scream.

– Lizzie.

– I put the hat and scarf and gloves on Daddy because it's cold.

She said it sullenly, sulkily.

– Honey, what do you mean? Tell me what you mean.

– Daddy's asleep in the cold.

Helen ran to her and Lizzie looked shocked, as though she might be hit – though she'd never hit her daughter; she'd never hurt her – and Helen picked her up and ran, crouching beneath the lower branches, her daughter's face against her neck.

– He's very cold, Mammy, said Lizzie.

The world around her was not the world at all, or not any world she knew. In a few more steps she was in the open, in the fairy ring, the small clearing covered with snow and the snow falling heavily about her. Helen walked to the middle of the clearing, then stopped and turned slowly in a circle. She was no longer shivering, no longer frightened or cold.

She couldn't go on. She would never, she thought, move from this spot. If she stepped forward or turned back the world would slip away from her. Lizzie – she could feel her daughter's deep, slow breathing – was suddenly sleeping, and Helen felt she was alone in a far country. Perhaps, she thought, the world might stall – perhaps she could will it to be so – and there would be no moving any more, no thinking or feeling. She would stay where she was and time would stand still, and she would never see Martin – her husband, who was young and beautiful and who she loved – she would never see Martin dead in the snow.

But it was beyond her will, and she felt what mastery she had, what grace she'd been granted, slipping from her, and she began to shake, her legs and arms and jaw, and a sound came up from deep within her, from a place older and truer than God, a sound that filled the world and felled the trees and cracked the mountains, goes on and on, will never stop.

Mary Costello

Mary Costello is originally from East Galway and now lives in Dublin. Her first book of stories *The China Factory* (Stinging Fly Press) was published to widespread critical acclaim in May 2012. Her stories have been anthologised and published in New Irish Writing and in The Stinging Fly. She was short-listed for a Hennessy New Irish Writing Award in the 1990s and was a finalist in the Narrative Short Story Competition (USA, Spring 2010) and in Glimmer Train's Open Fiction Competition (USA, June 2011). She received a bursary from the Irish Arts Council in 2011.

The Hitchhiker

For three hours they drove east without talking. The sun lit up the bare trees on the road ahead. They passed small, deserted villages, downcast and desolate after the winter. She looked out the window at a house or a garden or a tree, turning her head slowly and deliberately, indicating some proud, implacable stance. When he changed gears his arm brushed hers. A delicate silence hung between them, neither ceding to be the first to speak. In certain moments, however, in a yawn or a sigh, in the little concessional noises he made, she sensed something infinitely gentle, infinitely tender between them. It would not take much, perhaps a thought, for one of them to make an offering.

She remembered other journeys, travelling in the confined space of the car, when the hum of the engine led them to distant, vaguely happy thoughts, before the city lights brought them to their senses again. She thought of them as permanently in transit, forever journeying together like this. Years ago, just after they met, she had had to drive to Cork and back in a day, and he had come along on a whim. She had driven slower than usual, to stretch out time. She knew that the moment he left the car all good would go with him. She resented stopping off to eat, or sharing him with others in a public place. He crowded her thoughts and she was alert to every breath, every tensing muscle, every minute gesture. She was given over completely, soft and yielding on the outside, tense, febrile, consumed within. His hands rested calmly on his thighs that day, proud, indifferent; he would not give.

She thought him impervious, untouched by the pitch and charge of feeling in the car. Towards the end of the journey she looked in the rear-view mirror and saw the long line of road disappear behind her and somehow the agitation abated. She knew that something had passed between them, that they had divined some distant parts of each other. She looked out at the trees against the sky and she knew then her fate with him was sealed. She longed to mark the moment, take his hand, leave it on her lap, make something of it.

Outside now the small farms and stone walls of the west gave way to open fields and occasional groves of trees. He picked up speed on the open road through the midlands. She turned her head to look at him. It seemed that everything she knew or had ever known was within him, or had come out of him, or been deemed by him.

It was April and they had rented an island cottage at the edge of the Atlantic with the sharp white light and the waves and surf surrounding them. The island was in his blood; he knew its paths and its people. In the mornings he rose early from the bed and she rolled over into his space and listened for sounds – the kettle boiling, the time signal on the radio, the clatter of delft – in the kitchen. She heard him slip out of the cottage, his footsteps trailing away. She lay very still then, waiting for his return, to feel herself reconstituted again.

One morning she stood at the bedroom window and watched him on the strand below. He was looking out to sea as the surf washed over his shoes. How small and mortal he looked before the waves, with the sands darkening around him. She thought he might be drawn in by the dark undertow. She always feared losing him. She felt herself lean to reach him, to hear him, across the cold air.

"Did you get up last night?" he asked at breakfast. "I thought I felt you getting up."

She shook her head. He stopped stirring his coffee. "What?" he asked. "What are you thinking?"

"Nothing," she said.

She had woken at dawn that morning, exhausted and unnerved by the subterranean pull of her sleep. She slipped from the bed and put on her coat and went outside. She crossed the rough grass behind the cottage and rested against a rock. The horizon was streaked with pink as the sun broke through. Her shoes were wet from the dew. She had the feeling of being watched and she looked back at the bedroom window but he was not there. She turned to her left and there, a few feet away, stood a fox, silent and motionless. Her heart froze. His body was old and worn and wretched, as if he had been standing there since the beginning of time. The sun's rays pierced his irises. A flicker of recognition passed between them, some creatureliness that bound them together, the remains of something long gone from memory. She heard the lapping of the waves behind her. She saw the suffering in the fox's eyes. Then he stirred and lowered his head and disappeared through the hedge.

"I must have been dreaming," he said. "I was sure you were gone from the bed for a while."

On their last day they walked around the island, weaving their way in and out of tiny beaches and around headlands.

Small bleached bones lay on the sand, and he kicked one and kept walking and then scaled a low cliff.

She watched the gulls circling and screeching overhead. They came on bunches of primroses and she plucked some and held them up to him and told him of the May altars she'd made as a child. They followed a path along the headland and she turned and stood for a moment. She saw his eyes linger on the cliffs, the waves, the islands in the distance. She thought he must be thinking that this was the view his antecedents had had for hundreds of years, that nothing had changed.

They hung on to each other that evening. He cooked steak and vegetables and she sat reading by the fire in the next room. She heard his movements in the kitchen, and the tinkle of lids and the rush of tap-water. The radio played traditional music. He would be standing beside steaming saucepans, a fork in his hand, reel music in his head, poised to test the potatoes. He kept coming into the room, his sleeves rolled, setting the table, opening the wine, checking the weather and the waves beyond the window. Given up to each task. Humming softly, thinking himself alone.

When they sat down to eat he touched her elbow and said "Go ahead, start." They talked a little of the day. The music streamed in from the kitchen and she saw how the notes and the wine and the dying light softened him. Afterwards, she returned to her book. He remained at the table with a local newspaper spread out before him. Time passed and when she remembered him and looked up she was surprised, elated, he was still there.

"Tell me," she said, "Tell me about the others, before me. Before you met me."

He looked up, a little dazed.

"Why?" His voice was hoarse and remote.

She shrugged and smiled. She felt a little drunk.

"There's nothing to tell," he said.

"Please. Tell me. Tell me about … Ann or Catherine or Ruth. Tell me about Ruth."

"It was years ago. I forget all that, it's of no consequence." He gestured with open hands. "This, the here and now – this is what counts."

"You couldn't forget. People don't – they never forget things like that. They're too private."

"Leave them then."

His eyes were dark and tired and these words, Leave them then, threw her into disquiet. "I want to know," she pressed.

He rose and went into the kitchen. It was dusk now and the ocean seemed far off. He had said that name, Ruth, in his sleep in the early days and it had remained a faint abstract pain in a distant part of her. She was not privy to all of him.

"Okay then," he said, when he returned.

She closed her book. She could hardly make out his face. Suddenly she knew why she did this, why she pushed him to reveal his life before her. She wanted to map him, decipher him, turn over every inch of him, every disparate clue, and find the cause of him. Know the absoluteness of him.

"I was young, only twenty or twenty-one, when I met Ruth," he said. "I'd just bought my first car, an ancient old Ford with leather seats.

I wanted to go over west for the weekend. It was a hot summer and the city was killing me. I wanted to start living. I remember starting out in Dublin and not really knowing where I was headed. It could be Clare or Galway or Mayo. I turned the radio up real high. I had a picture of myself, you see – you know those shots of young American guys driving along the Californian coast in open cars with girls beside them, playing loud music – well, that was me!

"Anyway, out near Maynooth, there was a girl on the road, hitching. She was holding up a card with SLIGO written on it, and I thought, ah-ha, Sligo! So I slowed down and as she was getting in I was thinking… mmm, if she's ok, if she's nice, I'll go to Sligo, and if she's a pain I'll turn off at Kinnegad for Galway. So…"

"So… that was Ruth and she wasn't a pain."

He shrugged. "That's how I met her." He raised the glass to his lips.

"Go on," she said. "What happened then?"

"We drove to Sligo. She'd gotten off the boat from Holyhead that morning. She'd been working in London… and I think she'd been to France or Italy or somewhere too because she was very tanned. She was from Sligo town. She was very funny – I remember laughing a lot. On the way down she pulled out a bottle of duty free whiskey and we started drinking it straight from the bottle. Jesus… And it was such a hot day. We got to Sligo around lunchtime and I wanted to go out to Drumcliffe, to Yeats' grave, because I'd never been there, but she wanted to go straight to Rosses Point. She made me drive past her parents' house first so she could see it again. Like she was checking it was still there, or something. It was a tall stone house in the middle of the town… She made me slow down and she went really quiet as we drove by…

Then after a minute or two she was happy again.

"We bought food and drink and spent the day on the beach – the far beach – at Rosses Point, lying in the sun and swimming and talking. The sky was the bluest I ever saw it that day … She was very young and very... well… a dreamer. We were all dreamers in those days... I have photographs from that day somewhere – or maybe I threw them away… I called her The Hitchhiker. I'd say 'Hey, Hitchhiker, I'm hungry...'"

She had seen the photographs among his things. They were mostly of the landscape, but one was of the girl. She was young and tanned and warm-looking. She had short, dark hair, and a beautiful pixie face and she was sitting back in long grass with Ben Bulben behind her. And what must have been his shadow on the ground beside her. They must have left the beach and walked off into the fields for that photograph, she thought.

It was dark but neither of them moved to switch on a lamp. The flames of the fire had died down.

"I used to go down to her place at weekends for the rest of that summer. She played the piano, nocturnes. I didn't know what a nocturne was then. Three months after we met we got engaged. We were just going from weekend to weekend, like two kids. She'd be noisy and funny one weekend, and the next – so volatile… inflamed. She was very bright and very… fragile… damaged too. She wanted a child with me… She bit me on the face once, really hard..." He paused and brought his fingers to his cheek as if feeling for the tooth marks and she knew he was, for an instant, coming into her presence again.

"The night we got engaged a crowd of us went out to a place, The Blue Lagoon, outside Sligo, and I remember thinking as she was dancing there with me, in my arms… I remember having this feeling – like those moments you read about in books – a revelation – that nothing else mattered, or would ever matter, and maybe I'd never feel that way again..."

His voice trailed off. He got up and stood at the window. "For all I know she might be dead now. But even if she isn't, even if she's alive and well and walked in here this minute, I wouldn't have a word to say to her."

She saw him again at the water's edge, with the bleached bones strewn on the sand. She remembered the empty space in the bed and the fox's eyes at dawn and the cries of the gulls and the piano notes and the beautiful pixie face, and she thought there was something in all of them that she must fathom. She thought if she were patient, if she fixed hard on one image, and then the next, she would unscramble the signs and penetrate their meaning, and understanding would surely, eventually, come.

"You never told me this," she said. "What happened?"

"She went back to England, or somewhere. I think she'd come home in the first place to get over someone, a man."

He left the room. A sean-nós song drifted in from the kitchen. She pictured him standing under the light, his arms by his side, the notes and words of the song washing over him, and a face conjured, a memory resurrected, tracking him down.

***

They are passing through the strung-out towns west of Dublin – Clonard, Enfield, Kilcock, Maynooth. Last night's name hangs there haunting the air, sounding an absence. The oncoming lights dazzle her. Beyond the roadside is impenetrable darkness. She has brought it on herself. She steals a glance at him, at the face, branded. He has been marked by many. She closes her eyes. Was there ever one marked by her? Not many, not him.

She is suddenly cold. She cannot conceive of an end to this journey, or the tasks awaiting them: the switching on of lights, the unpacking, the preparation of food. She knows its end will dislodge something small and crucial and irreplaceable. She stirs and releases her seat-belt and reaches behind for her coat. The car loses momentum abruptly, drops speed. She catches her breath. A row of red and white barrels signaling road repairs looms before them. Her stomach lurches. They have veered across the road into the opposite lane. Blinding white lights are coming at them. She calls out his name, harshly. His body jerks forward. "What?" he says, in a strange, ghostly voice. He had drifted to sleep. His eyes are startled, his voice the lonely dawn voice that delivers him out of sleep. He swerves and the car glances off the barrels and she cowers and covers her head, her ears. There is a streak of light on his side and the blare of an angry horn, and then the thump and crunch of something on her side – a ditch or stones or bushes – all coming together in an instant, and then gone.

They are stopped on the hard shoulder. The lower half of the sky is amber. Cars are going by, too merrily, on the other side. Up ahead are house lights, and beyond, the city spread out. He leans in with soft eyes and touches her arm and speaks small, comforting words.

She watches his mouth moving and his face and she has a sudden vision of him, his corporeal body, shrinking, contracting, growing back in time and shape – in skin and bone and hair – until he is a youth, and then a boy, and then on back, receding downwards and inwards, until he is a plump, smiling infant and fading out until finally there is nothing left of him but a nub and he disappears, vanishes entirely. And then his voice breaks through and startles her, and he is back and whole again, and she raises her arm and opens her hand and slaps him hard and sharp on the face. And again. Thwack. Because something has been lost and she wants no part of him now, no part of his look or his touch or his words. Because she is tumbling into darkness, all into darkness, and she wants to fling open the door and stumble out into the undergrowth. She wants to crawl into some secret mossy place under trees and hole up there for the night, and reach the farthest, quietest end of herself, and sleep the deep sleep of forgetfulness.

He puts the car in gear and they move away. She is reminded of a film and it is the final scene. A man and a woman are driving through a forest in rain, their last ever journey. There is no talk, no music, nothing except the constant flapping of the windscreen wipers over and back, over and back, and outside, ahead of them, shafts of sunlight filtering down through the trees, so white and blinding and terrible.

Emma Donoghue

Born in Dublin in 1969, Emma Donoghue is an award-winning writer, living in Canada. Her novels are *Room*, *The Sealed Letter*, *Landing*, *Life Mask*, *Slammerkin*, *Hood* and *Stir-fry*; short-story collections *Astray* (Autumn 2012), *Three and a Half Deaths* (UK ebook), *Touchy Subjects*, *The Woman Who Gave Birth to Rabbits* and *Kissing the witch;* and literary history including *Inseparable*, *We Are Michael Field* and *Passions between Women,* as well as two anthologies that span the seventeenth to the twentieth centuries.

Urban Myths

FROM: motoole@iol.ie
TO: hrajan@udu.edu.ie
RE: SO sorry

I'm mortified I missed my first supervision, Dr Rajan, there was a mix-up, the Secretary did give me the info on a sheet but it got tucked into my Mature Students Welcome Handbook … Anyway, I just wanted to make my apologies and ask if I could reschedule for the middle of next week maybe? I am keen to start work with you, and have done a lot of thinking about my thing already. Sorry, my thesis I should say, but I find the word a tad intimidating, so have decided to think of it as just a 30,000-word sort of essay thing!

All the best and huge apologies again,
Maureen O'Toole

FROM: hrajan@udu.edu.ie
TO: motoole@iol.ie
Re: Re: SO sorry

These things happen, Mrs O'Toole, especially at the beginning of term. (Twenty minutes into my undergraduate seminar on The Folklore of Place Names, this morning, a young woman stood up, announced that she was meant to be in Anthropology, and fled from the room.)

In my experience, as soon as one gets into the swing of an MA 'thing', the somewhat arbitrary word-count ceases to hold any terrors. Should I gather from your email that you have already formulated your area of inquiry to some extent? I see from your application that you are interested in Maternal Archetypes Among Celtic Peoples.

I will be happy to meet you at your convenience during any of my office hours, as follows: Monday 12-2, Tuesday 10-12:30 and 3-5, Friday 9-11.

A small point, my name is not Rajan but Rajani, Dr Hakim Rajani; you were no doubt misled by the format of faculty email addresses which include only the first five letters of the surname.

FROM: motoole@iol.ie
TO: hrajan@udu.edu.ie
Re: whoops again

Sorry sorry sorry, I'm sure you're sick of Irish people getting your name wrong! Not that of course you mightn't be Irish yourself, I wasn't assuming, it's only that I was in the Dept. half an hour ago and the Secretary happened to mention you just arrived last year from India. How do you like rainy Dublin?

Thanks for the reassurance about the MA 'thing', I feel a bit rusty as you imagine, since it's 20 years since I was here doing my BA (in Psychology, never used it). Like Woody Allen in *Sleeper*, you know? – waking up to a strange new world.

I'm afraid Monday or Tuesday would be tricky, could we make it Friday at 10?

Actually, I dropped that Maternal Archetypes stuff ages ago, it's all been done. What I really want to write about is – are urban myths about, well I suppose you could call it sexual revenge? Women having bizarre vengeance on men who abandon them, you know the kind of thing.

Since we're on the subject of names, it's actually not Mrs O'Toole, please call me Maureen.

FROM: hrajan@udu.edu.ie
TO: motoole@iol.ie
Re: title

I do beg your pardon, it says Mrs Maureen O'Toole in the student list; I will ask the Secretary to correct her records. Should that be Ms?

I do like Dublin well enough although, for academics, generally the job is the thing.

I certainly know *Sleeper*, a very witty cryogenic take on the motif of the sleeping hero (Arthur, to name only the most obvious example).

Your proposed topic is intriguing; how did you come to choose it? I do have a concern as to whether I am the most suitable supervisor, given your change in direction. My background is in Early German Folklore (my doctoral research was on animal proverbs) and I must confess to having little familiarity with the kind of contemporary, international material you mention. But in any case I am certainly available at the time you mention.

FROM: motoole@iol.ie
TO: hrajan@udu.edu.ie
Re: topic

It began when a friend emailed me a few of these urban myths and I found them so clever and surreal and ... basically they make me laugh. Just this morning I came across one about a woman who cut the crotches out of all of her ex's trousers. Not the trousers of all her exes I mean, but all the trousers of her (one) ex. Of course I've made a few false starts – when I stupidly Googled 'Men' + 'Punishment' I was offered some hard-core porn sites!

You're as suitable as anyone else to supervise me, I think, Dr Rajani, because Professor Jarrell says there's nobody in the Dept. who does modern studies, or 20th-century even. The word is that you're one of the shining stars of Folk Studies and I'm a lucky girl to be working with you!

Further confusion about names, sorry, what I meant was that I was Mrs O'Toole until recently. Separated, not widowed, in case you were wondering (or probably too polite to ask). I am thinking of reverting to my maiden name (Lannigan), there's a lot to decide as you can probably imagine. No kids, so at least that's not an issue, name-wise.

Didn't people believe that King Arthur would wake one day when his country needed him? I certainly don't delude myself about that, Ireland doesn't seem to need anyone over 30 these days. Tir-na-nOg you might say (land of youth, do you know the phrase?), or land of jumped-up gobshites in 'financial services' earning four times what their daddies ever did...

FROM: hrajan@udu.edu.ie
TO: motoole@iol.ie
Re: office hours

Just a reminder that my office is F113, the very small one at the end of the corridor (beside the Ladies).

FROM: motoole@iol.ie
TO: hrajan@udu.edu.ie
Re: encouragement

I can't tell you how much I enjoyed our first supervision though I was must admit I was startled to find (given your glittering CV) that you are half my age, but then everyone on this campus seems to be, so as a 'Mature Student' (euphemism for wrinkly) I will just have to get used to it.

Thanks SO much and sorry I hogged you by staying till the end of your office hours, I hope there weren't lots of other students trying to see you. Thanks as well (again) for all your wonderfully encouraging words. I've actually been taking some stick from friends/family along the lines of 'an MA in Folk Studies isn't going to help you get back into the job market' but I happen to be passionate about it and as you put it so well, passion is the fuel of the mind.

FROM: hrajan@udu.edu.ie
TO: motoole@iol.ie
Re: your project

Maureen, I do have some concern about your reliance on the internet, but of course you are only at the preliminary stage of gathering stories and I can see that traditional sources would be of little use. But I am attaching a short reading list to help you formulate your methodological approach when it comes to analysing the motifs.

Re: 'half your age', like all the Irish, you exaggerate! I have been told I have a misleadingly babyish face.

FROM: motoole@iol.ie
TO: hrajan@udu.edu.ie
Re: theory

Thanks a million for the reading list. I wonder could I come in on Monday at 11? Oh hang on, sorry, I just checked, you don't start till 12 on Mondays, but I'm seeing my solicitor at lunchtime, I'll have to figure something out…

Just found a good one about a woman forwarding all her ex's most explicit emails to his entire company. Do you think her spreading the news (as it were), i.e. copying and circulating his emails corresponds to, or should I say comments on, his 'spreading his seed'? I've always thought it funny how such phrases imply that the man is following some kind of hardwired biological order to save the species rather than just relieving an itch…

FROM: hrajan@udu.edu.ie
TO: motoole@iol.ie
Re: in haste

Monday at 11 is fine, in fact, Maureen; I am usually in my office at that time doing paperwork.

TO: motoole@iol.ie
FROM: hrajan@udu.edu.ie
Re: Hell hath no fury, as the poet Congreve put it

Well, this is indeed a fascinating corpus (I did as you suggest look at www.stringemup.com). And I found it far more extensive and elaborate than I would have imagined. The transferred violence, the castration symbolism in most cases (legs cut off suits, bent golf clubs or stopped-up fountain pens, also perhaps the chilli sprinkled in the underpants) seems rather too obvious to require analysis but is still fascinating by virtue of its ubiquity. I very much look forward to seeing what you will make of this project, Maureen, you have (among other strengths) a remarkable sense of humour. You should perhaps ask yourself, what need do these narratives of woman-paying-man-back (and never it seems the other way around) serve, why does our society, at this moment in its cultural development, find them so gratifying?

FROM: motoole@iol.ie
TO: hrajan@udu.edu.ie
Re: 'remarkable sense of humour'

I'll take that as a compliment, Hakim! Thanks so much for this morning's session, I would be completely lost without your guidance, there's so much material and so many variants and I feel like a complete blunderer every time I attempt to write a sentence of my 'thing'... academic language doesn't come easy I'm afraid ....

FROM: hrajan@udu.edu.ie
TO: motoole@iol.ie
Re: your concerns about style

Maureen, I feel that you are worrying unduly. For instance, in your draft proposal, when you refer to 'Certain characteristics of widely circulating apocryphal, oral narratives concerning the termination of affective relationships', it might be more helpful to speak simply of 'urban myths about break-ups'. On the more specific matter of your vacillating between 'men who have done them wrong' or 'men who have done wrong to them', may I suggest 'men who have wronged them' (*cf* Strunk and White, the fewer words the better!).

It has been remarked by linguists that the Irish apologise constantly, and I note that your emails never fail to include some variant on 'sorry'. I can assure you that you are a very able student and have nothing to apologise for.

FROM: motoole@iol.ie
TO: hrajan@udu.edu.ie
Re: language

OK, I'll ease off on the sorrys – sorry!

But language (academic or not) all so biased, isn't it, Hakim? Further to our discussion about 'seed-spreading', I've been thinking about ones like 'stud', that compare the man to a breeding animal, not like words for female promiscuity like 'slut' which aren't about reproduction at all, but prostitution (money and morals) which don't get applied to his seed-spreading at all! In fact there is no insulting word in English for a fella who can't keep his dick in his trousers (pardon my language but I can't think of a politer way of putting it) unless we call him a whore and that's just a sort of joke that backfires against women because it implies that a slut of either sex is behaving in a classically female way!

You asked why the stories are never the other way round, well I have a simple theory. If a woman messes around on her fella and/or leaves him, he can just belt her, no need to be clever about it.

FROM: hrajan@udu.edu.ie
TO: motoole@iol.ie
Re: bias

I have been giving your last email much thought, Maureen. While soi-disant 'scholarly objectivity' has of course been exploded as a construct (the white male deluding himself that his can ever be a neutral eye), it remains the case that sometimes we can over-invest in our material to a certain extent … or rather, that our analysis might benefit from taking a little distance from our sources. I see no problem with the feminist slant (angle, I should say) of your approach, but I wonder if perhaps your passion for this particular topic is making it slightly difficult for you to put it in a broader folklore/popular culture context? Just a thought.

I hope you had a pleasant weekend. Are you enjoying being back at university, more generally? Is it difficult to achieve the much vaunted work/life balance?

FROM: motoole@iol.ie
TO: hrajan@udu.edu.ie
Re: being back

God yes, I'm enjoying it, not just the general buzz but also the feeling of my mind stretching for the first time in ages. Doing paperwork for my husband's export business (well, I would have called it our business, a family business, but his solicitor doesn't agree) was hardly stimulating to the old grey matter. I really should have had a proper career, it's not as if I was busy raising kids – we had no luck in that department despite medical intervention, thought of adopting but it's a gruelling business if you go internationally which you really have to these days and HE 'wasn't quite motivated enough' as he put it so charmingly. Sorry, this is probably TMI which my niece tells me is txt-spk for 'too much information', I'm just trying to explain how glad I am to be a student again. I don't know about 'work-life balance', mind you, it's really more a matter of plunging into work so I don't have to think about life, have you ever done that, Hakim? Sorry, none of my business.

Re: being 'over-invested', mmm, you're probably right. My sister says it's not a project, it's an obsession. I suppose I can tone down the language when it comes to actually writing the thing.

FROM: hrajan@udu.edu.ie
TO: motoole@iol.ie
Re: work v. life

Oh, indeed, it is a rare academic who is unfamiliar with that sensation of hiding in the library.

On the subject of time, perhaps you could look more closely at the group of urban myths you identify as being about its passage (such as the woman who rings the Speaking Clock in Singapore from her former husband's apartment and leaves the phone off the hook) – which stands for death, I would assume?

FROM: mlannigan@iol.ie
TO: hrajan@udu.edu.ie
Re: note new address

Wow, that hadn't actually occurred to me, Hakim, I was reading them a bit more literally as representing the years she's spent with this worthless bastard, washing his socks or whatever. By running up a huge phone bill while he's off in the Seychelles sucking the new girlfriend's toes she wants to literally make him pay for all the time she's wasted on him when she could have been having another life, setting up her own business or whatever ... But of course it could be death too because she's that much closer to her own death now, isn't she, and need I say the 'market' for not-so-young woman is way more brutal than for the men who've lied to them and used up all their energies then up and left them. (I don't have a documented source for that last claim, it's just common knowledge!)

I'll pop in tomorrow to talk more...

FROM: hrajan@udu.edu.ie
TO: mlannigan@iol.ie
Re: note new address

New address noted. May I say, it seems like a positive step to take.

Re: choosing your angle, I believe your thoughts about what these narratives reveal about cultural anxieties around gender roles may open the most fruitful path. (Oh dear, what a mixed metaphor!) The grass seeded in the carpet, the prawns sewn into the curtains – these bizarre forms of revenge the woman takes on her absent betrayer speak eloquently of a link between femininity and an unnervingly fecund/decomposing Nature.

FROM: mlannigan@iol.ie
TO: hrajan@udu.edu.ie
Re: Nature

SO right Hakim, whether it's the grass sprouting like some crazy green fungus over his entire flat with its chic new Balinese matting or the prawns rotting and stinking behind the curtains but he can't tell where the terrible smell is from, it's all the same thing: she's invaded the sanitized sanctum of the nouveau 'bachelor' pad and fecked it all up! Stained it, you might say, with her outrage and her unwanted 'want'. Or no, maybe she's made HIS disgusting behaviour visible (and smellable, if there's such a word) – maybe it's HIS crimes that stink to high heaven? (isn't there a bit in the Bible that goes like that?) maybe it's HIM who destroyed the domestic peace by cheating on his marriage vows? (or implicit agreement to be faithful if they're not married) In which case, he's the prawn, damn, that doesn't fit with the fecund/female stuff. Sorry this is a mess, Hakim, I shouldn't really email you until I know what I'm talking about but it's such a relief to let it all out while my thoughts are flooding through my mind and I haven't had enough sleep, I always get a bit wired when that's the case. Sorry, sorry. Whoops, not meant to be repeatedly apologising in the Irish way!

FROM: mlannigan@iol.ie
TO: hrajan@udu.edu.ie
Re: last email

Forget all that. I don't know which of them is the prawn and what does it matter?

Sometimes I think I'm just pathetic, a lazy housewife who's spent her best years watching telly now deluding herself she can write a 30,000-word thesis, and my topic, what was I thinking and who am I kidding, when you come right down to it it's just variations on a joke, one of the many forms of time-wankery cluttering up the internet. My sister was right, this isn't healthy. I think I might withdraw and try again next year maybe, I'm so sorry Hakim (yes I know but sometimes sorry is the only word that will do!) to have wasted so much of your time.

FROM: hrajan@udu.edu.ie
TO: mlannigan@iol.ie
Re: withdrawing

Maureen, I am worried about you. Not about your thesis – since you bring to your subject a quality of fervour (obsession by another name) which, properly harnessed, will only make it more intellectually rigorous. But about you in yourself. Forgive the intrusion, but may I ask if your marital breakdown is of recent date?

FROM: mlannigan@iol.ie
TO: hrajan@udu.edu.ie
Re: breakdown

Well, you could call it that – a marital breakdown – but again the words are misleading, it's not a car that just coughed to a halt on the motorway one day. And 'break-up' sounds spontaneous and natural as well, like an iceberg cracking in two (though we know nowadays that there's a reason for that, it's called climate change…). I would say that my husband is the one who BROKE our marriage of nearly 20 years, six months ago now, by shagging (or, he insists, 'being seduced by') the neighbour's au pair, a 19-year-old from Budapest who chews her cuticles. I know it must sound as if I'm still hung up on him, believe me I'm not, he is a loathsome peddler of Oirishy (shamrock/harp/leprechaun) bric-a-brac and Miss Hungary is welcome to him. It's all this aggro with the solicitors that's getting on my nerves, I can't believe the piddling amount he's going to be forking over per month while (I happen to have seen it in his drive) he has a brand new Jeep in a particularly crass shade of yellow and it would serve him right if I did a Vivienne Eliot on it. Do you know that one, it's not an urban myth it's a fact, T. S. Eliot (the poet), his (first) wife poured melted chocolate through the letterbox of Faber & Faber where he worked. I can't work out what the chocolate symbolised – faeces, or am I being too literal? I wonder how many bars of Cadbury's Dairy Milk it would take to cover the Jeep. Sorry (again) Hakim, you didn't ask for all this, I'm just free-associating here, you're very easy to talk to somehow (in any medium), you don't judge, I think that's it, and you have a kind of kindness and a gravitas I've never met in anyone under 30. Are you much under 30, I wonder? I do know I'm a bit of a nutcase these days. I'm not so much of a nutcase that I don't know it. Could I come in tomorrow sometime? Damn – you don't work on Wednesdays. Or rather you don't have office hours, which probably means you're working on your real work (something Early German?) which is actually important work unlike listening to or reading my muddled ramblings. You may also have a life (!), a wife and children here (or back home?), I have no idea, sorry.

FROM: hrajan@udu.edu.ie
TO: mlannigan@iol.ie
Re: breakdowns in various senses

My dear Maureen, the irrationality and unhappiness of your tone worries me very much. If I may speak frankly, a doctor would probably advise you to take pills of some sort to help you though this difficult transition, but in my own experience work (even of a somewhat obsessive nature) can be as effective a medicine.

As it happens I am single and 32, a matter of grave concern to my parents. So I cannot draw on the wisdom of experience when speaking about marriage. But it sounds to me as if you have wasted enough of your Cadbury's on this man already. If I may offer an applicable proverb, which is common to Early German and to many other traditions, the best revenge is living well.

FROM: mlannigan@iol.ie
TO: hrajan@udu.edu.ie
Re: oh I know

Oh I know I know I know, Hakim, he's no loss. And hating him is the last tie I have to cut. I just need to find a way to do it. A suitable punishment – like one of my urban myths. Set fire to his yellow fucking Jeep, or something … (sorry) He can't be let get away with this, jumping from one woman to another like a frog between lily pads! And did it have to be a 19-year-old with tits up to her chin? Bad enough if he'd gone for somebody else my age, but to look in their window and see them laughing together over their beer bottles, I feel like such a raddled bitter old bag –

Must run.

FROM: hrajan@udu.edu.ie
TO: mlannigan@iol.ie
Re: punishment

Maureen, perhaps you should rely on karma (divine justice, you might call it?) to mete out the punishment for you? After all, the 'laughter' is hardly likely to last. The young woman from Budapest is not likely to devote herself to such a man with devotion and zest the way you did. I think you can feel confident that sooner or later, your former husband will be hurt as much as he has hurt you, but (unlike you) he will not have so much spirit left in him.

I wonder would you like to come in for supervision today or tomorrow?

FROM: hrajan@udu.edu.ie
TO: mlannigan@iol.ie
Re: supervision

I have not heard back from you, but I am still available to meet; just call my office. I hope everything is all right. I hope you have not gone to your former husband's house.

FROM: hrajan@udu.edu.ie
TO: mlannigan@iol.ie
Re: ?

Maureen, I urge you to reconsider before it is too late. Any act of arson would be highly dangerous and (especially on such

an expensive vehicle as a Jeep) could have disastrous conse-
quences for your future. I beg of you to talk to someone (your
sister? a doctor? and I repeat, I am available anytime) before
you do anything rash.

FROM: hrajan@udu.edu.ie
TO: mlannigan@iol.ie
Re: ??????

Maureen, where are you? I asked the Secretary for your cell-
phone number but she claims not to have it. I suspect that she
has it but that there's a policy of not giving it out, which is
absurd given that I'm your supervisor and have reason to be
terribly concerned about your welfare.

Maureen, please please please get in touch.

You have no reason to feel like a 'raddled bitter old bag',
or indeed a vengeful archetype in an internet joke. You're a
beautiful woman with a life ahead of you, which will contain
many forms of intellectual and personal happiness.

This bastard is not worth it!!!

FROM: mlannigan@iol.ie
TO: hrajan@iol.ie
Re: it's OK

Jesus Hakim, I'm SO sorry (sorry, I really do have to say sorry
here) to have given you a fright, I think the server was down
yesterday so I didn't get your four emails till they came all
together this morning. Yesterday I was in the library all day.
I just tried to ring your office but you're not in yet. I swear I
was never really going to set his Jeep (or anything) on fire, you
mustn't take the Irish too literally, we're all talk.

Let me know you got this –

FROM: hrajan@udu.edu.ie
TO: mlannigan@iol.ie
Re: apology

It is my turn to apologise, Maureen, for my overreaction. (I think perhaps it is I who am in an irrational and unstable state.) I am going to ask Professor Jarrell this afternoon if he would mind stepping in to replace me as your supervisor.

FROM mlannigan@iol.ie
TO hrajan@udu.edu.ie
Re: no!

That's ridiculous, Hakim, you were only being nice. I don't want you to stop being my supervisor.
    For my number, see below.

FROM hrajan@udu.edu.ie
TO mlannigan@iol.ie
Re: nice

I was not only being nice. I spoke (emailed) in a completely inappropriate way.

FROM mlannigan@iol.ie
TO: hrajan@udu.edu.ie
Re: inappropriate

Do you mean the bit where you called my ex a bastard or the bit where you said I was beautiful? Because the first is just a fact, and as for the second, I don't think it's ever inappropriate to tell someone she's beautiful.

FROM: hrajan@udu.edu.ie
TO: mlannigan@iol.ie
Re: appropriateness

According to the University's code of conduct, it was an exploi-
tation of my position of trust for me to tell you so yesterday,
but by the end of this working day (since Professor Jarrell has
reluctantly agreed to relieve me of my supervisory role) it will
only be inadvisable. So if that's all right with you, at 5 pm I will
call you and tell you so again.

Roddy Doyle

Roddy Doyle has written nine novels, including *The Commitments, Paddy Clarke Ha Ha Ha* – for which he won the Booker Prize in 1993 – and *Paula Spencer*. He has also written two short story collections, six books for children, and plays and scripts for screen, television and radio. His adaptation of Gogol's *The Government Inspector* ran at the Abbey Theatre for eight weeks, from December 2011. His latest books are the short story collection *Bullfighting* and *A Greyhound of a Girl* for young readers. He lives and works in Dublin.

Karaoke

This was going to be the last place, the table they'd stay at till it was time to get up and find the beds. The women strolled past; mothers, grandmothers, girls learning to walk like their mothers. There were men too, but Sam was drunk enough to be able to look only at the women.

It had been a long night – a good day.

The dead places came alive on Saturday. The lesbians' bar had been empty all week but there were three other people in it tonight.

– Jesus, it's packed.

– All of them at the pool table.

They'd called it the lesbians' bar because the woman behind the counter had short hair and didn't smile. One of the men at the pool table – there were two men and a woman – had followed Sam out to the jacks. Sam heard the guy walking behind him in the narrow corridor. Then he stood beside him at the urinal. But Sam still managed to piss – he was pleased with that. The guy beside him said something. A strange looking man, too old for his clothes and dyed hair. Just one word – Sam couldn't make it out.

– Wha'?

– Cocaine?

For fuck sake.

– I'm not sellin' any, Sam had said.

– No, said the other fella, the Spanish guy. –I sell.

– No, said Sam.

– No?

– No.

– Your friends, they like?

– No way, he said. –Don't even ask them.

It was sound advice, although it had sounded rough. None of them had ever done drugs, except the odd joint, way back. Lester had nearly lost his daughter – hallucinating, screaming, trying to tear through the kitchen wall with her fingernails. She'd passed out and the ambulance lads had managed to save her, a young one of fifteen out with her pals, and she'd come home in that state – some pill or other. That was ten years ago. She was grand now, lived in a house of her own down near Gorey somewhere, but Lester had watched her start to die on his kitchen floor. Drugs were a sore point, especially when they were pissed or on their way there. Sam didn't say anything to Lester or Shay when he got back from the jacks.

That had been a good while back, hours ago.

They'd made the decision – one last drink, then back to the apartment.

But it didn't happen.

Lester stood up.

– Karaoke, he said.

He was gone already, in among the strollers. Sam and Shay went after him – they'd no choice. Lester had the keys. Lester had the kitty.

– What's he fuckin' up to?

– Fuck knows.

They saw him go into one of the bars they hadn't bothered with before. Bar Karaoke. There was some kind of a hall, with a plastic roof and a palm tree. The door into the bar was done up like the entrance to a Spanish Santa's grotto. The music inside was loud and dreadful. The voice, a woman's, would have been grand at home in her bathroom. Here, amplified, rolling down the hall, it should have been illegal.

Lester was just ahead.

– Lester! Sam shouted.

Too late. Lester hadn't heard, or he hadn't cared. They'd have to follow. Lester had the kitty and the keys. Lester always had the kitty and the keys, even back in Dublin, when they all had their own keys. Lester was the man in charge. It rarely mattered, and it didn't really matter now.

Santa's lintel was low. Sam had to duck.

The woman with the microphone was probably forty. She was singing to about twelve other women, all about the same age. They looked like sisters, the lot of them. If it had been Dublin, they'd have been screaming, roaring at their pal making a sap of herself on the stage. Here, they just sat, looking. There wasn't a drunk face among them.

Lester was up at the bar. The only customer.

– I've ordered, he told Sam.

– Grand, said Sam.

He looked at the woman singing. She was droning along to one of those songs that could just have easily been Italian or Latvian – Eurovision music. She looked so earnest up on the little stage, like she expected an impresario, or Louis Walsh, to come through Santa's door with a contract. Or maybe it was the lyrics. She was back in school, trying to remember what she'd learnt the night before. Her head nodded slightly as she read and sang each syllable.

– This is shite.

– Brilliant, yeah.

They were having to shout.

The woman on the stage was finished, replaced by one of her sisters. She started singing the same song – same voice, same nodding. The same woman in a different blouse.

The barman arrived holding a glass you could have washed a baby in.

– What the fuck is that?

– Don't know, said Lester. – I just pointed to it on the menu.

– A fuckin' cocktail?

– There's one for everyone in the audience.

The barman came back with a second glass. He had to use both hands to hold it.

– I don't want a fuckin' cocktail, said Sam.

– Just drink the fuckin' thing.

– Okay.

It was a field and vodka – that was what it looked like. Or a lily pond, with a yellow straw. There was something not right, something just fuckin' wrong, about an adult man putting a straw into his mouth. But the glass was too big to get up to his mouth.

– How is it? said Lester.

– Grand, said Shay.

– Good, yeah, said Sam.

It was. It was lovely. But he didn't want it. He knew it was lethal; it was going to make him stupid. He was going to cry or fight or fuckin' sing.

They said nothing for a bit. It was too loud. They were staring at the women, trying to make sense of them.

Lester had the menu again.

– I don't want another one, Sam shouted.

– No, said Lester. –It's the songs.

He shouted at the barman.

– Here!

The barman was all sweat and smile. He leaned across the bar, so he could read what Lester was pointing at.

– You're not singin'? said Sam.

He looked to Shay for support, but Shay was sucking up his lily pond. Either that, or trying to fit his face into the glass.

– I am, yeah, said Lester.

– No.

– Fuckin' yeah.

– They're shite.

– *They* are, said Lester.

The latest woman was climbing off the stage.

– Mind me drink, said Lester, and he went across to the stage, hitched his shorts, and stepped up.

– Hello, Spain, he said.

Shay whooped into his straw.

– Here's one I wrote earlier, said Lester.

The barman pressed a button on a console behind the bar, and gave Lester the thumbs up. The music started – a squawk and then notes.

– Oh, for fuck sake.

It was 'Satisfaction'. And it – *he* – was desperate. One note in his fuckin' head, and it was a bad one. Sam wanted to go over and kill him. It was the drink, whatever it was he'd been sucking out of the bath beside him on the counter. He wanted to grab the mic from Lester's hand, to end it. To get them out, back to the apartment. They were heading out of beer, into spirits – out of drunk and into madness.

Shay beside him whooped. He was upright again, clinging to the counter.

– Good man, Lester! Up the fuckin' Republic!

The barman smiled at him, shook his head. Sam expected him to draw his open hand across his neck, like a knife – a warning to Shay. But he didn't. Shay leaned across the counter, kind of climbed onto it – lay on it, his hand outstretched, wanting the barman to take it.

– You an' me, bud! Up Spain.

The barman took Shay's hand – he touched it, lightly, then held Shay's shoulders and gently shoved him back across the counter.

– Franco was a cunt, amn't I right?!

Lester was trying to persuade the twelve Spanish sisters to clap.

– Come on! It's *real* music!

Something was going to happen. Nothing surer – it was already happening. Texts were being sent. Knives were being honed. A hole was being dug. Sam could feel the morning's headache. He was having it now because he wasn't going to see the morning. The barman was gone. The women were moving, shifting. There was action outside – coming in.

– Come on, said Sam.

– What?!

He looked around for another door.

– Come on!

– Why?!

It was a wedding. Coming through Santa's door. A gang of bridesmaids or something, all lively, lovely and laughing. They were younger than the karaoke sisters. And a gang of lads. They weren't hard men or assassins. They were in the good trousers and shirts, ties loosened – Spanish culchies. They were with the bridesmaids, or whatever the girls were, but not in the same way Irish lads would have been. There was nothing aggressive or even stupid about them. They hadn't been drinking.

Lester had given up.

– Fuck yis an' good night, he said, and he came back to the bar.

– What's the story here?

– Weddin'.

– How d'you know?

The guests – it was definitely a wedding – were still pouring in. They all turned to face Santa's door and started to clap, and the happy couple walked in.

– Fuckin' hell. See this?

The bride and groom hated each other. Their friends' applause was a defense against the fact. The newly-weds were holding hands, doing what was expected. But it was clear – there – in front of them. It wasn't a tiff or a misunderstanding; they weren't going to rip the good clothes off each other at the end of the night. The hatred crackled. They couldn't look at each other.

– There's a story here.

– There fuckin' is.

Lester had ordered three more baths. Sam didn't object. He wasn't going anywhere.

She was beautiful, and he wasn't. She was like your one, Penelope Cruz. Not nearly as good looking, but gorgeous all the same. Her new husband was like your man from *The Big Lebowski*. Not the Dude – Jeff Bridges. His pal – Lebowski's pal. Sam couldn't remember the name. It was the groom's beard. It didn't hide the fat under his chin.

– John Goodman, Sam remembered.

– What about him? said Lester.

– *The Big Lebowski*.

– Great film.

– Your man looks like him. The groom.

– You're right.

Shay roared across the room.

– Shut the fuck up, Donnie!

– Shut up, for fuck sake.

– The Dude abides!

– Here's your drink, look. Shut up.

– She's pregnant, said Lester. –She has to be.

It made sense.

– There's no other explanation, said Lester.

– Maybe he's filthy rich, said Sam.

– Ah, look at her but, said Lester. –She's lovely. She wouldn't marry that prick for money.

– Maybe it is John Goodman.

– I'm going to check, said Shay.

– Where are you fuckin' going?

It was too late to grab him. Shay was gone. Straight up to the bride.

– Oh fuck.

Then he was dancing with her. The other girls and boys got out of the way. And Shay brought her around the floor, to the one-note beat of a karaoke sister. Others joined in. Shay had started a dance.

– Takes the Irish to get the ball rollin'.

– Ah, don't start that aren't-we-great shite.

– It's good but.

– Fuck off, said Lester. -D'you think he'll try to get off with her?

– God, I hope not, said Sam. –He won't.

– He's been a bit weird but, hasn't he?

– Well, if he drops the hand, I'm gone. I'm not jokin'.

– Hang on, shut up.

John Goodman was right beside them, at the bar. He was handing bottles of San Miguel back over his shoulder.

And Shay was coming back.

– She's not pregnant!

He was right up at them now, still shouting.

– Definitely, she's not!

– Shut up, for fuck sake.

– She's fuckin' gorgeous!

– Shut up!

Shay saw John Goodman and started laughing. John Goodman was still passing back the bottles. Still angry, and affable. Sam could nearly hear teeth grinding.

He looked at the bride. She was dancing with someone else, laughing. She didn't look like a messer. She was lovely.

– Look at this.

John Goodman had put three bottles in front of them.

– For us?

– For you. Yes.

– Ah, thanks.

They tapped his bottle with theirs – one, two, and three.

– Congratulations, by the way.

– Yeah. Fair play.

– Thank, said John Goodman. –Thank you.

He'd stopped passing back the bottles.

– Expensive round, said Sam.

John Goodman smiled.

– D'yeh speak English, son? Sam asked him.

Since he'd hit fifty, Sam had been calling all younger men 'son'. He was the man who'd lived, the sage, the fuckin' chieftain, the man who knew enough. Although he knew fuck all. He knew his name and how to breathe and find his way back to the apartment. That was about it.

– No, said John Goodman. – Some.

– Grand.

They clinked bottles again.

– You're a lucky fuckin' man, said Shay.

Lester laughed.

– Jesus.

The four men looked out at the room, the mass of women and men, all young, all lovely. The bride was in among them. At home.

Sam looked at John Goodman. He didn't feel sorry for him. He felt jealous. It was weird, but that was it. He was jealous. He'd have given anything to be furious like that again, to give a fuck. To be hated by that woman.

– You'll be grand, he said. – D'you understand? You'll be grand. The Dude abides.

Dermot Healy

Dermot Healy is a novelist, playwright, photographer and poet. He is a Hennessy Award winner, and a recipient of the Tom Gallon Award, The Encore Award and The Irish American Literature Award. In 2011, he was short-listed for the Poetry Now Award for his collection, *A Fool's Errand*. His most recent novel, *Long Time No See* (2011) is published by Faber & Faber.

Along the Lines

He lived in an ancient place. His house of three rooms sat to the side of a fort. Stone walls ran through the fields.

His back yard was a field of whins and grey gravel. Beyond it was the railway line where a few trains a day ran over and back between Sligo and Connolly Station in Dublin.

He was always at the back door to watch them go by as he learned his lines. After the first train in the morning he made the porridge. After the second he ate the pancakes. The midday train meant a shot of bourbon. The one heading the other way in the late afternoon meant climbing on the bike and heading for Henderson's pub where the carpenters, plumbers and house painters gathered and met up with the local farmers.

They talked of nothing but money and local deaths, and shouted out laughter in a nearly insane manner.

He grew to hate that laugh.

It was not humour.

He could not enter the banter. He grew to hate that talk of hard times as more drinks were ordered. His face grew grim. They thought he thought he was above them. Sometimes his face would suddenly appear in an ad on the TV, and there'd be a momentary silence as they grinned and looked at him, and then at each other, and shook their heads before re-entering the aggression of the recession while he checked the time.

Good luck men, I have to go, he said, downing his glass of gin.

Goodbye Mister O'Hehir, nodded the barman.

Good luck Joe, called the plumber.

I would not like to be here after I'm gone, he thought as he stepped out the door.

Joe O'Hehir hopped on his bike and rode to The Coach Inn, which was surrounded by cars. He sipped his Sauvignon Blanc and ordered goujons of cod with chips, and then sat by himself for two to three hours watching the old folk collect for meals alongside groups of young folk. Old professors, architects and electricians sat alongside ancient nurses, doctors and secretaries. A nun and priest led a funeral party all in black to a table. In the background Frank Sinatra was singing, then along came Dean Martin as soup bubbled in spoons and prawns slipped through leaves of rocket. Joe read his books on Ghosts and Mysteries, then headed back to his script and began mouthing the lines to himself.

Over the speakers came 'I Got You Babe', 'I Want To Go Home', 'Take A Load Off Sally'.

For weeks he'd disappear, take the train to Dublin and enter rehearsals, and eventually take his place on stage. He always stayed in the same B&B, a place filled with tourists and backpackers and computer screens. Amidst the entire furore his silence grew.

He'd stand under the bridge down the street to hear the train pass over his head. He reread old scripts in McDonald's Café. The hallucinations grew.

Then on the opening night of the play towards the end he dried up. The others waited. He stared out at the audience. It was a sad moment in the script, and the distress the audience saw in his face they read as part of the character's inner self as he approached the bad news.

Off stage, a cue was whispered.

It looked like a tear appeared in one of his eyes.

He lay his head down, and the other actors watched their mate's extreme trauma. In rehearsal the sadness lasted only a minute. Now it had reached three minutes of silence. Then suddenly he threw up his head and out of his mouth came all the mad laughs from Henderson's, the laugh at what was not a joke, out came scattered lines with always the Ha-Ha, Jesus there's not a penny to be had, Ha! Ha! Bastards, give me a half one, Ha! Ha! He bobbed to and fro tossing imaginary glasses into his mouth, read imaginary papers for a second. Look at what's going on down there, he said, prodding the non-existent article, Ha! Ha! They know nothing, nothing, do you hear me, nothing! Win a stroll in Christ! and he roared laughing as the curtain came slowly down and the lights went off, ten minutes before they should have.

I have inherited the gene, he said to himself as he ran down to his room, undressed and prepared to go.

Joe, stay there please, shouted the director. We need to talk. Badly.

Joe eyed him.

What happened? he asked.

Christine Dwyer Hickey

Christine Dwyer Hickey is an award-winning novelist and short story writer. She is the author of the Dublin Trilogy – *The Dancer* (short-listed for Irish novel of the year), *The Gambler* and *The Gatemaker* (1995-2000) – which spans three generations of a Dublin family from 1913-1956. Her bestselling novel *Tatty* was chosen as one of the 50 Irish Books of the Decade, long-listed for the Orange Prize and short-listed for the Hughes & Hughes Irish Novel of the Year Award. Her novel *Last Train from Liguria* was also a bestseller (Atlantic Books UK) and was nominated for the *Prix L'Européen de Littérature*. Her latest novel *The Cold Eye of Heaven* (Atlantic Books UK, 2011) has already received wide critical acclaim and been short-listed for the Hughes & Hughes Irish Book of the Year. Two-time winner of the Listowel Writers' Week short story competition, as well as a winner in the prestigious Observer/Penguin competition, her short stories have been published in several anthologies and world-wide literary magazines. She is a member of Aosdana.

Windows of Eyes

The girl forced her hands up out of her pockets, then further up to the back of her neck. They clutched the collar of her gabardine coat and drew it up as far as it would go. She wished she hadn't cut her hair now; her hair could have acted as a sort of sponge against the rain and the back of her neck wouldn't have to feel like a concrete block.

She came into Castlewood Avenue, taking the slip lane off it, before turning into the cutaway that led past the cottages. She had covered these streets already today, scuttling with them from Ballsbridge to here. Tight little corners and squeezed in cottages; back lane entrances to big houses out on the main roads. Barely enough room for a car to pass through, no fear of a bus with its windows of eyes.

Maybe it would look different now, going the opposite way, on the opposite side of the road. Maybe it would look different in the dark. But except for the occasional piddle of light from an upstairs window, it was the same. Same rain-stained walls; same broken bin outside same banjaxed garage door. The sky was a different colour now. That's all.

Her hands were shaking; she watched them fumble at coins on her palm under a pyramid of streetlight. There was a fiver in her pencil-case and four cigarettes left in the box: that was her lot. On her palm, enough coins to pay for a newspaper and a lighter, neither of which was necessary. But the thought of having to ask a stranger on the street for a light. And the thought, too, of sitting in a café without a newspaper to hide behind.

There were books in her bag – plenty of books – but she didn't want to be reminded of school or of tomorrow, and she didn't want either to look like a schoolgirl alone in a late night café. She came out of the cutaway on to Mount Pleasant Avenue.

Window after window of night-shaded darkness. Houses that were cut into makey-up homes; a cluster of bells to a door. Not a human in sight. Cars though, as far as the eye could see, head to toe, on both sides of the road. Cars that were sleek with rain and streetlight. She found something beautiful in the sturdy shape of them, their rain-polished shells and their promise of soft, dry interiors. One careless driver – that's all it would take – one forgotten door left unlocked. One out of so many. She could come back to it later, after the café, slip in, lock the door safely behind her. Some cars even had rugs in them. Plaid, hairy rugs you'd often see folded on a shelf at the back window. She could curl up on the floor. But she would need to be gone before daylight and what if she slept it out in her hair plaid parcel? Or worse, what if the owner was a shift worker? Someone who started the day before the night was over? There was no way of knowing. If she lived along here, she might have some idea of who owned which car and what time they set off; the Mondeo man with the briefcase that left on the dot of seven. The dental receptionist who hopped into her Mini Cooper at a quarter past nine. But her house was away from here. Twenty-one bus stops away and not far enough at that.

She decided to forget about the cars, about where or how she would sleep. Step by step was enough for the moment; moment by moment. Step by step, the next smoke, and soon the café.

She came to a pub on a corner. A curve of warm yellow light. Shapes dancing on a television screen high on the wall. The back view of a man looking up at it, one hand stretched towards his pint on the counter, the other on his hip. The slow movement of a nearby barman. At a table just inside the window, a young man – not all that much older than herself – was staring out at her. Why was he staring? He nudged his companion who looked up from his pint and then they both sent out an exaggerated wave and a sarcastic type of smile. Jeering her. She realised then that she'd been staring in – how long had she been staring in? – and that's why they were staring out. Cheeks burning, she hurried away; cold rain smacking on her face until the heat was replaced by a painful tingle.

At the top of the avenue she could see the main road; only a few cars passing now, silent intervals between them. On the far side of the road, a strip of dark grass, the big raggy heads on an alley of trees, the pathway, the bank; behind all that, canal water.

On the bank looking down, she stood for a while, pockmarks of rain on a skin of green water. She could see the hooked neck of a swan in the shadow of the bridge and hear a purr of music from one of the pubs on the street above. On the opposite bank a man in a tracksuit running under trees jabbed punches on the air; double right, triple left, double right again. The quarter chime from the town hall clock came out of nowhere.

She couldn't seem to remember which quarter it was – a quarter to, or a quarter past? Maybe half past then? But half past what? Ten? Eleven?

One cigarette per hour, that was the deal she had made with herself. After four cigarettes, it would be time to eat. How many had she smoked so far? Now she was all mixed up. Numbers and chimes rattled inside her head; the nuts and bolts of lost time. After all the hours of nursing the minutes, adding them up, reining them in. After all that, she couldn't even remember.

She turned from the canal bank and made for the road. A car was parked at the edge, a man's half-face looking out over a half-mast window. He said something to her. Something she couldn't quite catch….

She passed under the light. 'Sorry, I didn't quite…?'

The man moved his hand as if to swat her away. 'Doesn't matter, forget it,' he said, the window gliding upwards as he drove away.

It would get brighter, she told herself, the further she walked, the closer she came to Rathmines centre. The town hall clock was lit up anyway, lit up like a big fat moon. Returning the time to her – a quarter to eleven. She could see the dome of the church now, a giant military helmet, peering awkwardly over the rooftops.

Across the road was a square – a playing field really, black trees and black grass. Railings. She considered going over to it, looking for a space to squeeze through, maybe find a spot in the bushes where she could make a nest for later on. But the dark seemed too solid on that side of the street and the road seemed too wide to cross with her legs too heavy and sore to do anything other than stay on a long, straight line.

She was almost at the church and wondered about going inside. She could sit down on a dry seat anyway. Light a candle, hold her hands over its sharp little flame. Pretend to put money in the slot.

But there would be no sound to confirm that a coin had dropped and someone might notice the silence. She could count the statues instead, study their faces. But if she did go in, it would be her second time that day and what if the same priest was in there pottering around? He'd wonder what she was at. He might ask if she wanted confession. He might think she had some sort of a vocation and want to talk to her about God. Or he might ask other questions. What was her name and where she did she live and what was she doing out so late on her own?

She came to the gates and peered through, past pillars and portico; the four long iron doors had been locked for the night.

Further along. A bus in the distance. A familiar number on it, sharpening into focus. She turned her face to the window of an empty shop. The bus stalled behind her, sighed, then screeched off again. A jagged reflection of light on the glass and over the floor of the shop; bare shelves and old letters, dead flies and dust.

In Londis, people were buying small; small sliced pans, small cartons of milk. You could get twin sausages wrapped in cellophane. You could buy one egg. There were men in the queue with cement-sugared boots and a gypsy woman wearing chubby runners. She bought the evening paper and picked out the smallest lighter, dropping her money into a cupped brown hand.

In the doorway of a charity shop, she turned the lighter over and over in her hand and waited for the hour to chime.

The window display held its own story: an old-fashioned evening bag and a bookcase of books, there were candlesticks and a lamp, a spotty dress on a headless dummy. The hour sounded, chimes blooming and shrinking over Rathmines.

A negative print of herself on the glass. Pale hands moving through a tangle of smoke; cigarette floating to and from an unseen mouth watched with unseen eyes. Almost done, one more pull and the cigarette would be past the golden ring just above the butt. One half a pull and it would be over. She came out of the doorway and the rain had stopped.

There was a palm tree painted on the sign above the café and the words *Sunset Strip Café* written in a slant beside it. She remembered when she was small, her cousin telling her that this was a rude place where women took off their clothes and men whistled loudly. For years she had believed that.

She pushed the door in; glass smeared with fog and long trickles of condensation, as if it was raining indoors. A blurt of greasy hot steam on her face, making her feel hungry and sick all at once. A sting of fluorescent light in her eyes. She waited for the blots and squiggles to clear, then closed the door behind her.

A thin figure in pink polyester was clattering behind the counter. Scant hair tied at the back, black eyeliner. One eyebrow lifted as if to say… Well, what do *you* want?

Her order stumbled out and the waitress quickly caught it. It seemed like only seconds before a cup and saucer landed on the counter, followed by a pyrex plate with a slice of bread cut on the diagonal, the bread already buttered or more likely margarined.

The café was long and narrow; rows of tables cut by a long, narrow aisle. A counter to one side, another half-row of tables just behind it. Across the ranks, single occupants zig-zagged; one to a table. At the back wall, a pair of toilet doors; silhouette of a top hatted gent on one, lady-in-waiting on the other. A table near the toilets would be best. She could leave her stuff down and duck inside, steep her hands in hot water; stoop her head under the hand dryer, a blast of scorching air on the back of her neck. But it was a long trek to the end of the café with her bag dragging down on one shoulder and the fingers of both hands trying to keep a grip on the plate as well as the cup and saucer and the sudden heat drawing a long, watery snot from her nose.

Cup and saucer chattering like minute teeth in her hand, she slid into the nearest seat. She released her bag from her shoulder, let it slide down to the floor, then pulled a napkin from the dispenser on the wall and furtively dabbed at her nostril.

The man sitting opposite had his evening paper perched on the cruet set. He shifted the paper a few inches to the right, but otherwise gave no sign that he'd noticed her. He was eating a mixed grill, moving the food around his plate as he ate so that she caught rotating glimpses of his meal under the hem of his paper. The nub of a sausage, the frill of rasher rind, a daub of egg yolk, black pudding. Ramming the lumps into this mouth, slurping on the tea, topping it up from large pot here and there, he reached and chewed and sawed and chomped. His eyes never left his paper.

The waitress came over with a side plate of chips and a small pot of tea. Is that your lot? her smudged eyes seemed to say. She put the bill to the table, nailing it down with a vinegar bottle.

The chips felt hard in her mouth; hard and tainted with cheap oil. There was no pleasure to be had from them yet she had to control the urge to wolf them down. There was a sort of yearning at the pit of her stomach, and in her throat a compulsive gulping as if the throat itself was trying to independently grab hold of the chips. She told herself, slow down, slow down.

Nowhere to put her newspaper; the man opposite was taking up too much space. It had been a waste to buy it. She glanced at the bill – cheaper than she had expected it to be. Had she not bothered with the paper she could have afforded something better; chips on a bigger plate, an egg maybe. She looked down the café. All the tables occupied by men. Repeats of the man at her table. Newspapers and mixed grills; a trick with mirrors. A table to the side had just become vacant, but she felt somehow it would be bad manners to move to it now. Not that the man opposite her would notice or care. But the waitress would – closing time soon – she could see it in her tired, fluorescent-lit face.

Almost finished. Her hand reached for the last chip. No more than a couple of bites left on the slice of bread. The tea nearly gone. The waitress would have the lot whipped away from her in seconds and she'd be back out on the street. She lifted the teapot and shook out the last drop. All the hours that had been leading up this. All the quarter hours she had built up with minutes then crossed off in her head. Just to bring her that bit closer to here. To this tea and these chips, this hard slice of bread.

To a notion of warmth: in her belly, on her face, the flat of her hand when she patted the teapot. Now it was nearly over. And after this, what?

The man opposite stood up sharply, his chair scraping along the floor. He rolled his paper, stuck it into his jacket pocket then collected his bits: keys, pen, a folded tweed cap. He took a step away then came back for the bill stretching over the table and leaving behind him a yeasty whiff of beer and egg. His eye rims were raw, she noticed, the eyes dead in his head.

She looked down at the remains on his plate. A scatter of chips stained with ketchup; a chop that needed handling in order to be finished; a whole sausage and two dark turdish pieces of liver. It was the sausage that got to her. Thick, brown, glistening, uncut.

Her hand made a few cautious moves in the direction of the plate. Once it even touched the rim but immediately withdrew. She lifted the empty cup to her lips and pretended to drink, put the cup down again and spent a few seconds biting the side of her thumbnail. Her hand went down and over again.

Cold sausage meat, clammy on the roof of her mouth, rubbery and stubborn. She chewed on, jaws frantically clicking but the sausage refused to be broken down. The ping of a cash register behind her, the slow creak of the door, now the man, cap on head passing the window.

The waitress was beside her; polyester arm clearing the debris from the table. She didn't have to look up to know she'd been caught in the act. The warm mess sitting like something alive in her mouth.

Her hand reached down, lifted the flaps of her schoolbag, dipped in and patted around till the pencil case was located. Her fingers pulled the fiver out and left it with the bill on the table.

Damp coat slapping on the back of her legs along the now deserted street. She turned a corner and veered into the first doorway. She took the café napkin out of her pocket and spread it out on both hands, a picture of a tiny palm tree in one corner. Opening her mouth wide as a lion's, she pushed her tongue out as far as it would go, letting the mess drop down into the napkin; meat, gristle, a few flecks of sausage skin, her own warm, sour spit. The girl remembered then, the large, fat fingers of the man and the way the dirt of the day, or maybe even days, had been lodged into the creases in his knuckles and smeared on the cuff of his shirtsleeves and under his finger-nails in thick, black arches.

Declan Hughes

Declan Hughes is the author of the Ed Loy PI series: *The Wrong Kind of Blood*; *The Colour of Blood*, *The Dying Breed* (US: *The Price of Blood*); *All The Dead Voices*; and *City of Lost Girls*. His books have been nominated for the Edgar, CWA New Blood Dagger, Shamus and Macavity awards, and *The Wrong Kind of Blood* won the Shamus for Best First PI Novel. Declan is also an award-winning playwright and screen-writer, and the co-founder of Dublin's Rough Magic Theatre Company. Declan lives with his wife and two daughters by the sea in South Dublin, Ireland.

Gloria

On Christmas Eve morning in the doorway of his small house in the grounds of the Church of the Assumption, Father Gerry Conway asked me to find his daughter.

'I have the address,' he said. 'It's just down the road.'

He turned to a block of green post-it notes on the scuffed hall table and scratched on the top with a red pencil.

'Is she in danger?' I said. 'Is it an emergency?'

'Oh no,' he said. 'Nothing like that.'

He tore off a post-it note and thrust it at me and nodded, as if I were a messenger boy. I looked at the red legend on green paper, noted the seasonal colours, put it in my coat pocket and blew through my cupped hands.

'Why don't you ask me in, Gerry?' I said.

'Christmas Eve,' he said. 'I'm run off my feet, you can imagine. And sure you have the address.'

'That's right, I have the address. So I don't need to find your daughter. You already know where she is.'

Father Gerry Conway blinked hard. Liquor pooled in his pale blue eyes, seeped out and trailed across his pale grey cheeks. He looked as if he had been drinking, and as if he had a cold, and as if he had been crying. He did a thing with his eyebrows and pulled air in through his teeth, as if to say he was a terrible man for mixing things up.

'Did I say find? I meant, talk to her. And anyway, she may not be there. Although she probably is.'

'Talk to her.'

'Yes.'

'About what?'

Father Gerry Conway blinked again, and almost laughed, and I thought he might burst into tears. He did something else with his face then, and his hands joined in, frowning and clenching and grimacing, a man whose patience had been tried to the limit and beyond.

I stood and stared at him, my face as expressionless as I could make it, and waited for him to speak. Sometimes, it seems as if my entire working life is spent waiting for people to tell me things they'd prefer to keep hidden, even, or especially, from themselves.

The church bell began to ring. On five, without a word, Father Gerry Conway stepped to one side and bowed me in.

'I may as well make coffee,' he said, sounding weary but steadfast, and left me on my own in the main reception room.

There was a worn brown leather three-piece suite by the front window, a brown mahogany table and chairs by the rear window and a small desk tucked into the corner alcove beside the door to the kitchen. The carpet was a burgundy colour and so were the walls, which were hung with framed paintings of women: the Blessed Virgin Mary, and St Theresa of Avila, and St Brigid, and St Catherine of Siena, and others I didn't recognise. Some were prints and some were originals; some were Catholic in style and some icons in the Greek and Russian Orthodox tradition; all were the same size, about eight inches by five. Among them, there were framed photographs of a woman with ash-blond, bubble-permed hair in a pink jump suit, of the woman with a little dark-haired girl of about six, of the woman with the girl in her late teens or early twenties, and of the woman with a scarf on her head and shadows in her smiling, red-rimmed eyes. The girl was Deirdre, Gerry's daughter.

The woman was Mary McDermott, who lived across the road from me when we were kids, and married Gerry Conway when they were barely out of their teens, and died of ovarian cancer seven or eight years ago, not long before I came back to Dublin.

The coffee was instant, but it was hot. I sat across the table from Father Gerry Conway and looked at his gallery of madonnas and virgins and mothers and daughters and thought about the rows I'd been having with Anne, my girlfriend, and how I didn't know what was causing them or what they were really about, and wondered if we would make it through Christmas, or if we were already through and I just didn't know it yet.

'Something on your mind, Ed?' Father Gerry Conway said.

'There is. But it'll keep.'

'It might not. Things have a way of bubbling to the surface at Christmas.'

'Is that what's happened with you, Gerry? With you and Deirdre?'

Father Gerry Conway, with a broad face and pale blue eyes and a back-combed plume of salt-and-pepper hair that made him look like a Soviet-bloc apparatchik from the 1960s, tipped his great head to one side, as if considering the point, and then set his lips and nodded, not in answer to my question but as a prelude to what he had to say next.

'Did you ever play Pin the Tail on the Donkey, Ed?' he said. 'When you were a child? You know that game where you're blindfolded, and there's a cardboard donkey stuck on the wall, and they spin you round until you're giddy, and then you have to pin the donkey's tail where you think it should go? That's what talking to my wife used be like. Not all the time, mind. But some days.

'There was something she wanted from me, but I couldn't tell what it was. And the harder I tried, the worse it got. It was as if I was just meant to know, she shouldn't have to tell me. Loving her was supposed to have imbued me with sensitivity and intuition and wisdom. God help us all.'

With this, Father Gerry Conway burst out laughing, and I found myself joining in.

'Maybe she didn't know herself. What do you think, Ed?'

'Are you suggesting that women don't know what they want, Father?'

'Well. If I am – and that would only be from time to time – it's as a former husband, not as a priest, you understand. Don't want you giving scandal about me round the town.'

'A former husband and a current father. Father.'

A flush of pink appeared on Father Gerry Conway's brow. He took a sip of his coffee and grimaced at the taste, or at what I had said, or both.

'Of course, the other side is being inadequate as a husband and a father. Being, not exactly a failure, that would be to luxuriate in self-pity, just not very nice, or kind, from time to time, thoughtless and self-absorbed and inconsiderate and selfish. And making hurtful remarks, slighting and belittling, and pretending they were said without thinking, or that they were jokes, when you know and she knows that's a lie, and you're only compounding the hurt by expecting her to join in your pretence. The other side is, once a man knows a woman loves him, how far he will go to hurt her. As if he hates himself so thoroughly that the ultimate proof of her love would be if she hated him too, by witnessing him at his worst, hated him and loved him still.'

I felt the words from the Confiteor chime in my brain: *Through my fault, through my own fault, through my most grievous fault.* Is that how I had been with Anne? I couldn't say it wasn't. I hoped only at my worst, but I couldn't even swear to that.

'Did it really go as far as hate?' I said, not even trying to conceal the stake I felt I had in the answer.

'Maybe not. Love, hate. Occupational hazard on my part, the rush to abstraction. I suppose if we open ourselves to each other, we are vulnerable, there's always a risk.'

'And with your daughter … you fear you said something to hurt her? Something to make her hate you?'

'Fear? I *know* I did. I …'

He exhaled loudly, slapped his hand on the table and stood up and walked about the room, pantomiming his exasperation. He came to rest by the front window and turned to me, backlit by the low December light and began to speak as if reading from a script.

'The Church, God bless her, is so twisted with hypocrisy she may never make straight wood again. She wants men like me, because we're stable, and reliable, and have experience in the world, and of course because we're evidently not homosexual, since deep down that is what they believe is at the heart of the sex abuse scandal. It only wants us when our wives are dead, mind, which is more of it. But it will not relinquish its fear, its disdain of the flesh, from St Paul, from St Augustine, that pervades everything it says about marriage, about sex, about women, and that fear has wormed its way into my brain … and there I go now, trying to shirk responsibility. A weasel, blaming it on "the Church." Do you see, Ed? Do you see?'

'I'm afraid I don't, Gerry. You lost me there.'

'The Church –'

'Gerry, you're standing up there by the window with your fists clenched and the veins in your neck going like a priest in a film. Sit down over here and never mind the Church. Tell me what happened to your daughter.'

Father Gerry Conway looked me in the eye for the first time, and bit his lip and flashed a quick smile.

'That's right,' he said. 'That's right. Thank you, Ed.'

He joined me at the table and stared silently into his coffee cup for a while. Gerry Conway. He'd been my patrol leader in scouts. He was from Fagan's Villas, where my parents had grown up, and was as tough as you needed to be to survive that neighbourhood. He had always seemed older than the rest of us, with a natural, unassuming authority that was hard to resent. His father was a plasterer, and Gerry worked with him during holidays, and went into the building trade when he left school, building houses here and there until the boom came and he was well placed to cash in.

Maybe if Mary hadn't died, he'd've kept dealing and lost his shirt and ended up owing millions like the rest of them. Instead, he sold up and got out just in time, and went for the priesthood, a mature man with experience of the world. I wondered if he had been hasty in his decision, if he was a rebound priest, and if he'd wake up one morning and behold his gallery of women, saintly and otherwise, and realise he had made a terrible mistake.

'My daughter … Deirdre is pregnant. She lives in London. She called and said she wanted to come back, come home, to have the baby here. And I said of course, she was always welcome, sure the house is ready for her whenever she wants it. The old family home, Ed, it's lying empty, waiting for her. And she said she wasn't asking for my permission, she knew she was welcome, she was coming home tomorrow. That was last night. She called me last night to tell me she was pregnant and say she'd be here this morning. First contact in six months. And I … I was flailing a bit, trying to take it all in, and she was very … defensive aggressive, what's the expression?'

'Passive aggressive.'

'Yes. Except she'd left it too late to be passive. She'd used all the passive up before she rang. She was putting it up to me.'

'And what, you said something you regret? What did you say?'

'That's just it. I don't rememember. I can tell you what I thought. I thought, what are you only telling me now for, and is the father on the scene, and how far on are you, and are you going to be coming to Mass? In front of everyone. A priest's daughter, pregnant. Making a holy show of me.'

'You didn't say –'

'I didn't say the last thing, anyway. But it probably coloured everything else I said.'

'And what happened, did she slam down the phone, or –'

'No, we finished out the call, and I arranged to meet her at the airport. And there was no sign of her.'

'Maybe she didn't travel.'

'I drove past the house on my way back. I saw her in the window. She's there.'

'You didn't go in?'

'I didn't trust myself. Not to say some or all of that. 'A priest's daughter, pregnant.' God forgive me, is there a scold's bridle of the mind I could have fitted to prevent such thoughts?'

'Well. "The mind is its own place…"'

'"And in itself can make a hell of heaven, a heaven of hell."

'It's the tongue you have to watch.'

'Will you talk to her, Ed? You have a … a way of talking to people.'

'Is there a message?'

'Tell her the truth. That I was afraid of what I might say. That I love her, and I want the best for her. That … and ask is she going to be at Midnight Mass.'

'And will you be ashamed of her if she is?'

'I've done nothing wrong,' he said, shouted, in fact, as if goaded to distraction and beyond, and looked at me for … what? Comfort? Reassurance? Solidarity, man to man: the standing army of men who've done nothing wrong, besieged by all the women who disagree.

'We've all done something wrong, Father,' I said. 'I thought that was the church's starting point.'

'No, it's the detective's,' he said. 'Original sin is not our true beginning.'

'I misremember my catechism,' I said. 'What is, then?'

And Father Gerry Conway looked up at me from beneath his heavy brow.

'Love,' he said. 'Love.'

The family home was the one Gerry had grown up in, not the grand affair overlooking Dublin Bay from the property developer years. It had been renovated and extended but it was still a modest house. Standing in the doorway, Deirdre Conway looked more like the landlady than anyone who would live here. She had her father's thick hair, darker and longer; she wore it back-combed high and held in place with a black Alice band.

She nodded when I introduced myself, as if it were the most natural thing in the world for her father to send a private detective to talk to her. I followed her into a small kitchen that was flooded with sun-roof light, and we sat at a table laden with the remnants of breakfast and the many sections of the Christmas Eve *Irish Times*. Heavily pregnant, she was smartly dressed in well-cut navy and black. She smiled a lot, and despite her poise, which was considerable, she looked hot and tired and uncomfortable. When she spoke, her accent was convent school South County Dublin with an overlay of Kensington and Chelsea. There was gold on her fingers, but no wedding or engagement rings.

'Am I to take you as a clerical emissary, Mr Loy? That's really rather grand, isn't it? I thought the poor old Irish Catholic Church was in too much of a fix for a mere priest to afford staff?'

'I'm not being paid, Ms Conway –'

'Deirdre, please. And what does my father wish, to present his credentials?'

'I think he wants to apologise. He wouldn't tell me what for. And to tell you that he went to the airport to meet you. But of course, you weren't at the airport, were you?'

'Of course not. I'm due in a week. I had a pal fake a doctor's cert even for the ferry. Mind you, they never asked. You could rock up with a machine-gun in the car and they wouldn't even check the boot.'

'So why did he go to the airport?'

'I may have led him to suppose I was on the first Aer Lingus from Heathrow,' Deirdre said, smiling. 'Crikey, have you got your detective hat on? What does he want, to stick me for the petrol money?'

'When you called him. When you spoke. He said things on the phone he regrets. He wants you to know that.'

'What things?' Deirdre said, her smile still holding. I found myself smiling too, awkward with the absurdity of it all.

'I have absolutely no idea,' I said.

There was laughter then, from both of us, and silence after. I could hear a clock tick, and the hum of a fridge, and Deirdre Conway's breath in the warm kitchen air. And if it had a sound, and perhaps it did, I could hear myself, waiting.

'It's just fucking ridiculous, your father becoming a priest. A fucking *priest*. You know?' Deirdre eventually said. She was laughing again, but in a different way.

'After Mammy … Mummy, died … he came to visit me, you know? I went back to London, I'd been there after my finals and Mummy's cancer was very fast, the whole thing was done in four months. And my boyfriend was there, my job. I wasn't expected to stay and look after Daddy, even though maybe I could have taken time off work. But he said not to, he insisted, and I was twenty two, I could barely look after myself, I didn't know about … caring for someone. I didn't know how to do that. Still don't.

'And when he came to visit me – I'd been back a couple of times, Halloween and Christmas, and we went to Mass, and to Mammy's grave, it wasn't as if he'd become some kind of Holy Joe, but when he came – it was February, Ash Wednesday, I remember the black on his forehead – when he told me, what could I say? "Are you sure?" "It's a big step." "If you've thought it through." And I remember I was dreading it, because he's said a couple of times over the phone, "We need to talk," in a serious, I-have-something-to-say tone, and I thought, O God, he's going to marry that tart, there was a secretary who was all blonde and orange faced and South County Dublin bling, you know, and I was absolutely dreading it, but then when it turned out he wanted to become a priest, God! I wanted to say, no, it's creepy and weird and the you I know, the Dad I know, would be gone forever, marry the tart but please the fuck don't become a priest. But I didn't.'

'Have you had much contact since?'

'No. My choice. I just … and of course, I work hard, all that. But I just didn't want to … even his ordination, I … I especially didn't want to go to that. God. He's written to me every week, I have a suitcase of letters. Describing his 'journey.' And he understands how I feel, I think. He has every right to be … if he is …'

'He isn't.'

'Upset with me.'

'He's upset with himself. Well. Maybe a little with you for only telling him about the baby now. But mostly, upset and angry at himself. I don't really know why.'

'His letters … he tells me how much he feels he's failed me. That he had a calling, and logically, I was grown up. But that I maybe needed him to be around, and he didn't realise. I rarely reply, once or twice a year. Never needed money, I've done well. And it's your twenties, you really don't want to be around your parents, do you? The people I know are either working like maniacs or drinking and drugging like monkeys or both. It's like, in your twenties, you get to do what you dreamed of in your teens. Only it seems I must have dreamed of working in the city and then getting pregnant by a chap I didn't … couldn't …'

Deirdre Conway came to a halt then. She was still smiling, and she didn't seem to do tears, so I could only tell she was upset by the increasingly unsteady sound of her breathing. I felt a chivalrous impulse to protect her from distress. I resisted it.

'I've been back and forth three or four times in the last while, want the baby to be Irish, consultant at the Blackrock Clinic, saw him this morning. But I've never been to see Daddy. Never.'

'Will I tell him you'd like to see him now?'

'Two lies for the price of one,' she murmured.

'You haven't come all this way not to,' I said. 'Not this time. Unless the father …'

'Yes. Unless the father's parents live in Dublin too.'

'Does the father know?'

'You'd think he should, wouldn't you? The father. Cormac, his name is. You'd think Cormac'd know. And not have to fucking ask me. So of course I said, "No." "God no" was, in fact, how I put it. "Er, am I," stumble bumble, "you know," mutter mumble, "actually like, the father?" "God no!" is what I said.'

'Because he should have just known.'

'Of course.'

'Were you in a relationship?'

'Not with him.'

'And so what … after a fling –'

'It wasn't a fling, it was a ride. At a party. Well, more than one, at more than one party. Maybe it was a fling, but … Christ, that doesn't matter, does it?'

'He should have just known?'

'A girlfriend said I only kept the baby to get out of the relationship I was already in. Dreadful creep. Maybe she's right. You look tense, Mr Loy.'

'This isn't exactly my forte.'

'Counselling girls in trouble, I shouldn't imagine so. Where are the bloody Catholics when you need them?'

'Does the father … would he be interested?'

'He was awfully keen on me. Even after he thought the baby wasn't his.'

'But you … you didn't want a man in the picture. Before your father knew. You wanted it to be between him and you. And then you found you couldn't tell him. Is that right?'

Deirdre Conway looked towards the door, and her smile faded, and she suddenly looked exhausted.

'Maybe you should go to Midnight Mass,' I said.

'Midnight's late, for a girl in my condition.'

'They start it at 11.30 these days. That way, you could see each other without necessarily meeting.'

'Yes, like lovers at the opera. Midnight Mass at half eleven, how bloody Irish is that? Will you be there, Mr Loy?'

'I hadn't planned to be.'

'If my father hasn't hired you, can I?'

'To go to Mass with you?'

'Not even to go with. Just to be there. And perhaps afterwards, to hang around. If there's to be a meeting. Which there may or may not be, depending on how I feel.'

'You'd want me present. When you meet your father. Are you sure?'

Staring fixedly at the door, Deirdre Conway said, 'If there's a single thing you think I'm sure about, perhaps you could write it down and let me read it, Mr Loy. Because I'd love to know what it is.'

When she turned to look at me, her eyes were full of tears.

I spent an hour on the internet. Between Google, Facebook and Linkedin, I established that Deirdre Conway had gone to school at Holy Child, Killiney, studied law at Trinity College, Dublin, and that she worked as Head of Enforcement and Corporate Compliance at the London Metal Exhange. I came up with two Cormacs in her orbit, a solicitor in Cork who had been in her graduating class and a Leinster fan in London who worked at the LME. The solicitor was married to Jenni and had three kids; the Leinster fan, Cormac Quinn, tried to make it back to Dublin for home games and seemed to have no declared ties, apart from the St Michael's boys he met up with at the RDS and his parents in Booterstown. Another hour with the telephone directory and I had rooted a hungover Cormac Quinn out of bed.

He was a nice enough guy, if a bit taken aback to be told he was about to become a father, and once I'd assured him that I wasn't threatening or judging him or acting as a go-between, appeared very keen indeed to see Deirdre Conway.

I had arranged with Anne that I would come over to her house and do the whole Christmas Eve build-up. Her ex-husband had gone to New York with his girlfriend, and I got along well with her daughters, and if I sometimes felt I was in extended try-outs for a part in which I would be poorly cast, it looked to me like Anne increasingly felt the same way. But she had made it clear how important Christmas Eve was to her and the girls, and how upset they were that Kevin wouldn't be around, and how great it was that I would be there. So I wasn't looking forward to explaining how I would have to duck out and attend Midnight Mass six miles down the road. One of the many things I like about Anne is that she always listens to your reasons, even if it's just to give you enough rope. So there was a long silence at the other end of the phone while I explained all about the priest who had a daughter who was about to have a baby, and how sad it was making everyone, and where I came in. Where I came in was the bit I was having trouble with, and I kind of dwindled into silence, and waited for Anne to say something.

'Well. Why don't we come with you then? The girls' first Midnight Mass,' she said.

'You sure?'

'Why not? Hardly sounds like one of your dangerous cases.'

'No. The worst I suppose there's likely to be is tears, and recriminations –'

'But sure, isn't that Christmas?' Anne said, and hung up.

When I was eleven or twelve and allowed to go to Midnight Mass on my own, that is to say, with my friends, there were always drunks who had spilled across into the church once the Christmas Eve pubs had flung them out. These drunks felt they had to 'get Mass,' as we used to say, but they evidently didn't *want* to get Mass, and in any case, they were in such a ferment, their rebel angels having been invoked by all those tasty compliments of the season, that one of them always ended up making a scene, during the sermon, say, which was funny, or once, during the consecration, which was less so; there were bloodstains in the holy water font that year.

There were no such scenes this Christmas Eve; no recriminations either. There were tears though. In my experience, there always are, Christmas or no. Father Gerry Conway rang during the afternoon to thank me, and to say Deirdre and he had spoken on the phone, and things were grand, or they would be, grand being the Irish word for mind your own business. I don't know whether he was trying to warn me off showing up at the church, but I hadn't made the arrangement with him anyway.

I had a couple of glasses of wine with dinner, and suggested we take a taxi, but Anne said she'd drive; she didn't seem to be drinking much the last few weeks, which maybe hadn't helped matters between us.

We got to the church early, and found Deirdre Conway already there, seated about halfway down. We sat across the aisle from her. She acknowledged me with a brisk nod. When she saw Anne's face, she smiled broadly at her. Anne smiled back, and almost laughed. It was as if the two women were sharing a private joke.

I asked Anne how she knew Deirdre Conway, but she had suddenly become very attentive to Aoife and Ciara, and then the choir struck up *O Come All Ye Faithful* and we were off.

If there were drunks, they were keeping their own counsel. We sang the carols and said the prayers and Ciara, Anne's younger girl, had a nap on my shoulder during a long eucharistic prayer, and we went to communion and so did Deirdre Conway, and old ladies in the front pews who had known my mother all but pointed at her but didn't. Before the blessing, Father Gerry Conway said he hoped we would all have a happy Christmas, and that he certainly would, as his daughter had come home, and would soon be having her first child, and after a suitable hush, there was a round of applause, in which even the old ladies joined, and Deirdre Conway was crying and Anne and Aoife and Ciara were crying and who knows, I might even have shed a tear myself. It was Christmas, apparently.

Outside in the church yard, Father Gerry Conway was accepting people's congratulations and a tall man in the kind of clothes people who work in the City of London think are casual with the latest hideous scarf Leinster Rugby had inflicted on its season ticket holders was talking to Deirdre Conway. When Deirdre saw us, she came over and whispered something in Anne's ear and laughed, and Anne laughed too.

'How do you two know each other?' I said.

'We don't,' they said in unison, and laughed again. The light fell across Anne's face, and I saw how vivid her complexion seemed, the lustre of her hair, the glow of her eyes. She looked like herself, only more so, almost impossibly real, and in the instant I understood, I thought I might lose my balance.

'The Blackrock Clinic,' I said.

'The great detective!' Deirdre Conway said, and she and Anne laughed some more. Then Father Gerry Conway joined us, and Deirdre introduced Cormac to us all, and Cormac and Father Gerry Conway said something to each other about the Leinster-Ulster game to be played on Stephen's Day, and I turned to Anne.

'Should I have just known?' I said.

She shook her head.

'I only knew myself today. Only let myself know.'

She took my hand and smiled, and I smiled back. There were a lot more things we needed to say to each other but we didn't say any of them, not yet.

'Is the baby a boy or a girl?' Ciara asked Deirdre Conway.

'Ciara!' Aoife said. 'God! Embarrassing!'

'A girl,' Deirdre Conway said.

'What are you going to call her?'

Deridre Conway looked at her father, and at the father of her child, and then she put her hand on the swollen curve of her belly as if she were already caressing the infant she carried.

'Gloria,' she said. 'I'm going to call her Gloria.'

Arlene Hunt

Arlene Hunt is a unique voice in Irish crime fiction. Her dark and atmospheric stories perfectly capture the grimy underworld of Dublin and beyond. She began writing at the age of twenty-seven, and has written six novels: *Vicious Circle, False Intentions, Black Sheep, Missing Presumed Dead, Undertow* and *The Chosen.* Now thirty-four years old, she lives in Dublin with her husband, daughter, three cats and a faithful basset hound.

The Doorbell

The doorbell rang at twenty-past-three on a cold, damp Wednesday in December.

On hearing it, Mrs Ralph Lawson pulled her cardigan tightly around her and knotted its belt at her waist. She walked across her bedroom floor and peeked through the window to the garden below. When she saw who was there, she sighed and returned to the dressing table.

It was not that she was afraid to answer the door; that was not it at all. But she did not yet wish to shoulder the burden that had been placed on her shoulders by the Fates.

Instead, she sat at her dressing-table and considered all that the ringing of the doorbell signified, this electronic harbinger.

She could, she supposed, ignore it and pretend she was out, gone to the city perhaps. She did that on occasion, spending the day with her sister, Irene, shopping, drinking tea, enjoying the perks of being who they were.

But that was silly wasn't it? Why bother putting it off?

Well, there was of course the small matter of the rest of her life.

It rang again:

Ding-dong, ding-dong.

Hateful sound, why on earth had she agreed to have it installed? There was something obscene about it, something cheap and tawdry. She missed the old knocker, a lion's head holding a ring in its mouth. That had produced an excellent sound: sharp, no nonsense, *masculine*.

She picked up a hairbrush and pulled it through her hair. The result irritated her. When had her hair grown so wispy and brittle, she wondered. So faded?

She leaned forward and scrutinised her face in the central of the three mirrors. Her bone structure was something of a saving grace, holding aloft the ravages of time on sharp angles and arched brows. Her mother's gift: a lasting legacy.

Men had once lusted after this face, she thought, turning her head this way and that, observing one line and then another. They had flirted nakedly at parties and social gatherings. Ralph was never jealous though, for some reason the threat of a rival did not inspire such a passion. She teased him about it once, telling of an upfront and frankly lewd offer, seeking perhaps in his reaction some validation of her own thoughts, but he would not be drawn and when pushed, laughed in a distasteful way, and said, 'I don't care what *they* do.'

Oh bloody fool, she thought, powdering her face sparingly (it gathered in the creases if she was too heavy-handed), of course he didn't, he knew what he had in her; a dutiful wife, a dedicated helpmate, willing to play the part of adornment, content to be whipped out, polished and displayed at his leisure.

When had it changed? When had the gold become brass? She was young looking for her age – everyone said so: not yet fifty-five, her body was trim and lean from a lifetime of careful diet and regular exercise.

What shifts of sand had led to this impossible situation?

Ding-dong.

Oh that wretched sound, so jarring and persistent.

At twenty-to-three on that same damp Wednesday, her world had been as it had always been, solid, on the level. She had not known of his plans, his mighty betrayal. She had not yet stood, shocked and frightened, in her kitchen, reeling from his cruelty.

Oh, at twenty-to-three she had been Mrs Ralph Lawson, grower of award-winning roses, committee stalwart and valued member of the community. At twenty-to-three she had been an intelligent, vivacious, attractive wife, one any man ought to be glad to have.

Any man it seemed, except Ralph Lawson.

It wasn't that he had betrayed her, though he had, most certainly, it was as though he had murdered her, slaughtering her very identity with a few thoughtless words.

She had been preparing dinner when he came home and entered the kitchen. He looked feverish, as though he was running a temperature. He made no move to give her the customary peck on the cheek; instead he lowered his briefcase to the floor and squared his shoulders. A sudden foreboding filled her. He had been out of sorts lately, distracted and edgy. Was he about to tell her he had resigned his position at the company?

'I'm leaving you.'

Such a short sentence, hardly a sentence at all really. She smiled, thinking he was playing some kind of weird joke.

'What are you saying?'

'I'm leaving you.'

'Leaving me?'

'Yes, Emily and I are in love.'

Another short sentence: but this one with considerable *oomph* behind it. Like an arrow shot from a crossbow at a short distance.

'I am moving in with her,'

Another arrow. Then the *coup de grâce*: the fatal blow.

'Today.'

Emily? Then she remembered. Emily, young and pretty, glorious really, with her wide mouth and curling tresses the colour of autumn. Bursting from her clothes with plump vigour.

Emily.

What a curiosity.

'Emily? The nurse?'

'Yes.'

'The one who treated you for the panic attack?'

He sucked his mouth into an unattractive moue.

'Angina.'

Ah, of course, he did not like to be reminded that his problems stemmed from his mind and not his body.

'I'm sorry,' he lied, 'I hope you know I never meant to hurt you.'

Dignity stopped her from begging; fortitude from crying.

If abandoning her and making a mockery of their lives together was how he was planned to repay all her years of exemplary spousal care then let that be his cross to bear. No, she would not understand; no, she would not forgive; no, she would not be the better person.

She would not now – or ever – plead with him to save their marriage.

Ding-dong.

She pictured Emily in her mind's eye, easily visualising this robust, earthy creature, probably now waiting on tenterhooks in her flat over the chemists on the main street.

Though she had never been inside the flat, she imagined it to be full of knick-knacks, cheap curtains and scatter rugs. Rooms painted cheery colours, filled with shabby furniture; but comfortable though, Ralph liked his comfort.

Emily had to know of course that today was the 'big' day. She and Ralph must have thoroughly discussed it beforehand when deciding how best to deliver the news. Emily might have suggested a softer approach, but Ralph would not have seen the point, nor – truthfully– would she have appreciated such behaviour. Ripping the emotional plaster away cleanly was less degrading. It was also Ralph's *modus operandi*.

So, here she was, her wound fresh and stinging. Mrs Ralph Lawson in name only.

Ding-dong.

Expertly she applied a coral-coloured lipstick, smacked her lips together and slicked a second coat over the first, careful to avoid her teeth.

Her appearance no longer displeased her. She was still Mrs Ralph Lawson: wife of the CEO, grower of award-winning roses, trim and young looking. She drew back her shoulders and tilted her chin.

Satisfied, she opened her bedroom door and made her way downstairs. Shadows moved beyond the hall door; large, unfamiliar shapes that pressed against the bubbled glass.

Ding-dong.

The smile she had practised for so many years slid automatically into place as she opened the door.

'Hello.'

The two men looked at her, unsure expressions crossing their faces.

'Did you call for an ambulance?'

'I did, it's my husband, he's in the kitchen. Please, follow me.'

She led them through the house to the rear. Ralph Lawson lay where he had fallen, his treacherous face ruined from scalding water, a number of par-boiled potatoes scattered by his body.

'I am Mrs Ralph Lawson,' she said, as the men bent to the body. 'Mrs Ralph Lawson.'

Colm Keegan

Colm Keegan lives in Clondalkin, Dublin. Since 2005 he has been short-listed four times for the Hennessy new Irish Writing Award, for both poetry and fiction. In 2008 he was short-listed for the International Seán Ó Faoláin Short Story Competition. He won the All Ireland Poetry Slam in 2010. In 2011 he was nominated for the Absolut Fringe's 'Little Gem' Award for the play *Three Men Talking About Things They Kinda Know About,* which he co-wrote, and will be touring in Spring/ Summer 2012. He regularly reviews for and contributes material to RTE Radio's Arts program, *Arena.* His poetry collection *Don't Go There* will be published by Salmon in May 2012.

Yes

Winter brought a frost that killed the autumn dead and stopped the waterfall. Over days cold froze the ripples in the plunge pool. Tiny spines of ice reached up into the cascade – small stalagmites became spiralling beams that grew to be as thick as torsos, then a single mass, large and hungry for the water that fell upon it as it rose. Rising ice met falling ice. The flow became crystal. Ice owned the river and so it stayed.

Further upstream, there was a lake, and beyond that the river again – thinner, shallower and bordered by thick firs laden with snow. Wyman was crouched there, at the edge of the river, breaking frozen grass under his knuckles as he pressed his fist into the earth for support.

He placed one foot onto the ice and then the other. Reaching the middle of the river, he chanced a stretch that hurt his cranky back. A low curse floated from his mouth as he looked around. The sun shone hard from its cold midday distance. From the high jagged mountains to the mossy banks, everything was edged with cold silver. He blew on his hands, feeling his fingerless gloves dampen with his breath.

He coughed, pulled the collar of his coat around his ears, sucked meat from his teeth. He missed his warm bed, the small stove heating the dust mote blackness, spines of morning light shining in the window. He stepped forward. His right skate almost slid from under him and began to move, finding a familiar rhythm, scarring the ice and drawing lines in the thin sheet of snow.

He thought of his wife:

The night of their anniversary the car and their marriage had felt like the same cage. Wyman was driving and he was drunk. They hadn't said anything since the meal they'd shared. The meal Wyman refused to admit he had ruined. He was driving too fast.

'You'll kill us both one of these days,' she had said. Wyman had ignored her and rested his eyes. The car had veered quickly, hit something, shot into the air and flipped. He had opened his eyes to an upside-down world. A rushing sky of tarmac and hanging lights, an infinite ground of city-lit cloud. Gravity yanked the car back to earth and the road smashed into the car roof to crush it. His wife's side took all of the damage.

Wyman pushed the thought away. The ice was craggy and wrinkled with frozen ripples along the bank, smooth in the centre where Wyman chose his route. Ignoring a small, disturbing spring in the surface, he crouched and picked up speed. He felt a slight incline in the land and was grateful for it. The rhythm of the blades was glassy and sweet in his ears.

A startled heron shot up from the bracken to his right. Ice dust glittered as it rose into a cloudless sky. Wyman connected with the bird's effort, the bird's wings pushing it upwards as his feet pushed him on. He passed the spot where he'd first encountered the river. It had been long before the snow, with the river in flood. He had run from the road into the forest, drunk with concussion, blood pouring from a gash in his forehead, branches whipping him as he stumbled on without stopping. He had taken off his bloodied jacket and shirt and waded in to the flow, waist deep until he had to swim. On the other side he climbed out, all blood washed from his body, crawled into the forest where he lay down and slept.

The heron was a speck in the distance now. The river became a long, luxurious curve as it turned to the east. Wyman kept the same pace, stayed low, one leg crossing the other as he negotiated the bend.

The morning after he swam the river he woke to birdsong, wind moving through the canopy, leaves falling. He found the ruins of a makeshift dam and crossed back to the other side of the river. Collecting his clothes, he found a small hunter's hut among the trees. Inside were empty shot glasses, two broken chairs, a rusting bunk, damp matches on a long dead stove in the corner. Again, he fell asleep.

He woke at dusk, starving. He left the hut and wandered the area. Found a path that led him to a tumbledown cabin. He thought it derelict at first but when he stumbled, disturbing branches stockpiled for firewood, he saw a shadow at a window. Something held him back from the door. He returned to the hunter's hut and sat on the bunk, watching the treetops sway through the small window, the clouds move slowly above with their undersides tinted by the city at the foot of the mountains.

Next morning he heard movement outside. When he opened the door there were eggs and bacon on a metal plate, steam rising from a tin cup of black coffee. He watched a woman disappear into the forest, walking in the direction of the cabin. She was tall but stooped, with long grey hair, wearing a many-coloured winter coat. The river straightened. Wyman kept to the right side to avoid boulders. The sun warmed the ice here. The granite was slick. The boulders translucent. The surface smoother.

Every morning the woman placed food at Wyman's door. He never questioned it. He got used to the mountains, but not to the guilt of what he'd done to his wife. His solitary life became routine. Every action a negotiation, his mind constantly working away from what he'd done. Each day built around trying to forget. But the heaviness stayed with him. It lived here in the trees. He breathed it in, heard it in the movement of the river. He felt it least at dusk when he sat in the cabin, listening to the trees, falling asleep watching flames dance in the stove. This became the rhythm of his life. Each empty day a welcome punishment. Then winter hit. A whip crack of bad weather that caught Wyman and nature itself by surprise. The snow disturbed his routine, changed the route of his walk, and he found the skates. At the end of a new route he entered a copse of juniper and cedar trees. The frost held the dead leaves in their branches, gold and red and stiff. He'd found himself in a clearing. Light flashed from the skates hanging from a branch, a frozen rag tucked into one boot. He plucked them and brought them home, cleaned them and threw them under his bed.

The valley was flattening out around Wyman. Soon he would be skating across the lake he had discovered the day before.

Yesterday, instead of the sound of his plate at the door he had woken to a search party crashing though the forest, sticks swishing the undergrowth, voices calling to each other. He dressed quickly and ran into the trees. They searched the hut and found his blanket, hot ash in the stove. He shadowed the group as they made for the woman's cabin. The leader of the men rapped on the door, taking off his hat and barking at the others to do the same. When the woman answered Wyman saw her face for the first time. He realised he had wanted her to look like his wife and was disappointed when she did not. He didn't stay to hear what they said to each other. Instead he walked up higher into the mountains, beyond the tree-line. He sat and looked down on the valley, his eyes following the route of the river, and discovered the lake, almond shaped with a fingernail of grey beach on Wyman's side, the boulders of a collapsed cliff spilling into the lake on the far shore. He watched the lake for a long time, wondering about the depth at its centre.

When he returned to the hut he took out the skates. He replaced the perished laces with string. He held them in his hands for a long time before trying them on. After a while he covered the skates and went to bed. Next morning, his food was placed at the door as before but he ignored it. Now Wyman skated across the lake he'd only seen from above. The ice was clearer here than on the river, the water being so still before it froze. It was almost transparent. Wyman looked through the ice and spotted a fish, a cutthroat trout. It kept pace with his shadow before quickly darting left and swimming out of sight.

Wyman skated towards the centre where he knew the ice was weakest. He wanted the ice beneath to fracture, a web of fissures to spread out from under his blades before the ice would break and he could sink forever.

The ice grew no thinner. He turned in a circle looking down, saw the dark blue of deep water, seams of white encased within. He stopped and stabbed his feet into the surface. One, two, three kicks. Nothing. He turned his head to the sky. The sun had started its descent towards the west. He looked upstream, thought of going back. But the river's current tugged at his gut. He skated towards the end of the lake, where the river cut a gorge through the mountains and became tighter.

Either side the valley grew steeper, the woods denser. Trees blocked out the light. Before the frost the river moved quickly, descending over lines of boulders in a series of steps. Once the air filled with the noise of the river's churning, the forest swirling under occasional mist. Now the soil, once alive with trickles, was cracked and hardened, all moisture held fast in the river and the ground.

Wyman sped over the flat parts then jumped, gravity hardly changing his momentum. His descent took on a new rhythm. The push and the jump, the push and the jump. The blades grazing arcs in the ice; silence and silence until Wyman thudded onto the next level. The water sometimes stirring, squelching up between the ice and mud at the river's edge.

He passed dead trees trapped in eddies, weather bowed fences, deer footprints on the bank. His ears popped. Beyond the slice of his blades, Wyman heard nothing but the huff of his breath. He passed through a stretch where the forest seemed to be tumbling into the river and ducked white branches bent low. A single leaf fell in his wake.

The steps grew closer together, the drops became taller. Wyman was going too fast to stop and didn't care. On either side the trees receded. The banks grew steeper. Frozen heather, grass and fern gave way to craggy rock.

Wyman reached the waterfall and skated into thin air before he could stop.

His belly skipped. For an instant he was weightless, moving through the air above the blue grey landscape. He was aware of everything – the trees standing still, the sky and its clouds above, the silent white of the waterfall, the sharp poise of its icicles aimed at the frozen plunge pool below.

The rush of descent sang in his ears. He braced himself, stuck his feet together, and, as he smashed through the ice, his right shin snapped at its thinnest point.

Pain washed over him. Cold bled into his clothes. An arc of bubbles spread out behind him as his momentum took him down. The plunge pool was so deep he never felt the riverbed.

'Say my name,' his wife had said.

She was propped up in bed, her green eyes looking into Wyman's. Her chin resting in her hands, hair still in pins from their wedding the night before. She was lying on her stomach with her feet crossed in the air. A fresh white sheet wrapped around her that Wyman had slid down towards the small of her back.

'Nope,' Wyman answered, smiling.

'Say it once, c'mon; "Elise", say it,' she said, laughing, half begging.

He wrapped his arm around her, slid his hand down her spine, whispering *No* over and over instead of her name. He let his lips follow his hand along her back. He thought he was being funny until he felt her stiffen. He looked at her but she turned away. He pulled her close again and nuzzled her neck, tucked her hair in behind the curve of her ear and whispered.

'Elise,' he had said, and in her name he imbued everything. All he ever wanted to be.

Wyman felt something unlocking with the memory. He didn't want to die. He righted himself in the water, swam upwards, making sure not to use his wounded leg, and broke the surface.

He tried to pull himself out but couldn't find purchase. The ice broken up by the impact floated in his way, restricting his movement. He struggled to make room by pushing it under the rest of the ice but it was too buoyant. He felt a thud vibrate through the ice, then another. He saw a piece come loose from the top of the waterfall and crash down just before he slipped under again.

The river tore the heat from his skin. He felt woozy. His body was failing him, the cold slowing his blood flow. His legs were numb. His body didn't know the difference between heat and cold any more. He tried to find the energy to swim back up. The water was filled with the rounded out, slowed down sound of hailstones, and cracks and plunks and a low constant rumble.

He made it back up. It took everything to stop himself sinking again; his nails scraping at the ice. He tried to inhale deeply, to prepare for the next submersion but the cold had his ribcage constricted.

The waterfall was breaking up, its lowest, thickest parts falling in on itself, huge slabs and beams of ice coming free. The air filled with the rush of water as the falls were released. Everything crumbled, tumbling down in a crash of powdery ice that made a huge wave, buckling the sheet that trapped Wyman and making a noise that boomed through the valley.

A man crashed through the trees to look at the waterfall, the leader of the search party. His mouth agape in awe. He spotted Wyman and started shouting. Two, three, four more people appeared. The man yelled directions and tied a rope around his waist, which he threw to the other men before he ventured out onto the ice and pulled Wyman free.

Wyman's hands were claws. He shivered wildly, could barely talk.

'I murdered my wife,' he said.

'Be quiet,' the man said. 'Your wife's alive.'

The man waved the others over as he wrapped Wyman in a blanket. Wyman tucked his hands in and closed his eyes.

John Kelly

John Kelly is from County Fermanagh. Among his published works are *The Little Hammer* and *Sophisticated Boom Boom*, both published by Jonathan Cape. A new novel, *From Out of the City*, will be published in Autumn 2013 by Dalkey Archive Press. His radio play *The Pipes* was broadcast on RTE. He lives in Dublin and works as a broadcaster.

Prisoner

I didn't go to the church. Or the reception. But I had promised Andrea, with whom I was a small bit in love, that I would make an appearance at some stage and wish her well. And so, for the first time in eleven months, three weeks and four days, I was sitting at the bar of the Marine Hotel, Spa and Leisure Complex, sipping a Lucozade and adjusting the noose on the only tie I owned – a rust-coloured remembrance of the day I got married myself. The last time I was a small bit in love. Of course The Marine was exactly as I had left it. Same glare, same smell of chip fat and polish and the same line-up (to a man) of gobshites at the bar having the same conversation they always had. For the talk at the Marine, even at a wedding do, was always of death – specifically the death of Finbar and what it would mean for Farn, a town obsessed with all things Finbar and, in particular, his forthcoming demise. He can't last much longer, someone said. Definitely on the way out, said another. And that's a fact.

And then Brendan, the barman of twenty-nine years standing, started stirring it, as usual. 'He's been dead this long time,' he said. 'And yis all know it.' And then there were the usual squeals of drunken laughter and outraged roars of denial. The snorts and the guffaws, the gulders and the obscenities. 'I'm just saying,' said Brendan, tugging three bags of bacon fries from the wall. 'I don't know who it was out there today but I'll tell you this much, it wasn't Finbar.' And then he winked at me and tossed the bags onto the bar. 'Am I right, Mr Corrigan?'

But I wasn't about to get involved in this one. Farn, an end-of-the-world hide-out for the displaced, the disgraced, the disturbed and the disappointed, is never too keen on straight answers and I have to respect that. It's a place where people prefer to communicate in several languages at once and, if words aren't subtle enough in the circumstances, then they resort to either telepathy, violence or semiotics. I opted for a simple fifty-fifty wobble with my free hand.

'Ah ta fuck,' somebody said. 'We'll all be dead soon enough.'

I knew, of course, that I was sitting in the worst possible spot. Once the guests were loosed it would be six deep in here, but my plan was to say a quick hello to Andrea and then flee the premises long before things got too messy, as they always did in Farn. I'd just show my face and split, making sure to avoid the new husband – a class of an architect called Rory who always pulled at Andrea's wrists in ways that made me want to deck him. Not that I would. I hadn't decked anyone in eleven months, three weeks and four days and, in fairness, that had happened during the very worst days of it, when a rage swilled inside me like a rough sea. In fact both myself and Fachtna Regan, the local Garda Sergeant (and the man I decked) were both so full of Powers that neither of us were sure that it actually happened at all. So no wonder Bernard was uneasy with the dark silence coming off me like a hum.

'Another Lucozade, Mr Corrigan?'

'For God's sake, Bernard. Mr Corrigan was my father's name.'

'Sorry, Matt. Do you want one?'

'Might as well. Push the boat out.'

I was determined not to think about Andrea so I re-tuned into all the morbid chatter around me. More about Finbar's life expectancy, his will to live, his pallor and his general demeanour. According to this shower, there was, it seemed, not even the slightest chance that he would see another summer, such as summers are in Finbarville or anywhere else along the Connemara coast, and they were probably right. Finbar was 35-years-old now and somebody would surely find him soon, washed up on the far shore, among the rotting razor clams, his good eye still fixed on the town and the reckoning to come. For even Finbar knew that his death would mean disaster beyond measure for Farn and for all who existed in it – this rum bunch of bullshitters who lived off their wits, their handicrafts and their endless stories of a friendly bottlenose dolphin who popped up one day and never went home.

'The band'll be starting soon, Matt,' said Bernard. 'Are you staying for a boogie?'

He was looking for reassurance. Fair enough. And so I reached for the most reassuring tone I could manage. Something chirpy yet neutral. Mature yet nonchalant.

'Oh, I'll be long gone by then,' I tell him. 'Maybe take a walk back along the shore.'

'Well Matt, it's up to yourself.'

'No, I'm grand. Seriously. Maybe I'll see Finbar. Although this lot seems to think he's toast.'

Bernard sniffed in resignation.

'Ah, poor old Finbar is fucked.'

'Do you think?'

'On his last legs. He must be. On his last flippers you might say.'

'He'll be missed.'

'He will. And have you seen herself yet?'

'I'll see her in a bit.'

'Well she's about somewhere. Looks unbelievable.'

And then the drunks rose up again.

'For fuck's sake, Bernard! Do you really think it's not him?'

Bernard tilted his head and swept the top off a pint with a butterknife.

'I'm telling yis lads, that one out there's a ringer. Some kind of domesticated pet from Florida. His real name's Diego.'

The drunks hooted and howled.

'Diego *is ainm dom*! Bernard, you're one terrible fuckin' man!'

I rolled the icy glass back and forth across my forehead and stared up at a framed glossy behind the bar. Finbar, as happy as any Connacht dolphin could be, arcing like a scythe into a sky cut from Greece and pasted above these local hills of postbox green, all pointed with the whiteness of sheep.

Surely there was no better gig for a dolphin than Farn in the summertime? Show yourself to the charter boats. Rise like a god whenever you saw the engines churn their little typhoons above your head, surface a few more times in some surprising manner, cock your good eye at the cameras and flash that falcate fin. Every so often, you go the extra mile and thrill the kids with loops and flips and then spend the rest of the day chasing seabass in the dark. Right from the junkyard quays to the wild Atlantic lighthouse at the point, Farn Bay was all yours. Plenty of grub. No grief. No predators. Just don't ever think about leaving. In any sense of the word. Remember Finbar. The sluice gates. The patrolling subs. The hulking portcullis at the *Slí Amach*.

That theory of Bernard's – that the bottlenose in the bay was really Finbar's doppelganger – has been around for a while. In fact it was often the stuff of bilingual speculation in the sorts of places I frequented when I came here first almost ten years ago, places where solemnly stupified men like myself regularly fell off their stools before lunchtime. Was it really possible, we used to wonder, that Finbar wasn't Finbar at all? That the dolphin we saluted every day was really from some marine sideshow in Miami? Some cynical loner glad of a change and delighted to have the free run of an entire Irish bay? Surely even the venal hustlers of Farn couldn't pull a stroke like that? Or maybe they could? Farn was after all, in cooking terms, a class of reduction. The very worst of Ireland's flavours intensified almost to their very essence. Treachery, melancholy, greed, bitterness, anger and shame, all boiling down in the pot along with a good handful of horseshit and a few sprigs of spoof.

And had Finbar really been secretly replaced by a stunt double? Well, nobody could say for sure but it was entirely possible. In fact anything was possible in Farn when there was money at stake and the conversation was *as Gaeilge*.

'And what about our man up in Leinster House?' said Bernard. 'You heard what he said. That there'll always be a Finbar in Farn. Even if we have to build one ourselves.'

More splutter and whelp.

'Ah, would you stop!'

'I'm just repeating what the man said.'

More migraine laughter and Bernard smirking to himself as he slipped a beermat under my glass.

'And what do you think, Matt? Do we have artificial intelligence in Farn?'

'I'm a blow-in, Bernard. No comment.'

'Well, speaking as one blow-in to another, I wouldn't put anything past them. This is one cute hoor of a place. And it's full to the lip with the cutest hoors in Western Europe.'

'Again, Bernard, no comment.'

Bernard leaned in close.

'And what the fuck are we doing here anyway, Matt? I only came for a weekend?'

'Maybe we were just lucky.'

'And how would you figure that? If you don't mind me asking.'

'That we got to pick our own prison.'

'Jesus, Matt. I'm sorry I asked.'

And then from the function room came the first sounds of the dance. A woman was trying to sing *Moondance*, one phrase flat, the next sharp – a dull, limping bass all that was audible of her backing. And before she even got to the part about the night's magic, the doors slid open and the ragged pack of youngfellas emerged, already on the prowl, but not yet drunk enough to dance to this or any other music. They headed straight for the bar, dunting and elbowing each other as they approached, all of them eager for dark fortification and bad talk. Bernard caught my eye. He knew that before long, deprived of even the simplest love, some one of them would start. A punch would be thrown, a scream would be heard and a pint glass would explode on the tiles. This was the way of it in Farn. It was part of the cabaret.

'Should we call the Guards now, Mr Corrigan? Or will we wait?'

'Maybe give it a few minutes,' I said.

The bar filled quickly and, as the racket swelled, I tried to ignore the convoy of pints now being passed over my head, as if there was some inferno nearby that needed putting out. Yes, of course I should have escaped immediately but what kept me there, if I'm honest, is that I wasn't quite ready for Andrea yet. I knew just how beautiful she would be and I feared that the sight of her in a wedding dress would maybe break my heart a little too much. And of course what I dreaded most was the moment when I would have to kiss her on the cheek, just like any other guest. Just another harmless well-wisher. Decommissioned, neutral and irrelevant.

And so I lingered there at the bar and started flirting with the stock. Furtive glances at the the bottles of Jameson, Powers, Kentucky Gentleman, Noilly Prat, English Market Gin, Dewar's Blended Scotch, Mount Gay Rum, Martell, Hennessy, Smirnoff and Stolichnaya. But there was no harm done. And even when the barman put a settling pint adjacent to my elbow I was able to calmly pass it back to the lad behind me without savouring the full, cool feel of it for even a moment longer than was wise. It was almost twelve months now and I was doing well. But all the same, Andrea in a wedding dress was going to be a tough one. A situation which would surely scream for frozen vodka with gleaming shards of ice for that extra kick. Anything, for that matter, which might, when the moment came, blast this final scene to smithereens.

When I first came to Farn, the drink served to keep me usefully occupied and the Marine gave me a focus and a regular place to go, for the chowder and *The Irish Times* as much as anything else. It meant a constant stool to sit on and the comfort of those excellent black pints, which seemed to encourage in me what sometimes passed for profound thoughts. And it suited me because, after all, I wasn't drinking to forget, as men often do, but rather to *remember* and then analyse my recollections with what sometimes seemed like insight. I would even write things down on margins of the newspaper or on the inside covers of Penguin Classics, although when I find these scribbles now, it seems that all I was actually doing was brooding. No great surprise really, given why I came to Farn in the first place and so deliberately stationed myself on a bar stool at the very crumbling edge of the country.

But then one day, Canavan, the Farn doctor, pointed out over several pints, that several pints on top of cornflakes was a poor diet for a 45-year-old, whatever that was in dolphin years, and that I'd be as well to slow up a bit. And then one other day, when he told me over a bottle of whiskey that I could be dead in five years, I cut back to red wine only (except at the weekends) and embarked on what I considered to be a sort of health kick. It seemed to work at first, but it was shortly after that, having hit the whiskey again, that I hit the Sergeant. And it was then I realised that I needed to make an extremely public show of transformation, and so I knocked the sauce on the head completely. Teetotal overnight.

Fortunately it seemed that I was more of a committed boozer than an actual five-star alcoholic, and so I embarked on a very strict regime and trained myself to sidestep all temptation. Passing on the Marine was straightforward enough (I was barred for hitting the Sergeant) but staying out of the rest of Farn's drinking establishments wasn't quite so simple – not when there were ten public houses on the Main Street alone, all facing each other across the street as if they were about to do the Haka. But even so, for the past eleven months, three weeks and four days I had managed to do just that. Walking up and down the street at speed, using the palms of my hands as blinkers. Mugs of tea by day, the odd Lucozade by night, a strict avoidance of all occasions of sin and going to bed early with long Russian novels.

And so the job was a godsend. Set down one of several pirate alleys which wandered down to the quays, Andrea's shop sold mostly to tourists – glossy travel books, local history, children's books in Irish and, of course, postcards of Finbar. I used to go in looking for second hand Penguin Classics but soon enough, as I daily hoked through the shelves, I realised that what I was really doing was indulging an old excitement I hadn't felt since I was seventeen. But, of course, even if I'd had the nerve to flirt with her I no longer knew how. That side of me, if not lost altogether, now seemed embarrassingly and hopelessly tangled and about all I could manage with any confidence was to shave every day and iron my shirts.

So then one morning as I was paying for a copy of *The Odyssey* (bought so I could make a lame joke about which of the Homers had written it) Andrea told me she was planning to open a small jewellery shop on Church Street and asked if I would like to look after the bookshop for a few months. I agreed immediately and she quickly hopped out from behind the counter and gave me an uneasy hug. My breath caught as her lips brushed my ear. She smelled of peach and oranges and, for a moment, my right hand rested lightly on the studded hip of her jeans. I closed my eyes and tried to inhale the very heat of her but I dropped the Homer and she stepped back almost immediately, clapping her hands in a low, comical swing, telling me that the shop opened Monday to Saturday at 9.30 a.m. on the button and asking if I was OK with that.

St. Finbar of the Dolphins, I thought. Star of the Sea.

'No problemo,' I said.

Then she picked a postcard of Finbar from the rack, kissed it, fanned her face with it, then put it back on the rack.

It was the start of the eighties when Finbar arrived in Farn. He cased the entire bay for a day or two, vanished for a week as if to go get his stuff, and then returned. Nobody really knew why he stayed but he did, for almost thirty years. Of course there were rumours of all sorts of dirty tricks employed to keep him there – the nets, the wires, the drugs, the electric currents shooting across the harbour mouth – but the truth seemed to be that, for whatever reason, Finbar had simply chosen (if any of us mammals ever really make choices) to settle himself in Farn, content to grin at the swimmers, play peek-a-boo with the boats and generally act the lig.

Of course for the burghers of Farn, Finbar was not so much a dolphin as a Golden Goose and his continuing presence was, very quickly, all about tourism and business. But in fairness to Farn, for some of the locals, those who weren't mercenaries, desperados and gombeen men, Finbar meant something else. They got to know him. They grew to love him. They swam with him. They introduced him to their kids. They hung out together in the dawn light and they claimed to see understanding in his eyes. He saved a boy from drowning, so they said, and a few insisted that he had such theraputic powers that the sick, especially the terminally ill, were sometimes brought to meet him. In fact I often swam with him myself when I was giving up the booze and, yes, it really did seem to help. Certainly, all that freezing water and the sleek torpedo of power beside me was a pure and indescribable thrill. There was more energy in that brief moment than in any splash of whiskey, or in any drink which dared to claim life itself as its actual substance. Even I could see that. Even then.

And so, yes, Finbar's death, for all sorts of reasons, would be a very hard blow for everyone in Farn. And now that it was imminent, people thought of little else. The day was coming soon. He'd be found on his side, gleaming on the rocks, washed up among all the plastic boxes from Killybegs and Baltimore. Or maybe some teenager in a kayak would rest her paddle and sob out loud as his island of carcass drifted by. Or worst of all, maybe someone who had been swimming with him daily for three decades would wade in as usual and be met by nothing but absence. No more that powerful rise and fall that always lifted the heart. No more those late sunset evenings when he launched himself skywards and thrashed the summer water for, what seemed, his own amusement and all of our delight. And so I raised my glass to the picture. *Sláinte* Finbar, *mon ami*. Poor old Finbar. Faithful as a hound.

I still had the glass to my lips when there was a sudden hush at the bar and, through the window, I saw Andrea step out onto the lawn. She was laughing and joking gently with the smokers, not caring that her dress was now trailing in the wet grass. And yes, she was indeed even more beautiful than I had feared. Her eyes. Her hair. Her swimmer's arms and shoulders. Her perfect muscled back. Her perfumed skin not Irish at all but Iberian. Andrea the dark-eyed, dark-haired daughter of the wrecked Armada, descendant of some half-drowned sailor from Seville washed up on the beach and married into Connemara in a village named for rain. And as she walked off alone, the whiteness of her dress fading into the darkness, the glow of her Marlboro Light swept through night air like a firefly.

'She looks amazing, right enough,' said Bernard.

Calypso in pearls, I thought, but didn't say.

'She does,' I said. 'She looks well.'

The script of Andrea's cigarette was still curling in the darkness when I was suddenly poked in the shoulderblade by an extremely drunk blonde who had the look of someone who wasn't used to getting dressed up. Nothing about her attempt at wedding day glamour was convincing. Her skin was a painted blancmange of orange, white, pink and blue and she could barely stand in her heels. Her earrings looked like bunches of grapes and when she finally spoke it was as if she was addressing a mob she couldn't quite make out. Lipstick on her teeth and thick powder on a coldsore at the corners of her mouth. She had been having an argument with her boyfriend and it seemed that I, as a local, had been chosen to settle it.

'You tell me,' she said. 'For once and for all. Is it really Finbar or is it really not Finbar?'

I was trying to keep track of Andrea's Marlboro but the blonde moved in against the bar, blocking my eyeline to the lawn, and then she just stood there swaying, trying to focus on my tie.

'Is it Finbar or what?'

'I'm sorry,' I said. 'I really don't know.'

Then she tottered backwards, steadied herself again, planted her elbow on the bar and literally snorted. An actual snort.

'My boyfriend says that Finbar's a robot. Know what I mean? A robot for fucksake. So you tell me now, because you live here, is he really Finbar or is he really dead? Or is he a fucking robot or what is he?'

I had lost sight of Andrea now. She was probably back in at the dance, cigarette on her breath, moving now to what what sounded like a Trinidadian version of *Suspicious Minds*.

'I'm sorry,' I said to the blonde. 'I really don't know anything about it.'

'For fucksake!' she said. 'Is he dead or what?'

I changed my tactic.

'Yes he's dead,' I said. Deadpan. 'Deader than a dead thing.'

'No fucking *way* man!'

'Been dead this donkey's years.'

She shook her head as if to clear it and her earrings lashed at her cheeks.

'That's like, so fucking sad!'

And then she started to cry and began rubbing her arms as if her trauma was an actual one. As if she'd just been given the worst news. Actual, important news where the pain is real and not purloined. Like, say for example, your wife leaves you in the middle of the night, out of the blue, just walks out of the house and doesn't come back, and that you have to try to start a new life but you don't actually have a home any more and you realise that you're going to have to keep swimming out beyond the waves for the rest of your life, looking landward at your own country but unable ever to come ashore because, say for example, your wife, who still lives in your house, is now sleeping in your bed with some guy who tucks his jumper into his fucking trousers. And not only that (and in fact this is even worse news and something really worth crying about) but there's now this other girl with whom you are a small bit in love but she has just married some kind of architect who keeps hurting her wrists – a square-jawed, golfing, fuckwit of an architect who drinks too much and has already passed out in the honeymoon suite. Maybe given some news like that then she might actually have deserved her moment of grief? But these tears now running down her powdered, freckled cleavage were nothing but fraudulent and low and I felt the urgent need to cut through them at speed. This was a play which needed to be interrupted.

'For fucksake,' I said, or maybe shouted. 'It's only a fucking dolphin!'

All eyes were on me then. The loner at the bar. The sobbing girl beside me. Everyone in the bar wondering what exactly I had said. Or done. And soon the boyfriend stepped forward with a leer on his face that was all too easy for me to read. Ponderous drunks are predictable animals and he gave me plenty of time to get up off my stool, turn around and intercept the incoming punch – a big culchie haymaker thrown with his right. But because he was as drunk as his girlfriend, and twice as slow, I was able to grab his fist with my left and hold it away to the side, leaving him exposed and undefended. Of course this was the very moment when I might once have landed a right hook which would have had him spitting teeth all over the floor. What I used to call the saloon punch, clean and direct like one Robert Mitchum might throw or John Wayne – the sort of punch which, for all its violence, retains for all of us a certain aesthethic appeal. But instead I just grabbed him by the knot of his polyester tie and gave him a couple of casual shakes as if to straighten him up again.

'That's OK now, Matt,' said Bernard. 'Let the lad go.'

'No problem, Bernard. Everything's grand.'

I was still holding blondie's boyfriend by the tie when a space cleared and Hubert Conneely, the father of the bride, stepped in like an emperor, which in many ways he was. As a Councillor, auctioneer and former headmaster he was a man of some authority in Farn and when he ordered everyone back to the dance, the youngfellas, all former pupils, stepped back in silence. Then he leaned in close to me as of to correct my homework. He reeked of Hennessy and After Eights.

'Let him go, Mr Corrigan.'

I didn't mind Conneely. He wasn't wasn't the first man in Farn to corrupted by his own small-town standing and he was by no means the worst. All those second-hand Penguin Classics had his name on them after all – Hubert B. Ó Conghaile – proof that at some time in his life he had been engaged in something rather more edifying than all his current maneou-vres.

'No problem,' I said, and I gently floated the boyfriend away from me and watched him stumble back into the pack.

Conneely shoved his hands into his pockets and ran his cow's tongue across his teeth. Bottom then top.

'Now perhaps, Mr Corrigan, you might be as well to leave.'

'Ah now, Hubert, in fairness,' said Bernard. 'That other fella took a swing at him and Matt here never laid a hand on him.'

But Hubert Conneely, the father of the bride, knew me only as the man who had decked the local Garda Sergeant and as someone who spent all day long getting paid to read his old Penguins in his daughter's shop.

'This is my Andrea's wedding,' he said. 'And I'll not have it ruined on her.'

I couldn't blame him. Of course not. As far as he was concerned I was as much of a liabilty on the wagon as I was on the lash.

'It's OK, Mr Conneely,' I said. 'I was just about to go. Thanks, Bernard. For letting me sit here.'

'Fair enough so. Goodnight, Matt.'

'Night, Bernard.'

Conneely stood aside and grunted.

'Goodnight, Mr Corrigan.'

'Oíche mhaith,' I said. 'Coladh sámh.'

It was a mild night and so I took the path from the hotel down to the shore, following the line of the drystone wall which separated the lawn from the rough fields of giant rocks and cattle. In the darkness, it was hard to tell which was which until some hulking shape suddenly shifted or stood. On the beach the sand was damp and as soon as my feet patted on the finest layers of tide, the oystercatchers angled off into the blackness, the whirr of wings and high pitched kleeks a prelude to the hush of the gentlest waves.

I walked to the water's edge, inhaled the Atlantic ozone and, as usual, checked the void for Finbar. No sign of him. Sleeping in his favourite place no doubt. His vaulted cave on the far shore. Or maybe he was back up at the mouth of the harbour with his nose against the gates and sending out his little clicks and whistles to any other dolphin who might come to his aid. Rescue me, he might be saying. Get me out of here. Can anybody hear me? These people are fucking mad.

I had been standing there for about five minutes or so, the faint sounds of the dance in the distance, when Andrea suddenly appeared beside me like a ghost and hooked her arm in mine.

'You must be the search party,' she said.

Maybe it was the darkness, or the waves, or the slight florescence on the water, or the fact that I was feeling sober and self-possessed but, to my surprise, I was calm. Unflustered. Unhurried. Unhurt.

'I was looking for Finbar,' I said without looking at her directly.

'Any sign?'

'All quiet. And how's you?'

She gently headbutted me on the arm.

'Married,' she said.

And then she tightened her arm on my elbow and we just away, off to the open sea forever and ever. Amen. And so it

And then she tightened her arm on my elbow and we just stood there scanning the darkness for movement, looking for our friend, the ailing bottlenose dolphin. Not a word was spoken at first. Everything just appreciated and understood. We were Andrea and Matt. The happy couple.

And it was me who broke the mood.

'Congratulations,' I said.

And Andrea sighed because I had ruined the moment with rather too much precision. But she held onto me even so and we remained as we were, staring forwards, facing the sea. Next Parish Manhattan.

'So,' she said eventually. 'Any advice?'

'As the new Mrs. Architect you mean? I think I might be the last person to be giving you marriage guidance.'

'Maybe not.'

'You know, I've just been talking to your father.'

'You didn't hit him did you?'

'Eh . . . let me think . . . eh . . . no.'

'Well, you should have.'

'He's not the worst, your father.'

'Do you really think so? Well, let me tell you something you don't know about my father. Do you know that my beloved father is the reason that Finbar stays in Farn?'

'That's a new one to me. And I thought I knew all the Finbar theories by now.'

'Well you don't know this one. And this is the correct one. When Finbar came here first there was this constant fear that he would leave again. He was a wild animal, after all, and whenever any other dolphins came into the bay my father and his cronies used to panic that Finbar would join up with them and high-tail it off to Hy Brasil.'

'Look, if Finbar had wanted to leave he'd have left by now.'

'Yes, well this is where my father comes in. You see Finbar *did* make a friend once. A beautiful lady dolphin from a visiting pod and the two of them were seen together out by the lighthouse for a few days running. Just the pair of them. Now pretty soon the idea spread that she was about to lure him away, off to the open sea forever and ever. Amen. And so it

---

This section is replacing last paragraph page 194.

was decided that something had to be done – in the interests of the local economy if you know what I mean – and so my father, *Master* Conneely, this man who you think is not the worst, stood on the rocks, took aim with a rifle and shot the lovely lady at close range. The whole thing done at dawn so that nobody would ever see those slicks of dolphin blood but my father and Finbar himself.'

'You're joking me, right?'

'It's no joke, Matt.'

'Nah, you're winding me up?'

'It's the truth. And the only reason Finbar is still hanging around Farn is that he wants to kill my father. And old Hubert knows it. Put it this way, he hasn't been in the sea since. He won't even walk along the shore.'

'Fucking hell, that's terrible.'

'Yep. If people only knew that every time Finbar comes out of the water and looks at all those faces staring back at him from the boats, all those children, all those tourists, what he's actually doing is looking for my father. Scanning the faces one by one and looking for Hubert Conneely.'

'And I always had this notion he was looking for me. It's stupid I know, but I often thought that my life and Finbar's were somehow connected,' I said.

'All the lonely men in Farn think that.'

'Fucksake, Andrea, I'm not a lonely man. I just mean that sometimes I wonder why he stays here, why he's always on his own, has he no home to go to or what?'

'Like an outcast or something?'

'Maybe. Or a pilgrim?'

'Or on the run maybe?'

'Well, I often wonder.'

'Well now you know.'

'That's a really fucking horrible story.'

'There you go.'

And then she pressed her forehead against my arm.

'Can I ask you something, Matt?'

'Fire away.'

'Why are *you* here? In Farn?'

'Oh, the usual. Starting a new life as far as possible from Chapelizod.'

'And are you happy here?'

'I'm grand.'

'I'll take that as a no then?'

'No, I'm fine. No. Yes. I'm very happy. No, of course I am.'

And then she stepped in front of me. Her eyes like chocolate now. The cool skin of her cheeks. All peaches and oranges. And her mouth.

'And what would make you happy, Matt Corrigan?'

'Don't ask me questions like that, Andrea Conneely.'

And then she moved in closer and her breath was all spearmint and white wine and Marlboro Lights.

'Andrea,' I said, 'this is not a good idea.'

And then she raised her lips to mine.

'Matt Corrigan,' she said, 'you may kiss the bride.'

And that's how I came to kiss Andrea Conneely on her wedding night. And not like just another wedding guest, not with some wellwisher's gentle bump on the cheek or a comical puckered-up pop on the lips – this was a real kiss, as deep as kisses can go when that very serious silence falls and the universe opens up in the dark. My hands travelled lightly over silk and stitchings and lacings and pearls and, as she withdrew again, Andrea's tongue flicked just one more time with a little groan, expertly designed to torture the both of us to death.

There was no moon that night, no Plough or Pleiades as I held her on the shore, steadying myself, looking for words or the appropriate caress. I wanted to touch her neck, her shoulders, her arms. I wanted to keep on kissing her hair, the sides of her eyes, and her mouth – once again – the faint click of her lips as they opened.

'Good thing that didn't happen,' I said.

'Wouldn't have been a good idea. No.'

'So nothing actually happened then?'

'Nope.'

'Just as well. Given the day that's in it.'

And then I held her as tight as I could, as if to protect her from what both of us were thinking.

'Sorry, she said eventually. 'I suppose I shouldn't have done that.'

'You know, Andrea, that I'm a small bit in love with you.'

'I think I must have had a little too much champagne. We all have.'

'It's true. A small bit in love.'

'Definitely a little too much of the old champers.'

As I watched her walk back up the glistening lawn, returning to the music, the racket and the marriage, I just stood there, still tingling from the kiss but already wondering whether kissing Andrea Conneely on her wedding night had been the best or the very worst thing I had ever done. Was I a happy man now, thrilled by the openness of what had just happened, by the sheer honesty and intimacy of it? Or had I just rendered myself some especially anointed outcast, a practitioner of the very darkest arts, obliged now surely, by his own actions, to be exiled yet further and forever?

But as I walked home that night from the Marine Hotel, Spa and Leisure Complex I had not yet understood that kissing Andrea Conneely on her wedding night, rather than sending me away, would keep me exactly where I was. Because now, a year later, as I scribble this in pencil on an A4 pad, stopping only to sell postcards of Finbar (still alive and still in Farn) I'm waiting for Andrea to arrive. She comes in twice a week, Wednesdays and Fridays at lunchtime and, without saying a word, she locks the door behind her and smiles. The storeroom, perfumed now by countless Marlboro Lights, is cosy and comfortable. There's a sofa in there with two goose-down pillows and a duvet she smuggled from her home. She calls me her prisoner. She tells me that I cannot leave.

Claire Kilroy

Claire Kilroy was born in Dublin and studied English in Trinity College. After a time as assistant editor of a TV series, she completed a Masters in Creative Writing at the same university. Her début novel, *All Summer*, was published by Faber & Faber in May 2003 and won the Rooney Prize for Irish Literature the following year. Kilroy's second novel, *Tenderwire*, was published in 2006 and short-listed for the 2007 Hughes & Hughes Irish Novel Award as well as the Kerry Group Irish Fiction Award. Her third novel, *All Names Have Been Changed*, was published in May 2009 to critical acclaim. She lives in Dublin.

First Anniversary

Sunlight. I winced and raised a hand to shield my eyes. An old man in overalls was stooped over me, breathing heavily as he peered into my face. His head was a great size, as big as a bear's.

'I'm sorry,' I told him. I'm not sure why, though it struck me as soon as I heard these words that on a general level this statement was true. I was a sorry soul.

The old man accepted my apology with a nod and turned to retrieve two mugs of tea from the ledge of the headstone behind him.

'Warm yourself up,' he instructed me, offering one of the cups. 'You'll be stiff now. And sore.' He had done this before. The old man knew the drill.

I was lying on my back on a bench. Jesus Christ, my neck. I sat up and accepted the cup. 'Cheers.' The old man nodded again and I slid along the bench to make room for him.

The morning sun was a dazzling gossamer blaze upon the dew. My hands were scratched, my knuckles scuffed. Mud under my fingernails, mud in my mouth, mud all over my good suit. I should have changed. Too late now. In the distance, a farm vehicle trundled the length of the adjoining field, disturbing a flock of scavenging crows. A squat colony of polytunnels huddled in the field next to that. The old man slurped his tea. Steam was spiralling from the cup.

'I couldn't get back out,' I said, by way of explanation.

'I know, son. The wall. It's not banked up on this side.'

As I had discovered. No bother to me climbing in. Climbing back out had proved another matter. I pressed my palms to the scald of the cup.

'You'd be amazed how many I've found in here over the years when I open up in the morning,' the old man added.

'Really?'

'It's always the men. The women handle their emotions better.' He scratched his chin. 'Plus, they're scared to wander around at night.'

'Right.'

The gravedigger instituted a silence then. It was an alert silence, a lacuna inserted into the conversation to indicate that I was welcome to speak if I wished to speak and that he was willing to listen. I am no stranger to silences of this nature, not any more. I kept my counsel and sipped the tea. There was a trowel of sugar in it. Builders' tea, tacky on the tongue. A rumble overhead as a plane crossed the sky.

I followed the line of the old man's gaze. Our bench was positioned in front of a grave. At the head of the grave stood a stone of pale grey marble, a tiny vase of white violets at the base. A posy, I suppose you might call it. *Elizabeth, 1975-2011*, read the inscription. *Deeply missed by her loving husband Conor and beloved infant sons Kevin and Paul; her parents Sean and Deirdre.*

'She died young,' the gravedigger observed, joining the dots between me and this grave over which I had kept vigil through the night.

'Yes, she did,' I agreed and lowered my head. Yes, I am afraid she did.

The gravedigger murmured his apologies for my loss. There was no good way to disabuse him so I let it go.

The alert silence settled once more and we contemplated Elizabeth's headstone until it seemed it was her face we were gazing at, smooth and pale. Elizabeth had risen and broken the earth's surface to see who had summoned her, a dolphin treading the waves.

Elizabeth considered our strangeness and permitted us to consider hers. She could not join us in our airy world and we could not join her in her watery one – not yet at least – but here we were for a spell, together in the April sun.

Nothing is ever over, I wanted to tell the gravedigger then. I found myself suddenly laden with observations, brimful of impassioned sentences, the spiritual nature of which took me by surprise, as I am not the spiritual type. The old man's silence had done the trick. It had opened a door. Nothing is ever over, not really, I wanted to assert. You may be over, but the impact of you is never over. There is always a trace, a presence, a *vestige* – do you know what I mean? I turned to the gravedigger. His head was thrown back, arms folded, eyes shut.

The birds were singing in the trees. There will come a point when I sit down to study their modulations so that I can tell the song of a blackbird from that of a thrush. There will one day come a time when I do all the things necessary, when I learn all the things necessary, to become a whole man again, a repaired man, a normal one, unguarded, but not yet. I am not there yet.

The brightness faltered. I glanced up – the sun was being swallowed by a cloud. A final blast and it was gone. When I looked down again, Elizabeth was also gone. Her pale stone no longer gleamed. She had slipped back into the depths.

The gravedigger hadn't noticed her departure. Was he asleep? A frown crossed his face and he opened his eyes to squint up at the cloud.

'I suppose I'd best be getting back to it,' he sighed, rising to his feet.

'Oh,' I said, and got to my feet also to … I don't know, to see him to the door. The two of us stood there awkwardly on the gravel path.

The old man inclined his head towards Elizabeth.

'I'll keep her plot tidy for you, Conor,' he assured me. 'I'll look in on her every day.' I stared at the cup in my hands. 'Just leave that there when you're finished with it,' he said, and threw a final respectful glance in Elizabeth's direction before shambling off in his baggy-arsed overalls.

Several mourners were dotted about the graveyard, all of them solitary and old. The frenzy of the small hours seemed remote in the morning light. I had been unable to find my wife's grave and had lurched from headstone to headstone in the dark, only to give up and discover that I couldn't scale the looming wall, a beetle trapped in a jar. *I'm sorry, darling*, her note had said. Not as sorry as I was. The gravedigger had been wrong about one other thing: women don't handle their emotions better. We only tell ourselves they do.

I bent down to brush the dried mud from my trousers. What had I been thinking, wearing my good suit? I should have changed. I knew all along I should have changed. And now it was too late. What was I to do?

Pat McCabe

Playwright and novelist Patrick McCabe was born in 1955 in Clones, County Monaghan, Ireland. He was educated at St Patrick's Training College in Dublin and began teaching at Kingsbury Day Special School in London in 1980. His short story *The Call* won the Irish Press Hennessy Award. He is the author of several novels, including *The Butcher Boy* (1992), *The Dead School* (1995), *Breakfast on Pluto* (1998), *Emerald Germs of Ireland* (2001), *Winterwood, The Holy City* (2008) and *The Stray Sod Country* (2010). He is also the author of a children's book, *The Adventures of Shay Mouse* (1985), and a collection of linked short stories, *Mondo Desperado*, published in 1999. He lives in Sligo in Ireland with his wife and two daughters.

Perfidia

My old friend Val Shannon had been appointed class teacher in John Briory School, Tower Hamlets. I had always sworn I would get my revenge – and now the time had come.

It was October 1987 and he was sitting in his classroom, pouring over his pupils' essays. – There's a phone call for you, the young boy said. – *Chris Taylor I love you*, Valentine heard himself murmur, pushing open the staffroom door. – The forecast is good for this evening I'm glad to say, the school principal remarked good-humouredly, before excusing himself and exiting the room. Raising the receiver to his ear, Valentine Shannon assumed it was Chris, his partner, who was calling – probably wondering would he be late. – Hello is that you Chris? There was no reply. – *Hello?* he repeated. Still nothing – which was odd. Not that he was unduly worried. At least not until the muscles in his neck stiffened abruptly and he became aware that there was a face pressed to the window, staring in at him. The student in question held this grotesque pose before dramatically disappearing. Valentine Shannon gripped the receiver. – Hello again – is that you Chris?There was a sudden hiss – it was just some static. Then silence once more, just before I whispered, ever so softly. – It isn't Chris, Valentine. It's me – your old friend. I was rewarded with a dumbstruck silence.

Returning to the classroom, a small item on the desk caught Valentine Shannon's eye. It was approximately three inches in length, crescent-shaped and pearl-white, like a scallop. He was about to pick it up when a firm knock sounded on the door. – *O for heaven's sake!* he snapped, *what on earth can it be this time!* He was just on the point of declaring that he simply hadn't the time for any more nonsense, any of these constant and unnecessary interruptions. Before realising that he was looking into the eyes of Mrs Beggs, the caretaker's wife. Who, in turn, was glaring back at him. Subsequent to this unpleasant encounter, he became aware that the item he was holding in his hand was not, in fact, a bone, as he had assumed, but nothing other than a simple plastic hair grip, obviously left there by one of the children. He felt so foolish, tearing out into the corridor to make a full apology to Mrs Beggs. But of the caretaker's wife there wasn't a sign and he continued to find himself at odds and out of sorts. Especially when he returned to the classroom and discovered there on his desk a scrap of paper on which had been scrawled the following words. Lyrics that, as yet, meant nothing to him, had no significance at this point at all. They read:

> *Nadie comprende lo que sufro*
> *Tanto que ya no puedo sollozar.*

To many it would seem that events in this world just simply occur, take place randomly without being even perimetrically connected. That, however, is not the case. There was a girl to whom I developed, I don't know how you might describe it – an antipathy of sorts, I suppose. With one's nature, presumably, being akin to the scorpion in the fable – in that restraint, put bluntly, is simply not an option.

It is no revelation that out-of-season seaside resorts can occasionally possess a brooding and fretful semi-threatening aspect. This I have always found to be the case with Margate, the traditional seaside town in Sussex, on the south coast of England. Once upon a time, its world-famous *Dreamland* ballroom had played host to thousands of bright-eyed dancers, young couples on the cusp of romance and possibility. But now as I surveyed it, like so much of the surroundings, what remained of it and the adjacent *Winter Gardens* was suggested nothing so much as a sad and weather-beaten reminder of an age of populist glory that had long since passed. It was close by this place that I encountered the teenager. Her name was *Anka* and she had come from Poland – becoming entangled with a tearaway, the usual story.

It gave her obvious pleasure to unburden herself in great detail as I was enlightened as to how she had found herself addicted to various narcotic substances – I didn't inquire as to what they might have been. I wasn't interested enough. But there was a kind of rogue insubordination in her eye that I found attractive and I gave myself to following her for some time. She found herself in the throes of some disagreement with this vagrant associate of hers – as it happened – in an emporium not far from the *Winter Gardens*. I had been shadowing them for some considerable time that night, and was becoming mildly irritated, until she eventually parted from the lean and hunter, almost feral-looking youth. I watched her as she stumbled along the seafront, laughing edgily and calling out into the darkness. As far as she was concerned now, she declared in broken English, she didn't care whether he lived or died. She was so inebriated that she was scarcely able to walk at all. Her hair was cut in the contemporary cornstalk style of the disaffected female and she had adorned her body with a variety of piercings. She was shrill and ecstatic as she sidled blearily down some concrete steps towards the underpass. Announcing to Margate's slumbering citizens how, in spite of them, she would achieve her dream of becoming a world-famous artist. No one understood but she would show them, she continued.

The underpass walls were decorated in intersecting whorls of spray-painted primary colours. She spent some time appraising these high-handedly – predictably sparing and contemptuous in her praise. She had no idea I was there until I emerged from my place of concealment. She saw that I had drink and I handed her the flask. – *Where you come from out of there?* she asked, her street pose masking a gathering anxiety. I stepped into the light in order for her to see me; my trilby tilted a little to one side. I told her that I too was interested in art. – Oh, are you? she said. – Yes, I said, I really am very interested in art.

As I cut her throat.

But such incidents are trivial when placed beside Valentine and the fate I have in store for my dear old friend, the assiduous scholar and teacher who served for some years as senior dean of discipline at the minor Irish seminary known as Glassdrummond College. He never once spoke about me there. What was I only a representative of the barely tolerated Ascendancy – and it scarcely helped matters that I, in my time, had been sent down from Oxford. *Education discontinued for personal reasons,* as tradition has it.

Not that I cared. I was full of the gales of laughter in those days and entertained scant regret for the company of my former college associates, those uncouth peers from crumbling country seats, those illiterate lairds and ambitious young barristers. I liked nothing better than to arrive into the village in my red Trojan convertible, calling for Master Valentine to take him for a spin. Before we repaired to the boathouse for our 'entertainments', as I liked to think of them – which included some light-hearted film-shows and a bottle of fine old invalid port. Even if I say so myself, I cut quite a dash back then, in my boater and crested blazer. And there simply, I'm afraid, can be no denying the fact – that Valentine Shannon's betrayal of me notwithstanding, I was immensely popular with the people of the village.

Not that any of that that matters. Certainly not now, when at the age of forty-five Mr Shannon has carved out a whole new life for himself and found a lovely young lady; the really quite extraordinary Miss Christine Taylor, feminist scourge of the establishment in the turbulent 1970s. A most unusual partnership, one cannot but be compelled to observe. However, I digress.

Even in the aftermath of the regrettable incident with the caretaker's wife, Valentine Shannon succeeded in persuading himself that he felt fine once again. Which pleased me greatly, of course, for it was a cast of mind admirably suited to my purposes. Inevitably, my rather potty brother Toby made it clear that he in no way approved of my behaviour. In fact he made it clear that he had no desire to see Shannon coming about The Manor at all. – He'll land you in the soup, you mark my words, he admonished me, and you will have no one but yourself to blame. They profess to like you but, given the slightest opportunity at all, they will willingly destroy you, for they despise everything we – and our people – stand for. And when they do, dearest Balthazar Vane, don't come crying to me, if you please.

Chugging around in that Trojan of yours, doffing your trilby and acting the gentleman. It could hardly be argued that my brother was incorrect – I had indeed been setting myself up for a fall. There are times when I consider the possibility that Valentine Shannon had planned the whole thing to flatter and ply me for everything he could get. And then, when the time was right, pop down to the station with his infernal story regarding certain 'goings-on' in the boatshed. I don't know – I really cannot say. All I know is the little Judas is going to pay. And, as he does so, happily I shall croon into his tender ear:

> *Nadie comprende lo que sufro yo*
> *Tanto que ya no puedo sollozar*
> *To you*
> *My heart cries out 'Perfidia.'*
> *When I find you, the love of my life*
> *In someone else's arms.*

This very same treacherous apostle who is now climbing into his Renault on a calm October evening in 1987, making his way home to the suburb of Barnet, turning on the radio as the weatherman Michael Fish firmly repeats his earlier assertion that hurricanes are quite unknown in England, and that the very idea of an incipient storm made him laugh. Any rumours there might be regarding incipient inclement weather were entirely ill founded, he declared, as Valentine smiled and drummed contentedly on the wheel. He had suspected as much, he thought somewhat smugly. A development that saw a smile coming to my face – why, it amused me so much that I might have been watching *Laurel and Hardy*.

Not that Valentine would remember that classic comic little duo, as he motored along contentedly thinking about his partner. Of course, whether he cared to remember it or not, there was a time when such inconsequential cinematic diversions had been very much on his mind. Why, he had even summarised the plot of one for the police. With the grave-looking local sergeant most assiduously making his annotations. Moving his lips as he pushed his stump of a pencil along his pad, through set teeth repeating: – *Viewing a picture featuring Stanley Laurel and Oliver Hardy.*

It wasn't so long after that little assignation that I decided a trial would be too much to face and piloted my Trojan to the bottom of the nearest lake – yes, the beautiful cherry-red conveyance that Daddy had left to both of us in his will. I remember feeling almost deliriously secure within its locked chambers as I floated heavily, wobbling there in the weedy, greeny stillness. But, in fact the truth is that I was heartbroken, actually. For there can be nothing worse than a calculated betrayal. How he could do it is beyond me still – sit there denying that he had ever enjoyed the entertainments. Tangoing giddily and quite innocently to the popular tune *Perfidia* as rendered by *Bobby Darin* and *The Ventures* amongst others; or surrendering himself to repeated screenings of *Betty Boop*, which he also loved. But now committedly and strenuously denied, the mendacious, self-serving cretin.

Whether he'd ever have met Christine Taylor without my intervention is a moot point. But meet they did and, against all the odds, the lovebirds turned out to have a great deal in common. Certainly a lot more than might have been anticipated, considering Taylor's feminist background. And her once strongly held ideological principles – the majority of which were now conveniently forgotten. Not unlike certain happy times in the boathouse. Where the former Christian brother had never so much as watched a single film, or ever so much as consumed a tincture of port, invalid or otherwise.

No, all of those experiences were now written out of history. – I have never yet met anyone like you, Valentine, Chris Taylor would shyly declare, I so much want our relationship to work. Because I know in my heart that it's really special. Where had her feminist commitment gone? A born-out-of-wedlock Down's Syndrome boy – he had soon put paid to that. And a few years of loneliness in a dingy Kilburn flat.

Making his approach towards Shaftsbury Avenue, Valentine Shannon turned the radio on again.

– *Will you get out of the way you stupid, fucking cunt!* Another fraction of a second and without a doubt he'd have hit the van. – You blind fucking bastard! he heard again as the wild-eyed tramp leaped across his bonnet. – What are you doing – are you trying to kill me? the derelict squealed, pressing his hirsute, weather-beaten face to the windscreen.

Valentine made an aggressive gesture, but to no avail. Then, out of nowhere, another similarly attired individual appeared who seemed partially disfigured.

Almost immediately, both men were screaming at one another, before becoming locked in a grotesque, violent embrace. – I'll kill you! hissed one of them, lashing out just as the lights changed and his vehicle shot forward. Changing gear, he heard one of the derelicts screaming after him: – You think Michael Fish is right, don't you, you bastard! Well that's where you're wrong. That's where you are fucking wrong! A north-westerly gale is about to tear this town apart! Valentine Shannon caught a glimpse of his face in the mirror. It was, he reflected ruefully, a countenance which, if it had demonstrated earlier a gathering inner resolve and repose, there was little evidence of it to be read there now. Which was only as it should be. Suddenly, a purple flash went soaring across the sky in an arc. Where had that come from? Then he saw that some of the power lines were down. He pressed his foot to the accelerator and shot forward again. It was nothing to be worried about, he told himself. Michael Fish knew what he was doing.

More than likely the tramps had been inmates from the local mental hospital, Valentine thought, recently released under this spurious care in the community programme, which the Conservative government were so fond of. – Don't get me started on that! he heard Chris growling. Taking his eyes momentarily off the road, to his horror only narrowly missing a pole. Just as the Renault stuttered to a halt. – O for Christ's sake! he snapped, smacking the dashboard with his closed fist, I only just filled the damned thing up. How could it possibly-! But try as he might, the vehicle obstinately refused to start. He searched in his pockets to find some change. Nothing.

Could it be possible that anything else would go wrong, he asked himself, jammed into the rattling train, hurtling along on the Jubilee Line. There was debris all along the line and fallen branches cluttering the embankment. To cap it all, he would probably now be caught travelling without a ticket. And, as if that wasn't enough, was now being compelled to endure the forced intimacies of the passenger beside him, some clearly mentally unbalanced individual who was pressing the works of John Milton on his fellow travellers. Valentine Shannon gripped the steel pole tight. It was all he could do to hold himself together. For he dearly felt like confronting the beastly fellow.

Who, as it transpired, succeeded from a background not at all unfamiliar to dear Valentine Shannon. He was smiling as he treated the coach to a potted personal history. – Yes, I attended Oxford in the days when she was still a city in aquatint. When the chestnut was in flower and the bells rang out high over her gables and cupolas. Well I remember drinking claret cup. So don't get it into your heads – especially you, my Irish friend – for you'd be making a very big mistake, let me tell you! He grinned inanely into Valentine's face, tilting his trilby rakishly to one side. Just as the carriage was plunged into darkness. Someone cried out in surprise – then a tense and rigid silence ensued. But the new circumstances gave no indication of bothering the trilby-sporting 'poet' in the slightest. As a matter of fact, he was now in full flight. – *By what best way are we to proceed, by open war or covert guile?* he quizzed. The passenger beside Valentine stiffened, as he demanded: – O for heaven's sake! Do we really have to listen to this? But the poet remained nonplussed. – This night your city will experience unique havoc. – Obviously you didn't hear Michael Fish, laughed someone pointlessly. Just as the lights came sputtering back on, almost as abruptly as they had failed.

And it was at that point that Valentine got a proper look at me, standing directly opposite him in the compartment. As I swayed there, grinning inanely, swinging back and forth as I stared unflinchingly at him. There was nothing immediately recognisable about my bodily aspect, but it was clear that he drew something from a slight contraction of the lips and eyebrows that made him manifestly uneasy, as I had intended. The train slowed and I doffed my hat just as I prepared to exit. Just as I departed I pressed my message into his hand. But it was only when Shannon emerged from the next station that he got the opportunity to examine the piece of paper. The suburb was like a war zone as he scanned the crumpled scrap. *This is the seal of my hatred on you, Shannon. Solo temblano de ansiedad estoy/ Todos me miran y se van.*

The sky above him was lit with fire. The street filled with abandoned vehicles and fallen trees. Then the heavens opened and a ball of chalk with roots attached went rolling past, beaten ahead by the powerful gale. In spite of his trepidation, he made an impressively valiant effort to rally. He crouched down and ran, as the guttering of a roof came crashing down, landing dangerously just beside him. The Wimpy Bar on Kingsbury Road was emptying fast as he reached across the table to lift his cup. But in his agitation, it fell to the floor. The woman sitting across from him might have been mentally disturbed as she processed the scene in the street with parted lips and wild eyes. Until, without warning of any kind, she slammed her small tight fist down on the Formica: – I don't care what anyone says! Michael Fish is always right! The Italian proprietor looked as though he had just been acquainted of some great sadness but was bearing his load with admirable fortitude. He feared, he said, that the enormous chestnut opposite was going to topple at any moment. Repeated calls to the fire department had produced no results, he said. He turned his back to return to the kitchen, just as the plate glass window came crashing in. – *You must go home pliss! Pliss all of you, you must go home!* he bayed hoarsely, frantically waving his arms in despondent appeal.

I will readily accept that are certain episodes contained within this narrative that serve no purpose other than that of providing amusement and diversion. In this regard I cite the instance of the abstracted pensioner who found himself blown into a pond in Kew Gardens, and subsequently died. There were many others. But, I digress. To return to Valentine Shannon, the degree of dismay which he was now experiencing was quite extraordinary. As he continued along the roadside with a form of frantic semaphoring that he hoped might secure some form – any form – of transport. That would take him home to sanctuary and his beloved. It really could not have been choreographed with more aplomb – as, out of the haze of rain appeared the humble Golf car, which contained Ronnie Clegg, who happened to be none other than Chris Taylor's best pal! Who would ever have believed such a thing? Was it any wonder that his spirits began soaring? What a wonderful thing to happen! It had only taken him seconds to recognise her, even through the wall of swishing rain. This was glorious, thought Valentine as they motored along. – I'm going to have to go really slow, said Ronnie, craning forward. Did you hear about Kew Gardens? By all accounts, it's completely destroyed. He shook his head. He hadn't heard. – What on earth is going on? she asked, looking strained. He was coming back to himself, however. He wanted to change the subject at all costs. – How have you been? he asked Ronnie Clegg, are you still doing supply? – These days I teach in Harrow-On-The-Hill, Ronnie told him. In a boys' school next to the college. What about yourself? Are you still in John Briory then, Valentine? He nodded and smiled and confirmed that yes he was. He felt so comfortable in Ronnie Clegg's company. She was like Chris in so many ways. – I'm only going as far as Stanmore, Ronnie explained, I'm going to see my mother who is sick. As a matter of fact I think she's going to die. Power cables webbed the tumultuous, flooded streets. Panes of glass lay shattered on the sidewalk. – I'm sorry, said Valentine.

Ronnie pulled up outside the house in Stanmore. Valentine's spirits leaped when he saw the photo of Christine on the mantelpiece. It was one of a group of girls standing together beside a flowerbed, on a beautiful summer's day. Christine was dressed in a zippered blouson jacket and striped tank top. He started suddenly as Ronnie arrived back. – This is Dawn, who looks after Mummy. A rotund woman in her middle years stepped forward to shake his hand. Behind her, the elderly lady in the wheelchair bared her gums and began to laugh, rolled forward across the carpet in the direction of the television, chuckling as her shoulders heaved. – *Fish! Fish! Fish! Ee Michael Fish!* she squealed, removing her slipper and flinging it at the screen, extending her neck as if preparing to inspect the intrinsic quality of the pixilated image of the apple-cheeked newsreader in question, before proceeding enthusiastically to drop a small blob of spit onto her hands, smearing it then across her face. – I saw the devil in Margate once, she announced, in calm, remote and quite indifferent tones, he was wearing a raincoat and a hat with a feather.

Dawn was going his way, she informed Valentine, offering to drive him all the way to Barnet. So grateful was he for her company as they drove along, that on more than one occasion he found himself prompted to touch her gently on the hand. He felt grateful to have been granted the privilege of knowing such women, he thought. To have them as friends – for that's what Ronnie and Chris – and now Dawn were – friends. Yes, Christine Taylor would always be his friend as well as his lover. His cohabiting lover, something that in his former life as a seminarian he never could have dreamed. He found himself blushing when he realised he'd used the word *Lover*. Because for so much of his adult life, such a term would have only had connotations with the most obscure girlish romances, or failing that, the world of illicit, somewhat vague obscenities. Once, in Glassdrummond College, he remembered he had confiscated a magazine entitled *Readers' Wives*. Within whose pages he had discovered the most appalling narratives, detailing the profane congress of silhouetted, writhing, 'suburban lovers'. It had belonged to a boy named Martin Boan, out of whose eyes the sun had once shone. He had actually directed him as the Artful Dodger in a school production of *Oliver!* Sadly now, this was what he was up to – reading filth the like of this. Martin Boan had gone wrong, I'm afraid. That was what Brother Valentine had felt that day outside the school lavatories. When he had heard the boy in question muttering provocatively under his breath; – *There goes Brother Valentine. I wonder why he likes Oliver so much. I wonder that now. I really do! Hur hur!* It was hard to believe he had even remembered it. But here it was, on this night of such a storm of all nights, coming up again. The scandal and the disgrace that had ensued had almost ruined him. Would have, probably, if he had not met Christine. The voices and accusations had receded after that. – He likes the artful dodger, the whisper would come. Oh yes, how does Brother Valentine love the musical *Oliver!* Yes, thanks to the moral support and instinctive empathy of people like Chris and indeed, his driver, any rage stimulated by the re-emergence of repressed memories began eventually to subside during those first few years in London. His fists unclenched and he dabbed the last of the perspiration from his forehead. It's over, he thought. At last I've made it home. Dawn smiled as she chucked the handbrake, pulling up across the road from his house. All along the street the trees had been torn up literally by the roots. A crashed car lay on its side beneath a bridge. Valentine waved one final time and began his ascent of the granite steps towards his house. Slotting his key into the lock, and calling out: – Christine! Are you there, Christine love? It's me, Valentine – I'm home! His heart jumping when he heard her reply in what were – although it didn't occur to him to make much of it – noticeably uncharacteristic, husky tones: – I'm in here darling. I'm waiting in the bedroom! she called. At first he was uncertain. Then he became a little 'excited.' He hadn't known her to be partial to such – how might you put it – games. What a truly extraordinary night this had been. – *Come on sweetie. There's a good boy!* Standing now in the bedroom doorway, he was in such a mood of passion and anticipation that he feared his heart might exit his chest. She was sitting with her back to him, brushing her hair with long, patient strokes, humming a little song on the edge of the bed. – O Christine darling! he pealed, leaping forward – just as I turned and revealed myself to him. It was fated that Valentine Shannon was never to be the same again. – *This is the seal of my hatred on you*, I whispered.

As he stood there – catatonic. Which I have to say had the effect of making me smile. As I stroked his cheek and gave a little shiver. – Look at you, silly, standing there like that. Have you nothing to say to your old friend? Hmmph?Poor old Valentine. It had already been ordained that not another word would ever pass his lips.

A decree then which, exactly one year later, in Friern Barnet Mental Hospital saw Brother Valentine Shannon ever so dutifully making his rounds once more, in what since the beginning of his custodial care he had become convinced was his noble alma mater, the glorious Glassdrummond College. Which was perhaps not surprising for, after all, was that not where he really belonged – and where he had been so happy, in those long-ago days, which seemed tinted in amber. And whose corridors he patrols nightly at the very same time, before retiring to his study to add yet a few more paragraphs to his memoirs, reminiscing fondly on his career in these hallowed halls – this 'Irish Oxford', as he likes to think of it, with its chestnut in flower and its bells ringing out high and clear over gables and cupolas, and the air heavy with all the scents of summer. This nursery bed of learning from which he had never been dismissed, certainly not discontinued for personal reasons, at least not for displaying an uncommon interest in a particular student. But of course not. Martin Boan had made it all that up. Which explains why he often now wakes in the night, on occasion screaming quite horrifically. With no friend left in the world who will believe him, except for me. For certainly Christine Taylor doesn't know what he's talking about – or didn't, in the days when she bothered to visit. Days which are, sadly, long gone now. It was only making him worse, she decided. Not to mention the effect it was having on her. – *He made it all up; honestly you've got to believe me!* I take his hand, once more tenderly smiling: – But of course he did. Just as you did, in your time, Valentine. As I explained to him how at last, we might be able to put it all behind us – stroking his poor, sad forehead as I did so. Before, just as it does each night in Friern Barnet, where to make restitution for landing one in the soup, he's likely to spend the remainder of his mortal days, with these frail and fragile lyrics falling from his ashen lips:

Solo temblando de asniedad estoy
Todos me miran y se van
And so I find my love was not for you
And so I take it back with a sigh
Perfidia's won
Goodbye
Goodbye

It was somewhat bitter – I won't pretend otherwise – that after all we'd been through, it had to end like this. With one's cherry-red Trojan lying at the bottom of a lake, and a relationship that had been so special sadly diminished by a regrettable, self-serving and wholly unnecessary treachery. The basest of perfidies, how else could one describe it? But now that we are together once again, I genuinely do feel that one day I shall find it in my heart to forgive Valentine Shannon, as I tilt my trilby, once again repeating those stinging, wrenching words:

With a sad lament my dreams are faded like a broken melody, as a staccatoing Stan and Olly somehow once more elude their pursuers, in grainy grey monochrome vanishing beneath a campanile, colossal against the sky of all time.

Colum McCann

Colum McCann was born in Ireland in 1965. He is the author of five novels and two collections of stories. He has been the recipient of many international honours, including the National Book Award, the International Dublin Impac Prize, a Chevalier des Arts et Lettres from the French government, election to the Irish arts academy, several European awards, the 2010 Best Foreign Novel Award in China, and an Oscar nomination. His work has been published in over 30 languages. He lives in New York with his wife Allison and their three children. He teaches at the MFA program in Hunter College.

As If There Were Trees

I was coming home from my shift at the lounge when I saw Jamie in the field. The sun was going down and there were shadows on the ground from the flats. Jamie had his baby with him. She was about three months old. She was only in her nappy and she had a soother in her mouth. They were sitting together on a horse, not Jamie's horse – he'd sold his a long time ago to one of the other youngsters in the flats. This one was a piebald and it was bending down to eat the last of the grass in the goalmouth. Jamie was shirtless and his body was all thin. You could see the ribs in his stomach and you could see the ribs in the horse and you could see the ribs in the baby too. The horse nudged in the grass and it looked like all three of them were trying to get fed. There's nothing worse than seeing a baby hungry. She was tucked in against Jamie's stomach and he was just staring away into the distance.

The sun was going down and everywhere was getting red. There was red on the towers and there was red on the clinic and there was red on the windows of the cars that were burned out and there was red on the overpass at the end of the field. Jamie was staring at the overpass. It was only half built, so the ramp went out and finished in mid-air. You could have stepped off it and fallen forty feet.

Jamie used to work on the overpass until he got fired. They caught him with smack in his pocket when he was on the job. He complained to the Residents' Committee because he was the only one from the flats on the overpass but there was no go. They couldn't help him because of the junk. They wanted to, but couldn't. That was two weeks ago. Jamie had been moping around ever since.

Jamie started nudging his heels into the side of the horse. He was wearing his big black construction boots. You could see the heels making a dent in the side of the horse. I thought, poor fucking thing, imagine getting kicked like that.

I was standing by the lifts and every time the doors opened a smell of glue and paint and shite came out and hit me. I was thinking about going home to my young ones who were there with my husband Tommy – Tommy looks after them since Cadbury's had the lay-offs – but something kept me at the door of the lift watching. Jamie dug his heels deeper into the horse and even then she didn't move. She shook her head and neighed and stayed put. Jamie's teeth were clenched and his face was tight and his eyes were bright as if they were the only things growing in him.

I've seen lots of men like that in The Well. The only thing alive in them is the eyes. Sometimes not even that.

Jamie was kicking no end and his baby was held tight to him now and the horse gave a little bit and turned her body in the direction of the overpass. Jamie stopped kicking. He sat and he watched and he was nodding away at his own nodding shadow for a long time, just looking at the men who were working late.

Four of them altogether. Three of them were standing on the ramp smoking cigarettes and one was on a rope beneath the ramp. The one below was swinging around on the rope. He looked like he was checking the bolts on the underside of the ramp. He had a great movement to him, I mean he would have made a great sort of jungle man or something, swinging through the trees, except of course there's no trees around here, you'd sooner get a brick of gold than a tree.

The ropeman was just swinging through the air and pushing his feet off the columns and his shadow went all over the place. It was nice to look at really. He was skinny and dark and

222

I thought I recognised him from The Well, but I couldn't see his face I was so far away.

A lot of the men from the overpass come into The Well for lunchtime and even at night for a few jars. Most of them are Dubs although there's a few culchies and even a couple of foreigners. We don't serve the foreigners, or at least we don't serve them quickly because there's always trouble. As Tommy says, The Well has enough trouble without serving foreigners. Imagine having foreigners, says Tommy. There's problems enough with the locals.

Not that Jamie was ever trouble. Jamie, when he came to The Well, he sat in the corner and sometimes even read a book, he was that quiet. He drank a lot of water sometimes, I think I know why but I don't make judgements. We were surprised when we heard about him shooting up on the building site though. Jamie never seemed like the sort, you know. Jamie was a good young fella. He was seventeen.

I looked back at the field and all of a sudden the sun went behind the towers and the shadows got all long and the whole field went much darker.

Jamie was still watching the ropeman on the overpass. The horse didn't seem to mind moving now. Jamie only tapped it with the inside of his heel and the horse got to going straight off. She went right through the goalposts and past all the burnt-out cars and she stepped around a couple of tyres and even gave a little kick at a collie that was snapping at her legs and then she went along the back of the clinic at the far end of the field. Jamie looked confident riding it bareback. Even though it was going very slow Jamie was holding on tight to his little girl so she wouldn't get bumped around.

In the distance the ropeman was still swinging under the overpass.

It was going through my head who the hell he was I couldn't remember. People were getting on and off the lift behind me and a couple of them stood beside me and asked, Mary what're you looking at? I just told them I was watching the overpass go up and they said fair enough and climbed into the lift. They must have thought I was gone in the head a bit, but I wasn't. I hadn't had a drink all day even after my shift.

I was thinking, Jesus, Jamie what're you up to?

He was going in rhythm with the horse, slow, towards the overpass, the baby still clutched to him only in her nappy and maybe the soother still in her mouth. I couldn't see. There were a couple of youngsters playing football not too far from the overpass and Jamie brought the horse straight through the middle of their jumpers, which were on the ground for goal-posts. One of the jumpers caught on the hoof of the horse and the goal was made bigger and the youngsters gave Jamie two fingers but he ignored them.

That was where the shadows ended. There was only a little bit of sun left but Jamie was in it now, the sun on his back and the sun on his horse and – like it was a joke – a big soft shite coming from the horse as she walked.

Jamie went up to the chicken-wire fence that was all around the overpass to stop vandals but the chicken-wire was cut in a million places and Jamie put one hand on the horse's neck and guided her through the hole in the wire.

He was gentle enough with the horse. He bent down to her back, and his baby was curled up into his stomach and all three of them could have been one animal.

They got through without a scrape.

That was when I saw the knife. It came out of his back pocket, one of those fold-up ones that have a button on them. The only reason I saw it was because he kept it behind his back and when he flicked the button it caught a tiny bit of light from the sun and glinted for a second. Fuck, I said and began running out from the lifts through the car park into the field towards the overpass. Twenty smokes a day but I ran like I was fifteen years old. I could feel the burning in my chest and my throat all dry and the youngsters on the football field stopping to look at me and saying, Jaysus she must have missed the bus.

But I could see my own youngsters in Jamie, that's why I ran. I could see my young Michael and Tibby and even Orla, I could see them in Jamie. I ran, I swear I'll never run like that again, even though I was way too late.

I was only at the back of the clinic when Jamie stepped the horse right beneath the ramp. I tried to give a shout but I couldn't, there was nothing in my lungs. My chest was on fire; it felt like someone stuck a hot poker down my throat. I had to lean against the wall of the clinic. I could see everything very clearly now. Jamie had ridden the horse right underneath where the ropeman was swinging. Jamie said something to him and the ropeman nodded his head and shifted in the air a little on the rope. The ropeman looked up to his friends who were on the ramp. They gave him a little slack on the rope. The ropeman was so good in the air that he was able to reach into his pocket and pull out a packet of cigarettes as he swung. He flipped the lid on the box and negotiated the rope so he was in the air like an angel above Jamie's head.

Jamie stretched out his hand for the cigarette, took it, put it in his mouth and then said something to the ropeman, maybe thanks. The ropeman was just about to move away when the knife came and caught him on the elbow. I could see his face. It was pure surprise. He stared at his arm for the second it took the blood to leap out. Then he curled his body and he kicked at Jamie but Jamie's knife caught him on the leg. Jamie's baby was screaming now and the horse was scared and a shout came from the men up on the ramp. That's when I knew who they were. They were the Romanians, shouting in their own language. I remembered them from The Well the day we refused them service. Tommy said they were lucky to walk, let alone drink, taking our jobs like that, fucking Romanians. They didn't say a word that day, just thanked me and walked out of The Well. But Jesus they were screaming now and their friend was in mid-air with blood streaming from him, it was like the strangest streak of paint in the air, it was paint going upwards because his friends were dragging on the rope, bringing him up to the sky, he wasn't dead of course, but he was just going upwards.

I looked away from the Romanians and at Jamie. He was calm as could be. He turned the horse around and slowly began to move away.

He still had the baby in his arms and the cigarette in his mouth but he had dropped the knife and there were tears streaming from his eyes.

I leaned against the wall of the clinic and then I looked back towards the flats. There were people out in the corridors now and they were hanging over the balconies watching. They were silent. Tommy was there too with our young ones. I looked at Tommy and there was something like a smile on his face and I could tell he was there with Jamie and, in his loneliness, Tommy was crushing the Romanian's balls and he was kicking the Romanian's head in and he was rifling the Romanian's pockets and he was sending him home to his dark children with his ribs all shattered and his teeth all broken and I thought to myself that maybe I would like to see it too and that made me shiver, that made the night very cold, that made me want to hug Jamie's baby the way Jamie was hugging her too.

John MacKenna

John MacKenna is the author of fifteen books – novels, short-story collections, memoir, biography, poetry and history. He is the winner of *The Irish Times* Fiction Award, the Hennessy Award, the Cecil Day Lewis Award and a Jacob's Radio Award for his documentaries.

Sacred Heart

He sits in his car. It's late in the afternoon and the last of the autumn light is being wrung from the heavens, dribbling down onto the flaky, rusted stubble of a long, wide field. He watches an old crow flail jadedly across the dull September sky in search of its rookery, and he thinks of his young daughter running carelessly along the sprawling summer beach, her sun-bleached hair flying like a thousand short kite strings in the brightness.

And he remembers the shadow of a gull on the warm summer sand.

'Look,' his daughter says. 'Look, there's a bird under the sand.'

'That's a sand gull,' he says.

'What's a sand gull?'

'It's a magic bird. It can fly on the sand or under the sand. You can see it but, if you try to touch it, it isn't there.'

She looks at him quizzically.

'See,' he says, pointing to the circling shadow.

His daughter watches the silhouette darken and lighten as the bird swoops and rises unseen above her head.

'What does he eat?' she asks.

'He eats the wind.'

'Does he?'

'Yes.'

'Why don't we see him every day?'

'Because he appears only to children who are very good and even then just once in a blue moon.'

She throws him that look again.

'The moon's not blue.'

'Sometimes it is.'

'I never saw it blue.'

'Do you remember the first night we were in America?'

'Yes.'

'Do you remember the moon when we came out of the airport building?'

'Yes.'

'Do you remember what colour it was?'

'Orange.'

'See. You'd never seen an orange moon before that but there it was. And you've never seen a blue moon but you will.'

'Tonight?'

He shrugged. 'You never know. It'll be there when you least expect it and when you most need it.'

'What does that mean?'

'You're full of questions,' he laughs, swinging his daughter high into the air, twirling her above the sand and sea, throwing her into the sunny sky and catching her as she falls screaming with laughter.

And out of nowhere, as it always comes, the memory.

He is dancing with his wife, her head against his chest, her body warm against his own, her hands light on his shoulders, his arms around her waist, the music moving them in some slowed-down version of a waltz, and he shivers in the burning sun and looks at his daughter and he feels a desperate, surging need to know that she will have happiness in her life.

'The sand gull is gone,' the little girl says.

'It'll be back.'

'Will it?'

'Of course. It always comes back to good girls. Always.'

She smiles and he hugs her and puts her back down in the warm shallows of the Atlantic water.

'You know the way you write in your little book every night?'

He nods.

'Why do you do that?'

'I'm keeping a diary of our holiday.'

'Why?'

'Because it's special – just you and me.'

'Are you keeping it to read to Mum when we get home?'

'No, but I could.'

'What does it say?'

'Lots of things.'

'Like?'

'Like about what we do each day, about the sea and the weather and where we've been and things I've been thinking and tonight I'll write about the sand gull.'

'Will you read it to me tonight?'

'Okay.'

'Will you read it to me every night?'

'Yes, okay.'

'Promise?'

'Promise.'

They paddle on, the sunlight surging over them like a reassurance.

'Don't forget to look for the sand dollars,' he says and they lower their heads and walk slowly, eyes scanning the shining sand for the elusive shells.

That night, as he tucks his daughter into bed in her air-conditioned room, she reminds him of his promise to read from his diary.

'I haven't written today's entry yet.'

'Well, read me what you wrote for the other days.'

'It'll be boring.'

'I'll tell you if I'm bored.'

He goes into his room and returns with a notebook.

'Is that your diary?'

'Yes.'

His daughter settles herself against the soft pillow and waits.

'This is from the first day.'

She nods. He clears his throat.

'"The heat when we came out of the airport building was like a wall. We'd been warned but I wasn't expecting it."'

'That's silly, it wasn't a wall,' his daughter says. 'It was just hot. If it was a wall, we wouldn't have been able to get out, unless it fell, and if it fell it might have squished us.'

'Told you it'd bore you,' he says.

'Read more. I'll see.'

'"I like the way the houses here are built into the woods. When they build, they use the landscape; they don't clear everything. They knock as few trees as possible and then they put up the timber frames and block-build around them. As we drove down from the airport, coming through the tobacco fields, the skies opened and we had a glorious thunderstorm."'

He pauses.

'That's ok. I kind of like that. Read me something about the beach. About us at the beach.'

He leafs through the pages of the notebook.

'Ok, here's something, but you may not understand it. "There are several houses strung along the beach, straight out of *Summer of '42*." That's a film, there were houses in it like the houses along the beach.'

'I think I know what you mean. You don't have to explain everything. I'll stop you if I want to ask you something.'

'Yes, Miss,' he smiles.

'Now go on.'

'"The heat on the beach is intense but the breeze makes it manageable. I've been careful that L doesn't get burned."'

'L. That's me. Why didn't you write Lynn?'

'I was writing fast. I was tired.'

'Oh, ok. Go on then.'

'"The only things that are annoying on the beach are the jets from the airfield down the coast. They come in loud and low and really should be farther out to sea."'

He notices her nod gravely.

'It's just that kind of stuff.'

'Well, why don't you write more interesting things, like about the sand gulls and the sand dollars and stuff. You can write them before I go to bed and then read them to me and I'll tell you what I think.'

'That sounds like a very good idea.'

'Now,' his daughter says. 'I'm tired.'

She reaches up, wraps her hands around his neck and kisses his cheek.

'Goodnight, Daddy.'

'Goodnight, sweetheart. I love you.'

'And I love you.'

She turns, nesting her head in the pillow, closes her eyes and smiles.

In the morning they go body-boarding in the shallows but his daughter is terrified by the sound of the breaking waves and he takes her back to the swimming pool near the apartment and that night writes his diary entry while she's in the bath and reads it to her as he tucks her in.

'"I miss trees here – deciduous trees. The sea is pleasant when it's warm but it's too changeable. Trees change, too, but differently, more slowly. And they have the sound of the sea in their leaves. The sea is not so constant; regular but capable of great unpredictability and viciousness and the power to swallow. In the forest the change is more gradual; leaves fall, trees fall but there's a peacefulness and a smell of growth, not threat. And saplings, leaves unfolding, flowers, even the smell of cut wood."'

'I'm sorry that you miss the trees,' his daughter says.

'That's okay. I'll get back to them.'

'And I miss Mum sometimes.'

'That's good, too, and you'll get back to her soon.'

Later, he sits in the tarn of light from the reading lamp. Outside, beyond his glassed reflection, the sky flares and fades with distant lightning above the rumbling sea. He turns a page of *Lifting the Latch* and reads of Stow and Adlestrop and

Oxford. The names are freshly beautiful in the American heat. He remembers them as villages and cities emerging from the English summer haze and he catches his own slight smile in the mirroring glass.

His daughter is playing in the shallows of the sea. Another young girl, more or less her own age, is playing with her. Together they build a sand dam and giggle as the surging ripples eat the walls away so that they can start again, a foot closer to the high watermark.

He stands with the girl's father.

'They give the impression that they've known each other for ever,' the man says.

'Yes.'

'I'm Ken, by the way.'

'Al,' he says, and proffers a hand.

'Vacationing?'

'Yes. For three weeks.'

'Couldn't have chosen a more remarkably picturesque place.'

'No.'

'Been coming here since I was a kid myself.'

'You're lucky.'

'Yeah, I guess I am, blessed with the good fortune of being born in the land of the true and the home of the brave and the beautiful.'

The girls move again, hunkering in the warm, slow water.

'By the way,' the man says. 'My daughter's given name is Melissa.'

'And this is Lynn.'

'You're European?'

'Yes.'

'English?'

'Irish.'

Ken nods and smiles.

'Always appreciated here.'

'Thank you.'

They stand together, watching the children play.

He watches his daughter building sand castles in the rising morning heat. He lifts a piece of driftwood from the beach and carries it to her.

'Sand only.' She waves him away.

He smiles and runs his fingers along the bleached and faded timber.

He thinks about how the sea wears everything to a smoothness – shells, stones, timber, wire and glass. How, by the time they wash up here, every jagged rim has been robbed of its roughness and its edge.

'Homogenised,' he says out loud but his daughter appears not to hear him.

Back in the apartment, making sandwiches for their lunch, he turns on the radio. Judy Collins is singing Jerusalem. He stands transfixed while Blake's words pour over him.

> And did those feet in ancient time
> Walk upon England's mountains green?
> And was the holy Lamb of God
> On England's pleasant pastures seen?
>
> And did the Countenance Divine
> Shine forth upon our clouded hills?
> And was Jerusalem builded here
> Among these dark Satanic Mills?
>
> Bring me my bow of burning gold!
> Bring me my arrows of desire!
> Bring me my spear! O clouds unfold!
> Bring me my chariot of fire!
>
> I will not cease from mental fight,
> Nor shall my sword sleep in my hand,

Till we have built Jerusalem
In England's green and pleasant land.

Later, at that time where day and night begin to merge, he walks with his daughter on the orange sand and they find a long scarf of seaweed.

'What's that?' his daughter asks.

'It's a small sea dragon,' he says, lifting the golden green ridges in his hands.

His daughter looks at him, searching for a give-away twist of the mouth but, finding none, she returns her gaze to the puckered shape that rests against her father's arm.

'It's sleeping,' he says quietly.

'Can it make fire?'

'Not the sea dragon. Fire and water don't mix. Do you want to touch it?'

The girl is uncertain.

'It won't bite,' he says.

She lays an uneasy hand against the slippery seaweed.

'It's soft.'

'Yes.'

'And it won't bite me?'

'No.'

Again, she touches the spongy, wet crests.

'Would you like to put it back into the sea? That's where it belongs.'

'All right.'

Gently he drapes the ribbon of seaweed across her palms and she carries it down to the murky sea and lays it delicately in the small waves. Together they watch it blend into the dark water, retreating with the receding waves until it disappears into the wide Atlantic.

'You're a lucky girl.'

'Why?'

'You've seen a sand gull and a sea dragon. Some people live their whole lives and never see either.'

'Do they?'

'Yes, they do,' he says and realises the night has fallen. 'Time for us to head for home.'

'Will we be able to find home?' the girl asks, suddenly aware of the darkness.

'Yes, we will. We'll follow the lights.'

Feeling the sand crabs scuttle across his feet, he swings his daughter onto his shoulders, turns his back on the black, uncertain water and moves towards the distant, lighted windows.

He is sitting at the table, writing about the sand crabs, when the telephone rings.

He considers not answering but he knows it will ring and ring, every two or three minutes until he does.

'Hello.'

'Hello. Al?' His wife's voice from halfway across the world.

'How are you?'

'Fine. How's Lynn?'

'She's really well. She's sleeping.'

'At this hour? Is she sick?'

'It's midnight here.'

'Oh yes, of course.'

Silence spans the thousands of miles.

'When will you bring her back?'

'Sorry?'

'When will you bring Lynn back to me?'

'Why are you asking this? You know when we're back,' he says quietly, forcing himself to be calm.

'I know nothing. Who's there with you?'

'Lynn. She's sleeping, like I said.'

'Why are you whispering? There's someone in the apartment, isn't there?'

'There is no one else here. I was sitting alone writing in my diary. Lynn is sleeping.'

'Put her on to me.'

'She's asleep.'

'There's someone else there.'

'There is no one else here, just the pair of us, as you and I agreed, Lynn and me, for three weeks. That's it. No one else.'

'I don't believe you.'

'It's the truth.'

'Are you feeding her properly?'

'Yes. She's eating really well. Lots of fresh air, lots of good food, lots of sleep.'

'And you're putting her suncream on?'

'Yes.'

'Factor fifty.'

'Yes.'

Another silence and he imagines the waves rolling over the buried telephone cables.

'You realise how much the legal fees are going to be?' his wife asks.

'I'll pay them. All of them.'

'You realise this is an act of gross selfishness?'

'Yes.'

'And I don't believe there's no one else there. I don't believe there isn't someone else.'

He scratches his forehead and sighs very quietly.

'We'll talk about it when Lynn and I get home. Back,' he corrects himself. 'I'll have Lynn ring you tomorrow at one; that'll be eight in the morning your time.'

'Will you?'

'Yes, of course.'

'And there's no one else there?'

'No one.'

'You said once you'd die for me.'

'I almost did.'

'I'm sorry.'

'I know. Me too. We'll ring you at eight in the morning, ok?'

'Ok. Goodnight.'

'Goodnight.'

They sit in a bright, clean restaurant and a smiling waitress comes and stands at their table.

'This young lady will have a burger and fries and a Sprite. And I'll have … could I just have a large salad?'

'My daddy is a vegetarian,' his daughter says.

'Is he, honey?'

'Yes. He was a vegetarian before I was born. Weren't you?'

He nods an embarrassed nod.

'This lady is busy, Lynn. She doesn't need my life story.'

'We saw a sea dragon last night on the beach and we put it back in the sea.'

'Well, ain't you the lucky girl. Been here all my life and I can't say I've seen one yet.'

'My daddy said I was lucky, too.'

'Your daddy's right.'

'And we saw a sand gull one day.'

'Wow. You're blessed!'

'Lynn,' he says, 'the lady is busy.'

'Are you busy?'

'Not so I can't hear about sea dragons and sand gulls,' she smiles a warm smile. 'But I'd better bring your Sprite or you're gonna run dry and then you won't be able to keep me entertained with your stories.'

The little girl giggles.

'And coffee for your dad?'

'Thank you.'

Later, they go to Safari-Land but he finds he doesn't have the $25 they need to get in. The woman at the admission booth looks at the $19 he counts out and shrugs and listens to his explanation about having left his money in his other jeans.

'Sorry, honey. No mon, no fun.'

They walk slowly to the car.

'We'll come back another day.'

Across the hedges and fences they can see the water slide and the rides he promised he'd bring Lynn on. He knows she's upset but she doesn't cry.

When they get back to the apartment, they play chess in the afternoon heat and, as the sun begins to sink, they go down to the pool and his daughter takes her first, tentative strokes and he remembers the day she first walked.

Later still, they ramble to the edge of the woods and watch the fireflies do their flame dance and they catch one in a jar and bring it back to the apartment and when his daughter falls asleep he opens the jar and releases the fly into the darkness that's beginning to blow a storm.

They spend most of the following day at the pool. His daughter is frightened by the rolling breakers on the beach, by the pounding of the waves after the previous night's slow gale. Only in the early evening, when the sky is clear and the heat is clean and the sea has calmed do they go walking on the beach. Mostly, they have it to themselves. Five hundred yards ahead of them the surfers skim to a standstill and then turn and paddle out again in search of a last few breaking waves, reminders of the previous night's turmoil.

He watches his daughter scrutinize the sea, nervous of whatever violence it still might hold. He inspects the pieces of flotsam and jetsam on the sand: a broken, plastic fish box; three battered kerosene cans; a plank of yellow wood; dead fish, their mouths wide open in a series of silent cries, and what looks like a human heart.

For a moment, he cannot believe what he's seeing. His daughter has wandered ahead, dragging a piece of timber from the shallows; she is writing her name in the sand. A giant 'L' and a tiny 'y' and two ill-fitting 'n's.

Bending he looks more closely and, yes, as far as he can tell, it is a human heart. He feels his own heart pound in his chest, its every throb a punch against his ribs. What to do: lift it and take it with him to the apartment? What then, call the police? Explain why he had moved it from its resting place?

'See my name?' his daughter calls.

'Yes, I see. That's very good.'

He walks to where she's standing, hoping that when he turns there will be no heart on the sand.

'Will I write your name?'

'Yes, do. Can you spell it?'

'Course. Silly.'

She drags the piece of timber through the damp sand, slowly carving the two letters.

'And mum's?'

'Yes.'

Again, she sets about the task, her tongue between her teeth, concentrating hard, working her way through the eight letters of her mother's name.

'Now,' she says, standing back.

'That's wonderful. You've done a great job.'

His daughter nods and hands him the piece of timber.

'Can we go back now? I'm hungry.'

'Of course.'

He steers her away from the waterline, away from the dark heart resting on the shore.

'Let's see if we can find a sand dollar on the way back.'

He sticks the piece of timber into the sand, well above the high watermark, an indicator for the morrow. For now, there is nothing he can do. He doesn't want to bring the heart to his daughter's attention, doesn't want to frighten her with this macabre gift from the sea.

That night he dreams the dream again. He sees himself, the second youngest man at the long table, hardly more than a boy. This is all he ever dreams. The reverie never takes him beyond this point and on to the other, darker days that followed. Instead, he sits with the others and someone begins to sing a soft song.

He knows this bit of the dream has come from elsewhere, from another time and place, when they would sing together. It comes from one of the nights at a desert campfire or an evening in winter when they were crowded into one room in someone's house. But, in this dream, the singing happens at the long table. It starts at the other end, Andrew's voice running like a low, slow river beneath the conversation, gradually making its way into the ears of the listeners, stopping their speech until the song can run freely, without the word-rocks getting in its way, until each of them picks it up and feels the lightness of its beauty begin to lift them. Always the same dream and the same song that seems about to explode, to drive them from their seats and lead them smiling through the marshalled, silent streets outside. Forever, he sits waiting for someone else to rise; he waits to follow, he knows he will not lead. But the song never quite reaches that pinnacle. Instead, it fades away, the words becoming sparser, the silent gaps expanding to fill the moments between those words until, at last, there is only the silence, and the room is as it was that night, full of fear and indecision. And then he wakes, as he always does, his body a berg of perspiring skin, his hair dripping sweat into his open eyes.

Outside, he hears thunder rising and falling, catches the sheets of lighting through the window of his room and hears the wind begin to rise.

The following morning, he leaves his daughter with her new-found friend Melissa, and Melissa's mother, at the pool and jogs to the point where the timber marker still skewers the warm sand. His stomach is churning, bile rising in his throat. He tries to remember how far above the tidemark the heart was resting. He wishes it gone but he needs to be sure, needs to go back. If it is still there, he has no idea what he'll do. Chances are the tide or a scavenging gull will have lifted it, yet it doesn't matter if the heart is there or gone. What matters is the fact that it was there.

The sea is calm, the tide retreating steadily. And, indeed, the heart has disappeared. He walks fifty yards in each direction, scanning the sand and the shallows but no sign of it remains. The surge of the sea or some wandering foragers have done their work and there is no longer what Ken might call a situation requiring resolution.

Standing in the shallows, Al vomits, the clear water diluting the green liquid, sucking it out into the deeper waves and the open ocean beyond.

That afternoon they drive to Safari-Land. To his relief, the woman at the box office is not the woman who turned them away. Inside, the park is virtually empty. He counts five people on the paths between the rides.

'Right,' he says. 'Where would you like to start – water slide, roundabout, bumper cars, dinosaur, elephant swing?'

'Can we do them all?'

'We can do them all. We have all afternoon. Twice if you like.'

She laughs.

'Really?'

'Really.'

'Mum would love this, wouldn't she?'

'She would.'

'Can we come here some time with her?'

'Let's hope we can.'

And now he sits in his car. It is late in the afternoon and the last of the autumn light is being tightly wrung from the heavens, dribbling down onto the flaky, rusted stubble of a long, wide field. He watches an old crow flail jadedly across the dull September sky in search of its rookery, and he thinks of his daughter running carelessly along the sprawling summer paths of the amusement park, her sun-bleached hair flying like a thousand short kite strings in the brightness.

And he remembers the shadow of a gull on the warm summer sand.

And the sacred hearts of those he loved and lost.

Belinda McKeon

Belinda McKeon was born in 1979 and grew up in Co. Longford. Her debut novel, *Solace*, was published by Picador in 2011. It was named Bord Gáis Energy Irish Book of the Year 2011 at the Irish Book Awards, as well as winning the *Sunday Independent* Best Newcomer award. McKeon lives between Brooklyn and Ireland and has written on the arts for *The Irish Times* since 2000. As a playwright, she has had work produced in New York and Dublin, and is currently under commission to the Abbey Theatre.

Something To Say To You

It was nothing to be proud of. Sitting on a flight to the funeral of a thirty-five-year-old man, daydreaming of the perfect skin he'd had at twenty. That boy, with his jawline that had always put Deirdre in mind of sand dunes; not that she'd seen any sand dunes other than the grassy lumps of things at Enniscrone. And Sam Russell had been no grassy lump. When he had walked – loped – into a seminar on the first day of term, late and long-fingered and nodding vaguely to the tutor by way of apology, Deirdre had not so much stared as stopped. *But.* That was what had come into her mind, the word *but*, as though to protest that there had been some mistake. Some hitch in the order of things. Some hope. He wasn't Irish; she knew that much. Irish boys didn't look like that.

The recorded fanfare blared to mark another on-time landing. Nothing to be proud of, either, the plane jolting and splaying itself down the runway. Even the trumpets sounded cheap.

It was Andrew she might more usefully have been thinking about. Andrew would meet her that afternoon at the train station in Cambridge; he taught at one of the colleges there and had offered Deirdre a place to stay while she was over for Sam's thing, as he had put it. Andrew was not going to London the next morning for the funeral. Andrew, Deirdre knew, was more than a little bemused that she herself was making such an effort. *I didn't realise you two were still so close,* he had typed in a chat message the evening Deirdre had written to give him the news about Sam, and to tell him of her plans to come over.

She'd tried to ignore that, switching to more talk of the circumstances, and of how sudden and senseless it all was, but Andrew had not changed. When he wanted an answer to a question, Andrew kept asking, in versions and modulations, each one more irritating than the one before, until you accepted that it would be easier to tell him than to hold the thing away from him, whatever it was. Your deepest fears. Your most mortifying insecurities. What you lied to yourself about. Whatever it was, Andrew always turned out already to have known. *You must still have been in very frequent contact*, he typed then, that evening, and Deirdre glared at the little green dot beside his name, and at the photograph of Derek Jacobi as Hamlet that he used as his profile picture, and she replied with the only words she could bring herself to use: *It's just so sad*. If you write back *Indeed*, she thought, I am never speaking to you on this thing again. But when the word came, as she knew it would, she kept going with the conversation, all the same.

Deirdre had thought about Andrew occasionally in the twelve years since they had seen one another. She had Googled him, of course, and had found out where he was teaching, and what he had published, and what he looked like sitting at a table covered by a very creased white tablecloth, reaching for a glass of water while a woman wearing a velvet choker pointed at him as though telling him to leave. That had been a panel discussion at a Shakespeare symposium in Glasgow, apparently, and that was how Deirdre discovered how Andrew looked now, at forty-six, which seemed to be alright. Greyer, and slumpier, and a good deal ruddier, but alright.

From there it was only a matter of time before she gave in and did the Facebook thing. She'd known he was on there; she'd seen him appear every so often on the pages of other college friends, commenting, questioning, sliding in his droll retorts. But she had refused to be the one to ask. A Friday night at home in Phibsborough, after a shitty week at the radio station, with another weekend begun in the most depressing way possible: a takeaway, a bottle of Eagle Hawk, four hours of soap opera and the *Late Late Show* with the accompanying Twitter stream. After midnight she was still up, still lurching around online, looking at clothes she couldn't afford and at babies who were the image of their parents, the people she'd known years previously. Glancing at Saturday's paper, pretending to read some of it. And then, before she could stop herself, clicking through to Andrew Smyth's Facebook page and requesting to add him as a friend. Jesus, that terminology. Could they have made it sound any more pathetic?

He'd taken more than a week to get back to her. It was a week that served to remind Deirdre that she had hated him by the end of all; that she had had good reasons for keeping her distance from him after what had happened between them. And then he had accepted her – again, really, they could find no other way of putting that? – and Deirdre had practically torn the computer screen apart to get in at his photo albums for a proper look. And there he was. Still with the close-cropped beard, the tweed, and the condescending squint. More crows' feet, which was what came of fifteen years of condescending squints. The grey hair was hard to get used to; it was like seeing a long-familiar image turned somehow inside out. And the Jacobi-as-Hamlet thing; well, Andrew had always been very kind to himself. He had always heaped praise on himself, and in college, none of the rest of them had known enough to contradict him; you didn't contradict the mature student. You looked at him a bit strangely, that was all, wondering what it was like to be that age. To see life from that slant. At Andrew's birthday drinks in the spring of their second year, everyone had thought it was hilarious to be able to quote at him those lines from the Kinsella poem. *For they are not made whole*, however it went. The age of Christ. Now Deirdre was there herself. And it was true. You weren't made whole. You weren't made anything close to it.

At Cambridge, Andrew kissed Deirdre's cheek, quickly and not quietly, and she wondered if he had heard how much like the word *Moi* it had sounded, the noise he'd made. She laughed, and he stood back from her, a little unsteadily, and studied her. He peered. He could have been a plastic surgeon, working out what needed to be done, what slits and stitches needed to go where.

Deirdre saw that he had no intention of being the first to speak. She had come here, she had suggested this, she had brought this about, and the heavy lifting was hers to do.

'So,' she said, before she could stop herself, and she saw it in his eyes, the old flicker of disapproval. Andrew, as ever, had his ideas about how conversations should begin.

It had been while she was looking through his photos online that Andrew had first messaged Deirdre. She had flinched; it was impossible not to feel that he had caught her, that he could see her, crouched over her keyboard, clicking through his family dinners and conferences and his middle-aged attempts at zaniness under a street sign in Stratford-upon-Avon. But in the little chat window at the bottom of the screen, he was friendly. Warm, even. More liberal with his exclamation marks than Deirdre could remember him having been. They'd talked for half an hour that evening, and then again later in the week, and then again and again, until the catching-up had long since been achieved, and they were still chatting, for reasons Deirdre decided not to think about at all. This was the case even as they talked about his divorce, and about her last relationship; they talked about his position at Cambridge, about his students, about his books and his awards. When Andrew asked her about her job at the radio station, working on the morning programme, she was ready with the right spin on things; she was busy, and in a senior position, and having to travel all the time. Well, the next time she found herself having to be in London, Andrew said, she was welcome to use his place in Cambridge as a base; it was only a short hop away, and the couch was surprisingly comfortable. *Thanks!* Deirdre typed, secure in the knowledge that there would be no such work

trip; Deirdre's work trips consisted of the walk from the studio
to the archives, if she was lucky even to get away for that long.
And besides, what work trip would require the worker to sleep
on a couch in Cambridge, rather than in a London hotel? But
these matters did not need to be raised. They were talking, they
were dipping into one another's days, that was all. Neither of
them ever mentioned web-cams, or video-chat; there was no
need for any of that nonsense. They were trying something
out on one another; they were leaning back twelve years, as
though that was something you could do. And then came the
email about Sam.

At work, when she read that email, Deirdre had cried in front
of her computer for a while, and had talked in empty phrases
to her colleagues about what a great person Sam had been,
and what a dear friend. She had warmed to her theme; it had
been a while since Deirdre had had reason to be the centre of
attention in work. She had talked about how she and Sam had
stayed in touch, had written to one another so frequently after
he left Dublin and moved back to London; none of this was
true, but it could have been. It could have been, if only Deirdre
had been less lazy, less prone to put off all the things she really,
sincerely meant to do. What was true was that they had written to one another once a year, or maybe twice, and that Sam's
emails to her had been lovely, and warm, and friendly, but
no more than that. Not really wistful; that word could not,
in truth, be used to describe his tone. But still. At work that
Tuesday, Deirdre went online to book a flight to London for
the funeral, which would be on Friday, according to the email
from Sam's gallery. It was January, and Deirdre was more broke
than she had ever been before, so Ryanair to Stansted was her
only option, and while the funeral was on the Friday, it would
be so much cheaper to fly to Stansted on the Thursday, and to
stay over Thursday night, somewhere close by. Cambridge was
half an hour from Stansted. And on Friday morning, there
were plenty of fast trains from Cambridge right to the part of

London where Deirdre would need to be. 'Need'. She made sure to use that word as she explained her plans to herself, and to her colleagues, and afterwards, as she wrote him a brief and sombre-toned message, to Andrew. *Favour to ask you*, she typed. *I hope you won't mind. But*, she typed. *But, you see.*

'You haven't changed in the slightest,' Andrew said now, and she heard how much more polished his accent had become; how much more he had learned in the last twelve years about how to sound as though you had never so much as set foot in East Galway, never mind grown up there.

'Remarkable,' he said, and he shook his head.

'Oh, fuck off,' Deirdre said, through a snort, and it shot through his gaze again: not just disapproval this time, but fascination. That you could be like this. Conduct yourself like this. Spluttering out obscenities in the train station in Cambridge at two-thirty on a Thursday afternoon.

'Let me take that,' he said, and he gestured towards her bag, which Deirdre pulled away from his reach.

'It's no weight,' she said, which was not exactly true; she had been worried, that morning, about getting it through as carry-on. 'Ryanair, you know how strict they are. And anyway. I have to bring it to London tomorrow, and I don't want to be lugging a heavy case to the church.'

'Goodness, no,' Andrew said, raising his eyebrows. 'That would not look good. You might look as though you'd arrived to make some kind of announcement.' He squeezed her arm, but he did not look at her; he looked ahead, to the taxi rank, where several cars were waiting. 'Poor Deirdre,' he said, as he nodded to one driver. 'I know you were dreadfully fond of our Sam.'

How Deirdre had been about Sam Russell, for almost a full year after first seeing him: mute. Idiotic. Paralysed by something that was too childish, too terrified of itself to be called lust: but that was what it was. The convent girl who wanted

Belinda McKeon

to fuck the English boy with the sandy-brown hair, and the
V-neck jumpers, and the beautiful skin, and the beautiful mumble, and who couldn't just admit this to herself and get on with
it. Or get on with trying, at the very least. For a while, Deirdre's
friends Sarah and Alison had encouraged her, conspired with
her, listened to her complaints about how she had fumbled
yet another chance to talk to Sam in the hallway before a tutorial, or on the ramp as he smoked a cigarette; Deirdre always
managed a hello, and a couple of sentences after that, and was
always, then, too distracted and too embarrassed by the growing heat of her own face to continue with the conversation,
and she always, essentially, ran away. Sarah, sometime around
the end of their first term, lost patience with this habit of
Deirdre's, and told her she was acting like a bloody peasant.
Alison was slightly more sympathetic; it didn't help that Sam
wasn't particularly interested in small talk, Alison pointed out,
leaving Deirdre to wonder whether this was actually an insult
in disguise.

But no. Alison was her friend. Alison said that Sam would
not bother to talk to Deirdre at all if he did not like her; hadn't
he come up to her in the library that time, to ask if she'd finished *Bleak House*? Hadn't he smiled at her when she'd shown
him her copy, unopened, with the spine uncracked; hadn't he
given her that sweet, slow smile of his? Hadn't he noticed that
morning in January when she'd come into Critical Theory with
a blistering hangover, and given her a comforting pat on the
shoulder as they walked out of the tutorial afterwards? Deirdre,
almost whimpering with the force of her headache, had made
it ten times worse by jolting her whole body backwards at his
touch. There's no way he would have noticed, Alison said, but
Deirdre had seen his face, how shocked he'd looked, almost
hurt, that anyone could take fright at such a thing. Well, stop
obsessing over what's happened, Alison said, and concentrate
on what can still happen.

And what happened was that Sam threw a party after
the spring essays had been handed in, in his basement flat in

251

Donnybrook, and that Sam himself invited Deirdre – that slow smile of his once again when she said yes, that slow nod – and what happened was that Deirdre went to the party and ended up in the corner with Andrew, thirty-whatever-year-old Andrew, her tongue in his mouth and her arms round his tweed and her crotch shoved up against his corduroy. He had listened to her while she talked about her essay on Victorian melodrama; apparently, that was all it took. Sam had been hovering somewhere nearby, and Deirdre must have been up to something, she supposed afterwards; must have been trying to make him not just sweet and handsome and interesting, but jealous, too.

'Jesus, you silly fucking cow,' Alison hissed to Deirdre in the corridor, as they queued for the toilet beside Sam's bedroom. Deirdre couldn't quite believe that she was standing there, within eyeshot of Sam's actual bed, but Deirdre, by that point, didn't believe very much of anything. Not what had happened with Andrew; not how Andrew, with what he had done to her in the corner, had just made her feel; not how unbearably perfect Sam looked, wearing an old suit which had belonged to his father, slipping between the rooms, welcoming people, putting his arms around them; not what the expression on Sam's face might have been, had he seen Deirdre and Andrew, which he must have, because everyone else at the party certainly had; and not that Andrew, mature student Andrew, *They are not made whole* Andrew, was waiting, over in the corner, to take her home. Now Sarah came into the corridor, with her American guy, and she mouthed something indecipherable at Deirdre. Not a compliment, Deirdre thought, anyway. Definitely not a compliment.

She had been with Andrew for ten months after that. Well, there had been advantages. He knew what he was doing. People looked at her differently when she was with him, and Deirdre was quickly able to convince herself that they were looking at her with a new respect. He shared books with her, and took her on coffee breaks from the library, and cooked her Italian dinners on the stove in his bedsit on Baggot Street. He didn't bring her places, so much, but she had not come to expect anything like that, so this was not really a problem. There was that one Saturday morning, when he was heading to Heuston to catch the train to Galway, to see the new nephew about whom he was so chuffed, and Deirdre had suggested that maybe she could come along too, and Andrew had looked at her for a moment, and had just swung his gaze away, then, without making any reply. After the ten months were over, there was a long period when Deirdre felt she was blinking too hard everywhere she went; when she felt, too, that she had to listen very carefully to people, to understand the real meaning of what they were saying. There had been someone else, for Andrew that was, but that didn't matter. And Sam: Sam was still himself, and still there, and still her friend. Just her friend. It did not do to be vulgar and imprecise about these things. The point had been made. The line had been drawn. There was no point in tripping messily across it.

'I got such a shock when I opened the mail,' Deirdre said when they were settled in the taxi. Andrew was pointing to as much of Cambridge as they could see through the back window: the churches and colleges, the ornate entrances, the cobbled alleyways, the golden brickwork laid all around. The students rode bicycles of the old-fashioned kind, and people actually dashed around the place clutching books and papers, in some cases wearing gowns. Really, Deirdre found herself thinking, was that really necessary?

'I mean, I thought maybe Sam had an exhibition coming up, or that he was giving a lecture maybe, and that someone was putting the word out. It just had his name as the subject heading,' she said, looking at Andrew. 'The email.'

'Mmm,' said Andrew, and he kept his eyes on the window and on the neat streets as they passed.

'I thought maybe they wanted me to get him a mention on the radio programme. Some publicity, you know?'

'Oh, well,' Andrew said now, and he exhaled a short laugh. 'Oh, I think …'

'No, I mean, I know,' Deirdre said, trying to beat him to the point he had already made. 'I know he was gone beyond that. I know he didn't need anyone like me to help him. I just …'

'Yes, there was that photo essay in the *The New York Times* magazine last year, for one thing,' Andrew said. 'He really was doing very well for himself.'

Deirdre waited, but Andrew did not ask, so she answered. 'SADS,' she said, drawing every letter out. 'The Sudden Adult Death thing.' Andrew did not need to know that, at first, Deirdre had not understood the term, had thought that the given cause of death was some kind of joke, some conflation of AIDS and the depression people got when they were deprived of too much sunlight during winter. 'The thing all the GAA players have been dying of lately.'

'Here, please,' Andrew said, and he leaned towards the front seat. He began to dig in his pockets. 'I don't think Sam had become a GAA man since last we saw him, somehow,' he said, with a tiny moue that Deirdre remembered now, that had always made Deirdre feel exactly this way. Exactly this small: this young, except that she did not even have the satisfaction of being young any more, not even in comparison to where Andrew found himself, to what Andrew had become. She knew that.

'Let me get this, please,' she said, as the driver rang the meter up, and she saw there would be no argument. 'It's so good of you to have come to the station,' she said to Andrew, handing a ten-pound note through to the driver. 'I know you must have better things to do.'

'So often these things just don't work out, don't you find?' Andrew said, and he shook his head. 'You make plans with someone, you talk about meeting up or making the trip to visit one another, and it just never happens. It turns out to have been all talk, and you work out that really, you never meant it at all, the invitation; that you were just extending it for the sake of politeness.' He opened the car door. 'And yet, here you are. True to your word.' He stepped out.

'Blimey, you're getting the welcome mat, darling,' said the taxi driver, over his shoulder. He handed Deirdre her change. 'Have a nice visit,' he said, and he winked.

There had been an evening, late on, sometime in the autumn of their last year, when Sam and Deirdre had walked the city for hours. It had been a Saturday, and the library had been busy that afternoon; essay deadlines and exams were close ahead. Deirdre had packed up when the bell sounded and walked across the square, heading for the 123 bus and her apartment on James's Street, her apartment with the view of the hospital and the smell of the hops from the brewery up the road. By then, she was able to smile when she saw Sam, and to talk to him as much as she pleased; somewhere along the way, she had grown out of the blushing, and the stammering, and the blanking on words. She could sit and catch up with him in the library; she could go to the Stag's with him, for a pint, just the two of them, or with other friends. By then, she and Sam were friends, and this was something of which Deirdre was very proud. That she was proud of it meant, she knew, that it was not really friendship for her, but something more loaded; something too carefully landscaped to be friendship. What was odd – what was almost embarrassing – was that the experience of getting to know Sam over three years had done little to contradict Deirdre's first impression of him, Deirdre's seventeen-year-old impression of him; you wanted to know more than your seventeen-year-old self, to know better, but where Sam was concerned, Deirdre could not truly say that she had been wrong, back on that first day. She could not say that her slack-jawed impression had been all that far off. There was nobody like him; that was simply how it was. And on that Saturday evening in the first year of the new millennium, Sam greeted her, and he smiled at her through his cigarette smoke, and he told her he was going for a long walk to try and clear his head before diving back into Marvell.

'Marvell, the bastard,' was how he put it.

'And you should come along,' was what he also said.

She'd love to, Deirdre said, because she was by then the sort of person who could say that, who could respond like that, who could seem cheerful and uncomplicated in the face of such a suggestion. Who'd read nothing into it. Who'd cause no trouble. Who'd get no wrong ideas, even if Sam should take her arm while they were walking, as he did. Even if Sam might look at her, as they sat on the cold benches along the canal, and laugh to himself, and shake his head in a way that friends did not – or if they did, you could give them a shove and demand to know what was funny.

It was all funny.

They walked down Westland Row and up past the spot where the old Art Deco garage had been demolished one night a few months previously; soon, the developer would be ordered to build an exact replica in its place. It was a bare site when Sam and Deirdre passed it, three orange extractors spinning and dipping towards its foundations. They went downhill at Holles Street, past an ambulance crew unloading an incubator and wheeling it into the hospital; Deirdre had looked into the small plastic box before it occurred to her that maybe this was something she did not want to do. Mount Street then, and the canal for a while, and Paddy Kavanagh with his pigeons and his epiphanies, and the bridge at Baggot Street, and the high proud houses on Waterloo Road, and the small, mysterious garden at the corner of Wellington Place and Morehampton Road. And a pint in McCloskey's, even though Deirdre hadn't the money for pints, and especially did not have the money to be buying both of them, but she wanted to; it was some point she wanted to make. And Sam's flat was still in Donnybrook, and only a few minutes' walk from where they sat talking over their empty glasses long after the barman had made it clear that he would prefer to take their empty glasses away. And dinner in his flat, Sam had said something about – would they go back and have some dinner in his flat? – but instead Deirdre said something about Herbert Park, and about the house on Raglan Road, and about other places they could walk to, other places they could see, and night was falling, but if you kept going down Lansdowne Road and down Herbert and down Sandymount, eventually you would come to the sea. And the Poolbeg chimneys gazed down on them as though they were seeing how things were, and how things would be, and how things could be wasted. And at the DART station, Deirdre hugged Sam Russell as though he were her brother, and she sat on the train and told herself that there would be others.

By which she meant there would be other days.

'Come along,' Andrew said, bent low to look at her through the open door of the taxi, and Deirdre nodded and grabbed her bag.

'I'm here,' she said, stepping out to stand beside him in the narrow street, shadowed by the high stone walls of his college, as another student swept past on another tastefully-rusted bike. A bell rang; the bicyclists were greeting one another, or warning one another, or letting one another know, at any rate, that they were also around. 'I'm here,' Deirdre said again, and she followed Andrew up to his rooms.

Mike McCormack

Mike McCormack (born 1965) has published a collection of short stories, *Getting It in ihe Head*, and two novels – *Crowe's Requiem* and *Notes From A Coma*. In 1996, McCormack was awarded the Rooney Prize for Irish Literature. In 1998, *Getting It in the Head* was voted a *New York Times* Notable Book of the Year. A story from the collection, *The Terms*, was adapted into an award-winning short film directed by Johnny O'Reilly. In 2006, *Notes From A Coma* was short-listed for The Irish Book of the Year Award. In 2010, John Waters from *The Irish Times* described it as 'the greatest Irish novel of the decade just ended.'

Mass for Four Voices

Introductory Rite

I'm not surprised she has refused to talk to you; I was her spiritual advisor for two years so I know all about her capacity for silence and withdrawal.

But she wasn't silent or withdrawn that day on the bog. I have never seen her so comfortable in herself. How she moved around handing out programmes, stood to chat with people she recognised ... I would never have thought she could be so relaxed.

I can understand why, in the wake of that performance, certain commentators insist on casting her in the role of a prophet.

But the difficulty with that is that it credits her with gifts and intentions beyond those she has claimed for herself. I can say with some certainty that Anna never had such privileged notions about herself or her work. Hers was the humility of the penitent, not the apocalyptic delirium of the prophet.

And people seem to have forgotten just how limited her ambitions were for that piece of work. When all is said and done the whole thing was basically an encephalogram transmitted to the sky over our heads, a real-time representation of her neural process while she was in a state of prayerful meditation – something new, admittedly, to the iconography of religious art. And whatever hopes she had for that piece, the idea that people might come away from it shook and shriven or that they were going to experience some sort of miraculous intervention – I find it difficult to believe she ever intended that.

You have to take into account also just how self-aware Anna was. She fully recognised just how ridiculous she sometimes seemed; she knew well that her work and her personality could be hectoring and verging on the hysterical. But that's the chance she took and maybe that's how it really is with prophets – they're an affront, they are unreasonable and they do not come to flatter us. And if they are doing their job properly they will draw down ridicule.

Penitential Rite
Confiteor
I married late and there was twelve years between my wife and myself. So all things considered, I had little hope of ever having a family. I thought it was one of those things in life which had passed me by, a chance missed, I suppose.

When Anna was born I was in my early fifties and fairly set in my ways; all of a sudden I had a lot to unlearn about myself.

I was happy at the prospect of having a family, happy in a way I could never have imagined. It was strange to have hopes and dreams outside of myself, expectations I would never have thought of. And of course I did my share of daydreaming, all those occasions at which I was going to play the proud father – first Holy Communion, debs, graduation, her wedding … And yes, I had a few of those days but of course Anna being Anna she lined up some very different days as well.

It's seven years ago now since I walked into that gallery and saw those self-portraits spread along the walls like the Stations of the Cross. I stood there looking at them and I thought this is my doing, my failure as a parent has driven her to this. Then of course you find yourself reading your life backward, looking for signs, for the writing on the walls and trying to find that one moment when things would have turned out different.

The heartbreak I felt the day she entered the convent was nothing compared to the loneliness I felt standing in front of those portraits. *Self Shooter with Botox* – I had not a clue what any of it meant. And seeing the gradual distortion of her face across those photos … it's one thing losing your daughter to

God, but it was another thing entirely losing her to something you know you will never understand.

Your own child driven to that kind of disfigurement … Christ.

Kyrie Elision

Why did I love her? God knows, who knows why people love? You just do and that's all there is to it. If you sit down and start thinking about it, picking through the bones of it you will very soon find yourself at your wits' end.

We met when we were in our late twenties. By that time she'd had that spell in the convent behind her and it was two years after those self-portraits. I had seen that exhibition but by the time I met her, the effects of all those injections had worn off. She was back to her old self as she put it, one and the same. Certainly her face had none of that laminated paralysis you associate with Botox. Seemingly it is absorbed back into the system over time. I never knew that. Anyway, it gave us plenty to talk about and we took it from there.

And of course I was well out of my depth with her. Straight away I knew that I had taken on more than I could handle. Sometimes she was penance to be with; it was like being in a relationship with an Old Testament prophet. That constant hail of ideas and her relentless pursuit of them – that constant harping on about Mayo as a place of atonement, all its shrines and pilgrim paths, all its visionaries – with the best will in the world there is only so much of that you can listen to.

As a Mayo man all I ever wondered about was whether we would ever win a championship again. Of course Anna professed to see the hand of God in that as well ….

Gloria

Legally and technically there was nothing difficult about Anna's commission.

The Second Cloud Procurement Act was drafted to regulate the traffic in unregistered clouds and the growing incidence of piracy. But the broader terms of this second act enabled certain agencies restricted access to commission clouds at nominal rates – NGOs, relief agencies, artists and so on. Many of us in the industry had lobbied for these changes because we saw these commissions as good corporate citizenship and good PR. Also, we were keen to work with someone like Anna; we were familiar with her work in Allergan Pharmaceuticals and we saw her as someone who could push the technology beyond the normal parameters of the industry. Frankly, the concept of clouds as freight carriers has been exhausted – beyond their use in irrigation projects we can now modify them to deliver oral vaccines and emergency nutritional elements to disaster areas. But could the technology be broadened out beyond the idea of freight and haulage? That was why we wanted to work with people like Anna. And, as it turned out, our intuition was correct; Anna's commission is now seen in the industry as the first step in a new type of mass medical imaging. Yes, I suppose you could call it a type of blue sky project.

Her requirements were straightforward – a one million litre alto-cumulous to be delivered on the 23rd of July to a designated GPS co-ordinate somewhere in North Mayo. Given that at any specific time we would have upwards of a thousand such clouds moored over the Porcupine Bank this was no problem. What was more interesting to our engineers was Anna's wish to have a rainbow substrate spliced into the cloud.

It was a novel request but not a difficult one – a colour morph that would mirror her neural patterning in real time – that was something we had never worked on before. It took a bit of time and there were a few twitchy prototypes but the cloud was delivered on time.

Liturgy of the Word
Creed

That part of Mayo was special to Anna; we're talking here about that area that lies north of Newport and west of Crossmolina, the whole north-west. Or the real wild-west as she called it, not some cultural reservation like Connemara nor sentimentalised like Donegal or Clare. To Anna this whole area was uncompromised and that's why she wanted to exhibit her work there; as she said herself, it was a site-specific piece.

Her fondness for the place goes back to those childhood summers she spent up there on her grandparent's farm. She was their favourite grandchild and she spent two months of every summer running wild and thriving on the sea air and all the little jobs she was given to do around the farm; those beautiful summers are what she remembers.

And as you know, she is fiercely protective of it and she does not like to hear anyone badmouthing it. She used to have great battles with my brother Kevin.

Like many more of his generation from that area he had emigrated in his youth and he had spent most of his adult life in London where he made his fortune in the building game; so he had little of any good to say about the home place. He'd say something to Anna like, 'A big wave should build behind at Blacksod and wipe the whole lot out as far as Crossmolina, the whole fucking lot.' He'd say something like that to get a rise out of her and of course that would start her off and they'd go at it hammer and tongs; it was great fun seeing Anna wound up like that.

Looking back though, I suppose all those arguments stood to her when she began to formulate her own ideas about the place.

Prayers of the Faithful

Towards the end of her second year in the convent and around the time she began having doubts about her vocation Anna threw herself into a study of the history of Mayo. Whatever the link is between these two events, be it causal or coincidental is something I have never been able to fathom. Whatever it was, Anna professed to see something unique in the psyche of this county. Pointing to all the shrines and places of pilgrimage she began to see Mayo as a place of atonement, a unique place of spiritual trial and endeavour.

'Look at it' she'd say, 'no other county is as blistered with penitential shrines and prayer houses and sites of pilgrimage as Mayo; this is a place of pilgrims and penitents and visionaries and anchorites and hermits and hunger strikers; atonement is our default disposition. And how did this happen, where did we get the idea that we were a people in special need of atonement …?'

Yes, she could go on like this, if you had the patience to listen to it.

Liturgy of the Eucharist Offertry

There were about three hundred people on the bog that Sunday, all of them curious but no one with any clear notion of what they were about to see. I was completely in the dark myself. Anna played her cards close to her chest where her work was concerned. And she was like that in other things as well, not just her work. It was hard to get close to her and sometimes I worried that this was because there was nothing really to get close to. Once you stepped inside a certain degree of intimacy you found yourself in a kind of void with nothing to show where you were and sometimes that frightened the life out of me. Then I'd find myself withdrawing from her and contenting myself with what little I got from her. This was especially evident when she was caught up in her work; coming up to a performance or an exhibition her concentration was total, almost unbreakable. These were weeks of rare intensity.

Sometimes, when she was in this work mode, she would go to her father's place and stay there a night or two. I'd get a call from her telling me that she was going to spend a few days with him. She was always a bit of a home bird and with her father now very old she was beginning to feel the responsibility of being an only child. Those little breaks always did her good, she would always return from them fuller and happier, as if some essential faculty had been replenished in her once more.

And of course there was always something of the little girl about Anna, something in her that never left home. And, as she pointed out herself, the performance piece was a variation on the old child's game of what-can-you-see-in-the-clouds?

We drove up early that Sunday morning. I knocked together a small stage for her, piles and decking, about ten foot square and planted it in the middle of the bog. By the time I had set up the cameras and the PA it was mid afternoon and she was ready to go.

Agnus Dei

It was easy to see she was at ease that day: the way she moved around, handing out programmes and stopping to speak to people she knew; she was comfortable in a way I had not seen in a long time. And that put everyone else at ease. Any anxiety people had was soothed away by how obviously comfortable she was with the situation. Any likelihood that she was going to hector or embarrass them as she had done in the past was quickly put to rest.

Of course everyone's gaze was fixed on the cloud, which was docked over the bog. She was lucky with the weather; this clear blue sky was broken only by this huge grey cloud over-head which looked monumental and expectant.

The program she handed out explained things a little. The piece was called *Mayo In Excelsis Deo* and Anna, drawing on the spiritual exercises she had developed as a novice was going to meditate on a few of her favourite devotional readings; with the aid of a headset which doubled as a sub-cortical probe she would transmit an amplified signal to the cloud which would model the ebb and flow of her neural tides when she was in a state of prayerful meditation.

Basically what we were going to see was a real time map of her temporal lobe while in a phase of deep prayerful medita-tion; the sky over our heads would be shaped by faith alone.

So she pulled on her headset, got up on stage and took out her missal. And we turned our gaze to the sky. In all, it took a little over an hour and while it was a low key affair with nothing in the way of drama or action it was undeniably compelling and beautiful. We saw her praying and watched the cloud gradually shift through the different tonal moods of her prayer, morphing through the colours of the rainbow. She had three chosen texts – the first five verses of John's Gospel, Rudolph Otto's famous passage on the numinous and she would finish by singing the Agnus Dei. After the first few minutes, when it became obvious that this would be a quiet affair, some of the audience settled into it by lying on the grass and gazing up at the cloud. It was a curious sight, three hundred silent people rapt to this colourful cloud. You can be sure that more than one person lying there took the chance to get an hour's sleep but for those of us who kept awake, we were able to follow it using the notes she had handed out to us. After about fifteen minutes the cloud had taken on a blueish pinkish hue, which I am assured is the proper colour of the brain, and was beginning to morph through all the moods of her prayers, which was something to behold.

There was a real sense of privilege among the onlookers, this woman sharing with us what was going on in her head. It was something which blurred the representational notion of what such images are about.

A small round of applause greeted her when she rose to her feet. She responded with a wave and a smile and then told us over the PA to put on our caps and coats.

We stood up then and by now our mood had coalesced and we were one happy congregation in this shared communion. We pulled on our coats and watched as the cloud elevated another thousand feet to where the air was cooled and the moisture in it condensed, and the heaviest and most localised summer shower poured down on our heads. I didn't notice it at the time but later on, when I was editing the footage for the official record I noticed that a few people emptied out their plastic water bottles and held them up to the sky. I'd say it is only a matter of time before there are all sorts of curative claims made for that water.

And walking off the bog that day I doubt if there was one person who did not congratulate themselves for having been there to witness it.

Concluding Rite

Of course the irony of the whole thing was that it added yet another shrine to the topography of Mayo. Word got around very quickly about her performance and within days people were visiting the site to have a look for themselves and to soak up the residual atmosphere. Over the remaining weeks of the summer the site became another place of pilgrimage in the county, taking its place beside Knock Shrine, Croagh Patrick and the Achill Prayer House as one more place where the divine had revealed an aspect of itself to the people of Mayo. The difference was that this was a place of ecumenical curiosity.

Christians, new agers, techno-mystics, sceptics and even those who professed that divided faith – secular spiritualism – all were drawn to the bog, compelled to wander around and look up at the blue sky, a site that was now seen by all to be mysteriously hallowed in art and devotion. Whether Anna saw this as the ironic failure of her piece I couldn't say; I suspect it may be one of the reasons why she has never spoken about it.

The last time I was up there, the site was signposted and a large crowd were wandering around amiably, looking up at the blue sky.

Siobhán Mannion

Siobhán Mannion was born in Ireland and grew up in Cambridge, England. Her family is from Clifden, Co. Galway. She holds first class honours degrees in English & French from Trinity and Film from UCD. Last year, her story *Lightning Bug*s won the Hennessy First Fiction prize, and she was named Hennessy New Irish Writer of the Year. She has previously been short-listed for the PJ O'Connor Radio Drama Awards and her most recent play, *The Big Picture*, was broadcast as part of the RTÉ Radio 1 Short Form season last December. In 2008, she was the recipient of an Arts Council Travel & Training Award to attend the Iowa Summer Writing Festival, and she has been a contributor to the *A Living Word* and *Sunday Miscellany* radio programmes. Her piece 'Peggy's House' was included in a *Sunday Miscellany* anthology. She is currently working on a collection of short fiction, and has had stories published in *Stand, The Moth* and *New Irish Writing*. She lives in Dublin where she works as a radio producer in RTÉ.

Looking for the Heart of Saturday Night

And you're stumbling…
           Tom Waits

Marion's dress rides up above her knees when she sits down. Paul first noticed this while she was perched at the end of their bed, putting on her heels. And he notices now when the automatic light flicks on in the car. Her coat covers all but the hem, a strip of shiny red. He turns the key in the ignition and reaches out so that his palm meets the sheer nylon of his wife's knee.

'We're late,' she says.

'I know we're late, love, but we need to let the car tick over for a while. It's thawed a bit but it's still pretty cold outside.' Paul turns his head towards the house and sees Julie, their babysitter, closing the curtains. Light shines through the frosted glass of the bathroom above. He dabs his finger where he nicked himself with the razor and feels a little blood pulse there again.

'We could always stay home, if you want,' says Marion, pulling her coat tighter.

'No, let's go. We need to get out.'

'Have you told anyone yet?'

He shakes his head. 'Nobody wants to talk about work at Christmas.'

'We'll be fine, love. We'll figure it out. And I can always go back to work early, if it comes to it.'

'It won't come to that.' He puts the car in reverse and swings it around slowly in the drive. Marion has parked her car, as always, slightly too close to his. This makes it harder to back out, but Paul doesn't say anything tonight.

'I like that perfume. Is it new?'

'No. I just haven't worn any in a while.'

He nods, holding on to her seat, inching the car out on to the road.

'I can drive if you want,' she says.

'There's no need.'

'Will you be okay? We don't have to go.'

'And ring in the New Year in front of the TV? I don't think so.'

It has been cold now for weeks. The snow fell for nine days straight; quiet assaults as the dark afternoons became night. When Paul had come down that morning, Marion was in the back yard. She squatted on the lawn, her nightdress tucked under herself, and he watched as she clawed two fistfuls of snow and threw them into a bowl. He pushed open the kitchen window to call to her, squeaks of ice breaking away from the frame.

'What are you doing?'

'It's for the baby. The pipes are frozen.'

He turned on the tap then, and it shuddered. On the glassy back step he slid a little, before crunching over to her and offering his hand. Her fingers were a shock to his skin and a dark pink watermark had seeped up her slippers.

'Come back inside, love. Here, give me that.'

She smiled, and they turned together towards the house. Ten minutes later, his office called.

'I can't believe they'd call you today,' said Marion.

'It's not official yet. They're announcing the cuts next week.'

'I suppose we knew this could happen,' she said, putting her arms around him.

In the afternoon they huddled on the couch. Paul kept the fire going, stabbing the embers and rationing the briquettes. Lola made noises from inside her mouth sucking the snow water boiled into formula. Marion pulled the teat away and Lola straightened, her feet pushing against Paul's elbow.

'It's okay, baba. It's okay. I'm just giving you a little breather.'

Lola reached up with her tiny starfish hands. Paul leaned over to kiss one of them. 'Lo-la' he sang, and she laughed. He stroked her on the cheek then and put his hand on her belly to jiggle her from side to side; her cream sleepsuit soft as a pelt against his palm.

The Kellys' house isn't far, but the roads are still bad. Paul feels the car go its own way more than once, but says nothing. He keeps it slow, and Marion stays quiet, concentrating on the road ahead. Eventually, they turn down the Kellys' lane. It is long and narrow, wide enough for only one car at a time.

'There's Frank,' says Marion. 'Who's that he's got with him tonight?'

Paul glances at the girl, who is tall with long hair, her gloved hand locked to his cousin's arm. In the headlights, they dissolve into single file, the girl's heels sinking into the snow at the side of the road.

'What do the younger ones see in him, do you think?' says Marion.

'I don't know,' says Paul. 'Frank's a good guy. Maybe that's enough.'

'He's still got a bit of a reputation though.'

'What do you mean?'

'All that stuff when you were kids. I don't know. Crashing cars and just being wild, I suppose.'

'*One* car. And it's not like anyone was hurt.' Paul moves into first gear so he can slow down without hitting the brakes. 'Anyway, what does that have to do with anything?'

271

'I'm only saying.'

'Well, don't. And don't bring it up with him.'

'Why would I bring it up with him?' Marion lets down her window. 'Frank! Get in.'

Paul tips the brake and the car swerves before stopping.

'Marion. Hello! It's hardly worth it, but sure we'll get in anyway.'

'And who's this?' says Marion.

'This is Abigail.'

'Hi, Abigail.' Paul and Marion say this together, so Paul says it again in case Abigail hasn't heard. 'Get in. It's cold out there,' he adds. Frank and Abigail slide into the back seat and the car stalls when Paul's foot comes off the clutch. 'Sorry, guys.' He feels his face heat up. 'There we go, that's it.' His voice is louder than he intended. Marion turns around to face their passengers.

'So, how've you been, Frank?'

Her elbow presses against Paul's arm.

'Grand. Grand. Don't you know yourself.'

'You've grown a beard.'

'Yeah, well. It's been a lazy few days, I suppose.' Paul glances in the mirror but his wife is blocking the view.

'Did the snow affect you much around your place?' Marion continues.

'Ara, we just decided to lie low for a while.'

There is a silence that lasts a few seconds.

'How's my godchild?' says Frank.

'She's good, thanks. We'll call in to you one of the days. We've a seven-month-old,' she adds, turning to Abigail.

'I know,' says Abigail. 'Frank has her picture on the fridge.'

'We haven't done anything about the christening yet, Frank. But we will,' says Marion.

The party is bigger than Paul anticipated; he had hoped the weather would deter some of the guests. Marion wriggles out of her coat and Frank hangs it up inside the door. Paul holds a bottle of champagne by the neck and slips an arm around his wife's waist; he can feel her hipbone under the silk. Marion leans in to him as they greet the crowd in the hall. Silver tinsel lines the picture tops, and inside a holly wreath on the table, a candle burns.

'Everything is so beautiful,' says Marion.

Paul watches Frank whisper something to Abigail, who puts her hair behind her ear and smiles. His cousin's hand slips down to the small of her back. Paul shakes his head and Marion looks at him, eyebrows raised.

'I'm fine, love. Really.' He kisses her on the cheek, tasting the powdery blush on her skin.

'You should talk to him, you know,' she says.

'Who?'

'Frank. He knows everyone around here. Maybe he could help.'

Three drinks in, Paul realises Marion is expecting him to drive home. He spots her standing on the hearth, her fingers touching the mantelpiece. Her other hand is cupped under a large glass of wine and her legs are silhouetted by the flames. On past New Years they had crashed on the couch or traipsed home at dawn. Last year, Marion was pregnant and drove a carload of people home. He wonders if she will be pregnant again next year. He is still looking at his wife when she traces her hand down the side of Frank's bearded face. He stares at them for a moment, then finishes his beer fast. When Frank laughs, Paul takes a step towards them. Marion sees him and waves.

'I'll let you know, anyway, what the story is,' he hears her say. Frank looks over and Paul changes his mind about joining them.

'Hey, Paul. How's the baby?' someone calls out in the kitchen.

'She's good. She's great,' he replies.

Through the crowd he sees Abigail at the fridge. He moves past everyone, reaches her. She has crouched down and he taps her on the shoulder, just beside the strap of her dress. She glances at him.

'Oh, hi,' she says.

'Oh hi yourself,' he replies. 'Need some help down there?'

'No. I'm just seeing if there's anything except beer.'

'I can get you some wine if you want.'

'No, I'm okay.' She stands up then and he wonders how old she is. Her eyes are green. She is looking at him and he realises he should say something. He can't think of anything.

'See ya later,' she says then, turning sideways to pass him, a can of lemonade in her hand.

Paul drinks some more until he is enjoying everything. He knows everyone here and what they want to talk about, and so he talks.

'How's work, Paul?'

'Oh, you know,' he says every time he is asked.

'Hey.' His wife squeezes his hand. 'The taxis are running again tonight.'

'I never said I'd drive home, you know.'

'It's grand, Paul. And you were right. We needed to get out. Want to dance?' She holds his face and moves her hips when she says this.

'No, thanks.'

'Suit yourself,' she says, swaying to the music on her way back out.

Paul checks his watch; it is hours later than he thought. When the whiskey comes out he sings. He opens his mouth and the words come out. And when someone turns off the music, he becomes the centre of it all.

He can see Marion in the hallway, candlelight shining on the buttons down the back of her dress. She turns around, flaring the dark red silk from her waist. She looks over at him, smiles. Paul closes his eyes into the song, and feels the words vibrate in his throat. He stands up so they can launch from somewhere lower down. There is humming then – he pulls it along – and feels safer than he has since Lola was born.

He opens his eyes for the clapping and the cheers. Then he waves them away, goes into the hall. Marion takes hold of his elbow and tilts into him open-mouthed for a kiss. She blinks slowly, her eyes bloodshot. Paul pulls back and she teeters.

'Jesus, Marion. You're drunk.'

'No, I'm not,' she says.

'I'm going to the bathroom. I'll be down in a minute.'

Paul flinches in the bright light, holding onto the sink. He juts his chin into the mirror and looks at the cut under his jaw. There is a second before he can focus. He licks a fingertip and wipes the dried blood off, then opens the door to see Abigail coming up the stairs. Her dress is long and green, and there is a piece of it missing between her breasts, where the fabric is stretched around a hoop dotted with beads. He tries not to look at the naked circle as it approaches. Abigail is barefoot on the carpet, a handful of dress clutched to her thigh.

'Hi, again,' he says.

'Hi,' she replies.

Paul looks at her mouth, which glistens in the dim light. He wants to press his thumb to it and wipe the colour off. Then he hears Frank's voice from downstairs.

'Paul, you're still here. I thought you left with Marion.'

Outside, the cold air comes at him. He needs to take another leak. He stumbles past a window and his foot bangs against a rock on the lawn. He stops to kick it and sees it is a tiny Santa Claus. Paul squints at it in the moonlight, unzips himself and launches an arc of piss over its head. It putters on the snow beyond and he relaxes.

'What the hell are you doing?'

He jumps at the nearness of his wife's voice, then shakes himself.

'Jesus Christ, Paul. Why can't you go in the house like everybody else?'

'Why can't you leave me alone?' he says, zipping back up.

Marion sighs, walks away.

'I didn't want you to say anything! Did you forget that, Marion?'

She stops and looks back at him. 'What the hell are you talking about?'

'Don't give me that.'

'If you mean losing your job, I haven't.'

'Oh yeah? Not even to Frank?'

'I haven't said anything to anyone. But I'm sure Frank could help'.

'Well, I don't need his help.'

'Oh, whatever, Paul.' She turns to cross the snowy grass and begins to pick her way through the cars. Paul watches her, shivers, then decides to follow. Her tracks are as small as an animal's and he covers them with his own. His wife has reached their car, the farthest from the house, by the time he catches up with her. The doors are unlocked and she is angling herself in when he takes hold of her arm.

'Wait. Marion, wait.' He pulls her outside.

'Leave me alone, Paul. I'm tired. I just want to go to sleep.'

'I'm tired too,' and he puts his arms around her, his face against her neck breathing in her scent. The two of them lean against the car. After a while he kisses her under the ear and she laughs. He moves around to her mouth. They kiss for a long time. Eventually Paul slides his hand inside her coat and under her dress, pulling down everything underneath. She presses her hips against his and he opens his trousers. Then he moves in and out of his wife, and thinks about what they are doing in the Kellys' garden. When his wife begins to make noise, Paul glances at the house.

'Shhhh, Marion. Shhhhh.' But he keeps moving, forward and back.

It is Frank's idea that Abigail should drive them all home. Paul leaves his glass on the mantelpiece when he hears his cousin calling goodbye to the crowd. He sways a little on his way back out to the hall.

'Sure, Abigail's stone cold sober,' says Frank. 'We can drop you guys off, and you can collect the car from my place in the morning.'

Abigail says nothing.

'Sounds good,' says Paul. The three of them cross the lawn together, their shadows thrown long on the ground. Paul opens a rear door to get in beside a sleeping Marion; his wife is curled up under her coat. 'Marion,' he whispers. 'Marion. It's time to go home.'

The car moves slowly. Frank says something in a low voice and Abigail responds with a soft laugh. Paul leans his head back. And then he notices the snow. There is so much of it, falling silently, through all the space around them. He wipes the window with the side of his palm, and when he feels his body move with the turn of the car he wonders if he has been sleeping.

'Do we have any beer in the house?' he says, tapping his wife on the leg. She stirs, looks at him and frowns, shakes her head.

'I'm sure Frank and Abigail want to get to bed, like everyone else,' she says.

'I'm sure they do,' says Paul and laughs. No one responds to this. He lets his head fall back again.

'Careful here, Abi,' says Frank.

And then Marion screams, slumping against him.

'Whoa! What happened?' he says.

'It's okay. We're in the ditch, that's all,' says Frank.

'Where are we?' says Paul.

'Look out the window. We're home,' says Marion, hauling her body away from him.

'I'm sorry,' says Abigail, very quietly.

'You're grand, love. You're grand,' says Frank and rubs her on the arm. They gather outside, holding their elbows, blinking under the falling snow. They watch Frank in the driver's seat; the car isn't moving.

'Just leave it, Frank,' says Marion. 'We'll get it sorted in the morning. It's too cold to be standing out here all night.'

'Are you sure?' asks Frank.

'I'm sure,' says Marion.

The four of them trudge up the driveway, Abigail holding Frank's hand. The porch light comes on when Frank steps onto it. He stands aside to let Marion put the key in the door. Julie comes down the hall towards them.

'Was everything okay? Did she wake up at all?' says Marion, pulling off her heels.

'There wasn't a peep out of her all evening.'

Frank wipes his shoes on the mat inside the door, and Paul does the same after him.

'Here you go,' says Marion, handing Julie some notes from her purse. 'But you'll have to stay over tonight. The roads are pretty bad again. Text your parents and I'll make up a bed for you in the spare room.'

They have switched on the lights all over the house. Marion sends Paul back downstairs with a sheet and a duvet. 'Pull out the bed for them in the sitting room,' she says without looking at him.

'What's wrong with you?' he says.

'Nothing is wrong with me.'

'I suppose you think the car is my fault.'

She sighs. 'It's just one other thing to worry about, that's all. Can we talk about this tomorrow?'

His cousin is stretched out on the couch. Paul leaves the bed linen down on the rug and jumps when Lola howls from the monitor on the table.

'What was that?' says Frank, sitting up.

'Nothing. Just the baby,' says Paul.

'Shhhh, baba. Shhhhh,' says Marion's voice before Paul switches it off. 'Here, make up your bed, will you?'

'It was a great night, all the same.'

'Glad you think so.'

'What's up with you?'

'Nothing. Unless you count me losing my job.'

Frank gets to his feet. 'What? When did that happen? Jesus, Paul, I'm sorry.'

'Yeah, well, it's not your problem.'

'Can I help at all?'

Paul lets out a mirthless laugh. 'Always the fucking hero.' Then they look at each other in silence. 'Why don't you just fuck off now, Frank?' says Paul after a while.

'Go and sleep it off, Paul.'

'Don't tell me what to do.'

'Christ. You were drunk then and you're drunk now.'

Then they see Abigail at the door.

'It's okay, love. We're just pissed,' says Frank.

Paul stares at the girl. 'Who are you anyway?' he says. 'And what are you doing in my house?'

'Take it easy, Paul. There's no need for that.'

'Nice dress,' he says, close to her ear, as he moves past her out to the hall.

'That's enough, Paul!' says Frank.

Lola has pushed herself to the end of her cot. Paul wants to pull her back but is afraid she will wake. He leans over to listen to her breathing, which he can't make out under the noise of his own. He reaches in to stroke the curve of her back and a sob hardens in his throat. He swallows. The voices downstairs get louder, and he hears Frank's above all the others. *It's no big deal, Marion. We were kids. I don't know why the hell he's bringing it all up again.* Paul wants to lie down in the darkness, but his body is rigid.

The door opens.

'Come on, Paul. Let's go to bed.' Marion beckons him from the hall, her hair tied up in a ponytail. 'Now. Come away from her,' she says, lifting her elbows as she undoes a button at her neck. She gestures with her head for him to follow.

The snow is still coming down. Paul stands at Lola's window and stares at the swirl. He can make out the shape of the car sticking up from the ditch; half in, half out. He wonders if it will be buried by morning. Then he sees the two dark shapes walking away from the house towards it. He pulls away from the glass and is momentarily confused by the curtain. He steps on something plastic and stumbles.

On the floor, he sits with his head resting against the cot.

'Lola,' he says under his breath. 'Lo-la?' He waits for a moment, then whispers. 'Happy New Year, my love. That's all.'

Peter Murphy

Peter Murphy is a senior writer for Dublin's *Hot Press*, and has contributed to *Rolling Stone* and *Music Week*. He is also a regular guest on RTE's arts review show *The View*, and has contributed liner notes to the forthcoming remastered edition of the *Anthology of American Folk Music*. He lives in Dublin.

The Gloamen Man

Well ne'er will I forget the night that me & Neddy saw the gloamen man I did not know it then I know it now it were the first sign that one of us days was numbert. I recall it were a hoor of a night the wireless were forecasten minuses as we med the last drop of a twelve-hour shift at Ballincual & turnt the van around & headet for the centerl deppa. Ned & me & a hunnert more like us worked the road crew deliveren the post that is hazardous work we is pros we keeps the show on the go come rain ner shine, bombs ner mines, in battle time & peacetime too.

It were commencen to snow when we headet back the wipers swep the windsheelt beyont which headlamps split the potholed road. We raised a hare he ren into the beams & scampert a while w/white tail bobben afore he dashed into yonder gripe. More snowflakes whirlt – that winter were a hard one fate it felt near centuries long, an ordeal ner a trial to be endurt, not ebber one would make it ay there would be cashelties. That were the winter Jimmy Kane the most contrary man in ole Hybern went arount the houses shaken the hand of ebber one he'd e're quarrelt with afore throwen a rope ore the crossbeam in his barn. Ay that were the kind of weather it were.

Neddy were behint the wheel that night he swervt to dodge the craters left by esploded mines he took them half-blind bends at speed the light were failen fast we was hell bent on getten back to the centerl deppa & clocken off for a jar. By & by we cem upon a stretch of road the Tramp's Heartbreak it were callt it went fer miles w/naira single light at which to make yer stop.

As I have already tolt ye it were twilight mebbe quarter-light, just afore true dark. Neddy slowt the van says I why are ye slowen down we is sitten ducks fer bandits says he what's that upon yonder road. A ways off in the gloom a figger were approachen, tallern any man, maybe eleven ner twelve foot tall. Neddy were staren it lookt like all the marra had bin draint out his bones I mane to say we knew it wernt real but here it cem, lopen closer, taken form

– Now afore I go on I will tell ye Neddy were my pal since we was pups. Ain't it peculer how you might see a lad ebber day for ten or twenty yearn & then one day as if by lottery sumpen happens & ye ne'er sees him agin. I recallt when we was chaps in school on party days when childer brang in crisps ner chock-ies Ned did not bring sweets he et carrots from a bag, offerd 'em around like eclairs, a quare card e'en then. Then when we was grown a bit we'd steal ole cars from the no-go zone, eyes peelt for the squadder & fer milisha men.

While I kep lookout Ned went prowlen with the petern can & siphonen hose, said he could taste fuel in his gob fer days. Some nights we'd motor all the way to the ferryport & park under them weirdy lights & skin up & harken to them bombs all fallen far away & we wondert how life would be in a place that were not nightly tore apart.

Soon after that ole Neddy joint the rebelts & went to fight milisha men in the bordertowns. It were oney for a spell but he were my pal & I allowt that I would miss him fate. The day he took the train we was sinken pints & shorts & roaren along to the jookbox in The Docker's on the quay, a Wexfert wake, a wonder Neddy med it to the stayshen. I watched that train depart & when it lookt like it had disappeart ore the edge of the worlt I returnt to the Docker's heavy in the heart & drank to Neddy's health till I cudden hardly spake.

Well soon after that I volunteert for service with the crew. As I have tolt you it were hazardous work but the pay were good comparet to the norm which were a pissance. Godspelt truth I had near given up on Ned I feart he were mebbe croakt in a ditch somewheres in the bordertowns but lo & beholt one day I got a postcart of an oldy homeless lad sat on a fruit crate wearing pilot's goggelts & playing three insterments at once it were from Ned he said grilla warfare did not agree with his constitushen he were comen home & I were very glad of that.

I securt him a place upon on the crew & we was partnert on the rounds. He were a great man to travel with for notten scaret him much he had no nerves it seemt. Mines ner IEDs twere all the same to him not a bodder on Ned I ne'er seen him shook until the night we saw the gloamen man.

Now on that night as the gloamen man drew near we reckernised he wernt what he seemt at first. Closer he cem & his true naycher were revealt he wernt no gowl ner fantem fate, he were no moren two milisha cadets out runnen on the road, one upon the nother's sholters for stamina ner endurence. Me & Neddy had a right ole laugh at that I mane to say it put the heart across us both. But as we drove on Ned remarkt how one of them runnen lads were the spit of a milisha prisoner they was forced to execute up yonder norn & he grew heavy with recollecten. Soon enough we returnt to base & parkt the van in the deppa's dock & slung them empty sacks in the storeroom & I hung the keys upon a hook.

– Will we get our cells a jar to steady them ole nerves, says Neddy-boy.

– O ay we will, says I.

Off we headet for the Vintner's Inn it were the oney place ye'd get a jar after a twelve-hour shift sometimes a lock-in 'til the mornen. Twere no moren a few mins walk but the snow were thick & the air seemt kinda muffelt.

Them stars above was normally so clear but on this night there were none as we could see to guide us to the Inn. On we traipst ye could not hardly see yr hand in front of ye them feels lookt like the surfess of the moon the white worlt shivert in its sleep.

At last we reacht the Vintner's Inn & gev the secret knock the landlort let us in. We stompt the snow offa our boots & ordert drinks & gev our cells a right ole jeer ore how spookt we was by the shape I callt the gloamen man. There we remaint a good long spell drinken & recyclen ole-time yarns till there were notten left but fumes. Afore ye know it we was rightly jart & that might account for what I saw ore Neddy's shoulder, not a ghost & not a shadda, more like akinda double esposure, like Ned's shape had sorta eckoed, & it left me rightly shook.

Ned got to his feet he said he were afeart that if he did not soon shift his carcass he might be trapped here in this Inn waiten on the shape of things to become apparnt & mebbe it nebber would so off he went.

I did not compny him home that night rest ashurt I have offen axt my cell why I did not. I were just about to shout the landlort fer another jar when a great esplosion shook the walls & rattlet the windas in their jambs. We ren out to see what happent there were notten to be seen but a smoken great hole in the road & red smears upon the snow.

Ay poor ole Ned had trod upon a mine & he were blown to smiddereens. Ne'er would I have beleevt that possible he had the sharpest peepers known to man it were the snow what done him in, covert the mine's mound & he nebber saw it unterfoot. They fount his boots two streets away I took one fer a keepsake & stasht it in the van these days I makes the drops alone.

Not a day goes by oney I thinks of Neddy & how things might of cem out differnt had we heeded the auguries when they was there afore us, not rashnalisen 'em not tryen to call 'em sumpen othern what they was. Them two runners who med up the gloamen man was a grave presentiment & Ned's doubled shadda were the final warnen my ole pal's name were callt his number cem up that night.

Offen times I dreams of that ole gloamen man but there is notten to be done I mane to say we are on this road we keeps travellen down this road till mebbe one day ye might say I don't reckernise this place, but no matter how ye might want to turn arount & go back the way ye cem or cut across grount ye've nebber walked until ye find another path ye may keep upon yer route the post may be delivert the drop be med & nebber mind if that ole gloamen man stalks yr shadda all the time, lopen through the twilight, bearen down & bearen down.

Nuala Ní Chonchúir

Nuala Ní Chonchúir is a short story writer, novelist and poet, born in Dublin in 1970 and living in Galway. Her third poetry collection *The Juno Charm* was published in late 2011 by Salmon Poetry. Her fourth short story collection *Mother America* was published by New Island in June 2012. Nuala's story 'Peach', published in *Prairie Schooner,* has been nominated for the 2012 Pushcart Prize. Nuala has won many short fiction awards including RTÉ radio's Francis MacManus Award, the Cúirt New Writing Prize, the inaugural Jonathan Swift Award and the Cecil Day Lewis Award. She was short-listed for the European Prize for Literature. Her début novel *You* (New Island, 2010) was called 'a heart-warmer' by *The Irish Times* and 'a gem' by the *Irish Examiner*. Her third short story collection *Nude* (Salt, 2009)) was short-listed for the UK's Edge Hill Prize.

Nuala keeps a literary blog at www. womenrulewriter. blogspot. com and her website is www.nualanichonchuir.com

Squidinky

Brine gets into your blood when you live beside the sea; it gets into your bones. You flow with a watery energy that carries you along. But you become tough and unwieldy too, like salt-cured fish. I haven't always been a shore dweller but ending up here with Luke made me feel at peace. I live above Squidinky, my tattoo parlour, and at night I hear the sea shushing and the tourists who patter by, drunk on beer and each other.

Lying in bed I pluck sleep crystals from my eyes, stretch until my bones click, then heave myself up because my bladder is leading me to the bathroom. To my daily surprise, the mirror above the sink tells me that I am old. Hovering in front of it I examine my shirred jowls and the yellow tinge to the waterlines of my eyes.

'Not too bad,' I announce, because if I say it enough it might be so.

Sunny days clang here: children beat buckets with spades, the ice cream van tinkles 'O Sole Mio' and parents whine and smile. There is such pleasure in letting all life take place outside my window to those who come to the sea in search of happiness and escape. They are right to come here. This is the home of happy.

I won't open Squidinky today; the skins of a few more people can stay blank until tomorrow – things are slow in the spring anyway. This is a day for walking and relaxing; for air in the throat. After my porridge, I wrap my slacks into my socks and pull on rubber boots. Luke's green cape coat will keep me cocooned if the wind is high.

Outside, the town is morning quiet and there's a tang of fish-rot. I head along Walk and Run Avenue to the top of the terraces, planning to end up at the pebble beach. I pass the ghost hotel that sits on one wing of the town; there's a ghost estate on the other. Refugees from Nigeria and the Ivory Coast used to live in the hotel but they are gone now, taking with them their turbans and kaftans, their firm-faced children. They had a church service above the Spar every weekend and it oozed joy: they sang and clapped and shouted. I often stood outside to soak it in after buying my few messages.

I continue along the avenue; pansies the residents have planted along the tops of stone walls curl their faces away from me like shy babies. I have the streets to myself and I savour the slap-and-echo of the soles of my boots on the footpath. The avenue feels long today but not in a bad way; it is uncluttered except for parked cars. I always relish that feeling of being queen of the town when I take an early walk. The sea glints through the gaps in the houses and I glance at it, anticipating the soothe of its blue expanse when I get to the beach.

The bench above the strand is occupied and I am put out. Who is this sitting on my seat? As I draw nearer, I see that the man on the bench is wearing socks and sandals. The first thing I always look at is people's shoes, don't ask me why. He turns to me and raises his hand.

'Hello!' he shouts, as if we are friends. I nod and go to take the steps down onto the beach but he pats the bench. 'Sit, sit. Come and take a seat here. Look at the view!' He tosses his hand at the bay as if he owns it.

'I'll sit for a minute,' I say.

This *is* my bench. Well, it's Luke's bench; I put it here for him after he died, replacing the wooden one with the fraying slats. On a cold day it is not as warm as the old seat but the Council said steel would weather better. I am possessive about this bench, about its position overlooking the bay and the two lighthouses – Luke's favourite view. I sit at the opposite end to the man and stare out to sea. A messy cloud, like the aftermath of an explosion, hangs over the horizon.

'If you just looked at that little slice,' the man says, making a frame around the cloud with his fingers, 'you'd think all was not well.' He lowers his hands. 'But of course, all *is* well.' He looks at me, his worn face alive with smiles.

'Is it?' I say. 'What about the economy? Bankers? The hospitals?'

'What about the here and now?' he says.

A young mother in pink runners barrels past with a three-wheeled pram; she pushes her sunglasses up on her head. Her child, a plump toddler, does the same.

'Sunglasses on a baby,' the man says, 'isn't it marvellous?' He rummages in a plastic bag at his feet. While he is distracted, I stand up. 'Have some fruit!' He hands me a red apple. 'It's a Jonaprince.'

I take the apple. 'Thank you,' I say and trot away.

He shouts, 'Cheerio!'

The man has tumbled my walk from its natural path and now I have to continue on into the marram grass and pretend that I don't mind. Soon I am tripping over the things the sea has belched up: barrels, lager cans, a wooden palette. I stop walking and pull wind into my lungs then let it out. Ducks in chevron flight skim over my head and I watch them until they disappear. I veer down towards the beach where oystercatchers poke about.

In the ladies bathing shelter, I sit and look at the apple. I feel like tossing it away whole but instead I polish it with the hem of Luke's coat and bite into it. The skin is bitter so I eat the flesh and spit the peels onto the ground. Luke's voice floats into my head: 'Spitting women and crowing hens will surely come to some bad ends.'

He always said that and I always answered, 'It's *whistling* women not spitting women.' Luke would shrug and we'd both smile.

I cannot even put a name on the feeling of missing Luke – it's too raw, too wide. All I know is that I am in a waiting-room and the world has receded. My heart opens and closes like a mouth that wants to speak but can't form the words. The days carry forward in regular ways – I ink people, I eat, I watch TV documentaries – but I push myself through weeks with a strength that seems to belong to somebody else. Mourning is hard work, it is long work; every twenty-four hours is a new lesson in learning the proper way to grieve. It's as though I am swimming through seaweed and just as the water begins to clear I whack into the hull of a boat.

I throw the apple butt onto the beach and the oyster-catchers scatter then regroup. The rocks below the shelter are decorated with doughnuts of amber lichen; they bring colour to the grey. Between the rocks, shell caches lie in sandpits – mussels and winkles, empty of meat. I heave myself up and exit the bathing shelter. The man is still at Luke's bench but now he is standing. I take a wide arc to avoid him. He will think I'm rude but, sure, let him off.

'Ahoy!' he shouts, waving his arms like a man signalling from the deck of a ship.

'Jesus Christ,' I mutter, throwing my eyes up in apology to Stella Maris who watches over the harbour from her plinth.

'Missus,' the man shouts, 'wait!' He putters up beside me. 'I'll walk with you.'

'I prefer to keep my own pace.'

'Not at all,' he says. 'You have "lonely" bobbing like a balloon over your head.'

He comes with me, his plastic bag rustling at his side, all the way down Walk and Run Avenue to my door. We don't speak and I feel foolish and annoyed; foolish for being irritated – what harm is he doing? – but annoyed with him too for disrupting my morning.

'Now,' I say, 'I'm home.' I fish my key from the coat's deep pocket.

'"Squidinky",' he says, craning to look at the shop sign. 'Well, if that doesn't beat all.' He sticks out his hand and I take it; he closes his other hand over mine and I see his knuckles are dotted with ink. 'Have a lovely day now, Missus. Be good to yourself.'

Once in the quiet of my hallway I am pleased as a pea-shooter to be alone again. I unpeel myself from Luke's coat and pop it onto its hook. It hangs like a collapsed cross and I twist it to press my face into the lining, searching for a whiff of him, the smallest scent. There is nothing there.

Luke would disapprove of all the time I spend alone now. It was he who kept up the friendships while I looked after the business. And because he was the one who rang people and greeted and mollycoddled them, after he was gone, I was forgotten. Our friends were his friends, it turned out.

In the morning 'O Sole Mio' drifts into my half-sleep. I think it is the ice cream van come a season early but it's someone whistling. The whistler trills the rising notes of the tune and drags them out; the sound is sweet wafting up to my bedroom. The words sing themselves in my head: *Che bella cosa na jurnata 'e sole.* What a beautiful thing is a sunny day!

I peep out the window and see the man from Luke's bench standing outside. Gulls lunge around him, their cacophony hardly keeping up with their bawling beaks. The man whistles louder to drown them out, then throws his arms up in surrender. He laughs.

When I open the door to the parlour he is still outside.

'Hungry,' the man says, and I'm not sure if he is referring to himself or the gulls.

'Can I help you?' I ask.

'I think so. I want to get a tattoo covered up.'

'Your knuckles?'

'No, no,' he says. 'Can I come in?'

I stand back and he walks past me, the same plastic bag rustling in his hand.

He takes a seat, removes his jacket and unbuttons his shirt. His story is revealed: he has been seaman, lover, convict.

293

'So which one do you want covered?' I say, taking in the blurred lines of mermaids, and Sailor Jerry pin-ups, the lexicon of names: Mabel, Assoulina, Grace.

He stands and looks in the mirror, pushes his shoulders back to right the sag of his chest. 'Do you know what?' he says. 'Give me a new one altogether.'

I haul a book of flash from the counter for him to look through. 'Where do you want to place the new piece?' I say, my juices up at the idea of giving him something to blend with the cascade of ink on his chest. I hold out the book. 'Here you go.'

He puts his hands behind his back, refusing to take it. 'I don't want some ready-made thing. I trust you.' He sits again, whistles a bar of 'O Sole Mio' and looks up at me.

'You trust me? You don't know me.'

'I know enough.' He slips off his shirt and shows his back to me; there are no tattoos. 'There's a man in Catalunya who collects tattooed skins. He says he'll buy mine when I'm done with it.'

'That's big in Japan,' I say. 'Well, maybe not 'big' but they do it there.'

'I've been saving my back until I met the right artist. I want the sun – a great furze and orange coloured ball of light. I want it to have a face.'

'I can do that.'

'I know you can. Like I said, I trust you.'

He comes every day after that and I work on his back; the sun's rays lick at his shoulder blades and armpits; its face frowns on the right side and smiles on the left. He asks me to put bones across the eyelids and a skull on each cheek.
'Everything has light and dark,' he says, 'even the sun. We'd be as well to keep that in mind as we go about our lives.'

My machine buzzes and he talks and talks. About his life as a seaman; how Barcelona was his favourite port; how he misses the sway of a boat under his feet. I mention Luke, little snippets: our trips to India; his love of musicals, especially when Esther Williams was involved.

'It gave him such pleasure to watch that Esther swim,' I say. 'Luke was a merman, most at home around, in or on water. He taught me to love the sea.'

'I'm that way myself,' the man says. 'Why don't we call it a day for today? Go out for a walk.'

I switch off the machine. 'Are you sure? All I've done is a bit of shading.'

'Haven't we all the time in the world?'

He sits up on the side of the tattoo couch; I wash him down gently with cold water and rub emollient into his skin. I watch him put on his shirt; he does it deliberately, with care, unlike Luke who was always in a hurry. I catch the scent of lemon off his shirt, that sweet freshness that always makes me feel hopeful and at ease.

We head along Walk and Run Avenue to the top of the terraces, past the ghost hotel and along the stretch where the residents have planted flowers on the tops of the stone walls. There are daffodils now, sweet and smoky and bright as the sun. We both stop to sniff them and we smile at each other, noses bent into the flowers' yellow bells.

Once at the beach, we sit on Luke's bench and look out over the bay and the two lighthouses. Stella Maris watches over the water and the boats, her arms raised in an eternal blessing. I take my new friend's hand in mine and he throws his arm around my shoulder; I lean my head against his head, feel the heat from his skin. He whistles a few bars of 'O Sole Mio'.

'Brine gets into your blood when you live beside the sea,' he says. 'It gets into your bones.'

We sit on, watching the oystercatchers and the ducks, the sway of the marram grass. The bench grows warm beneath us and the sea sways and shimmers under the wan glow of a March sun.

Phillip Ó Ceallaigh

Philip Ó Ceallaigh is an Irish short story writer living in Bucharest. The New Zealand writer Charlotte Grimshaw has described him as a 'clever Irish writer'. Michel Faber, in the *Guardian*, described his control of tone, dialogue and narrative contour as 'masterful'. Ó Ceallaigh won the 2006 Rooney Prize for Irish Literature and was the first Irish writer to be short-listed for the Frank O'Connor International Short Story Award.

Creation

I do not know how long I walked the city. The time it takes to forget who you are lost in the scenes of the broken world. The rosebush through the tunnel archway stopped me dead; blooms vivid red in the blasting sunlight of the courtyard, and the city went smoked-glass grey.

I walked into the blinding light. I entered the courtyard.

I was standing on a bright hillside sloping down to a bay and across the water was the mainland where I had had once lived. My love was standing beside the rosebush. It had been so long since I had seen her face and lain by her side but I understood that I had been lost and finally I had woken to the real world.

Giant butterflies moved in slow motion through the rose-bush and giant birds with lizard tails sailed across the sky, heading for the mainland, rabbits in their claws. Down on the beach, children were playing. They were moving towards the water, carrying inflatable rings.

Are the children safe? I asked, disturbed.

They float, she replied.

In the distance a man was sitting on a wall, mending a net, watching us.

My husband, she said.

That wasn't right. And the children? Whose were they? She shook her head, pitying my incomprehension.

Let the past be, she said.

I turned to see what she was looking at, over my shoulder. It was a small woman with long, lank hair, parted in the middle.

Her face was bloodless grey, corpselike, though she stood on the bright hillside with the rest of us.

That's your wife now.

You are my wife. I know you remember. You can't have forgotten.

But it was not clear that she did remember. I could have begged her. But what good is it to beg a woman?

Then I understood how I could explain it to her.

All this you see around you is wrong, I said. None of it makes sense. It is a dream. In the real world we are together. There is no other husband, no other wife. There are no lost years. Nothing is forgotten, nothing is misunderstood, and nothing in Creation stands between us.

She shook her head, and turned away. As she walked towards her husband she said to me, over her shoulder, pointedly:

Then why don't you wake up?

I will! I said, eager to prove it. I will!

This did not impress her.

Down in the bay the children were in the water. It was true, they were floating, and I could hear their burbling laughter and singing – there seemed to be three of them, then seven – and they were drifting away on their inflatable rings. If someone didn't do something they could float away altogether, gurgling and singing as they went.

I moved toward the table where the people were gathered, eating and drinking. They were people from my town. Some of them I had not seen in a very long time. Some of them were dead but they had come drinking with us again. One was a very good friend who was only recently dead. I waved to him but he was busy talking to a blonde girl and he did not notice me. Some people never change. She looked underage, but we would all be long gone before the police speedboats made it out here from the mainland.

There were so many stories I had forgotten to write, and there they were, listed on the page in front of me. I could see my love now, standing by her husband. They were holding hands. The grey-skinned woman hung nearby too, like a shadow. It would not be easy to shake her.

Then I knew what must be done. I would write it down. Otherwise the meaning would be lost in the flow of moment to moment and day after day, where people forget all kinds of things, including the origin of the world, love, where they left the scissors, where they mislaid the children (Where the fuck had those kids got to anyway? I could no longer hear them.) All those unwritten and unfinished stories were my undiscovered treasure on this earth. And I would add to them this story of my love not believing the truth, me explaining that it was a dream, and my pain at being trapped in the false world, unable to awake.

I sat at the table and with a sharp scratching pencil got it down, captured in little insect squiggles. I rode a surge of joy, that there were all those stories, about real life, of which I was the interpreter, the messenger boy to the Lord of Creation – but dammit these people were slopping drink about, a couple of times they nearly kicked the table over – the blonde girl had her blouse open and my dear deceased friend was sucking on her tits. The pages were disordered, falling from the table. I kept trying to recover my place. A woman pressed herself against me. You call this fun? I asked her, looking around for the woman I loved, but I could not see her anywhere, or her husband.

Still, I was not joining any orgy while I had all this stuff to write. There were still plenty of pages left and every broken sentence I cranked out was helping God light the stars and fill the oceans in the first week of Creation. These ghouls, these lascivious shades, could manage a little longer without me. I'd be back another day when my work was done and I'd hump them all to hell if they liked. I put my head down and laid down my hieroglyphs, and even when the little figures started to walk across the page and down the leg of the table and joined a column of ants heading for a hole in the ground I raced to create them faster than they could run away and I felt like I was winning.

It was the pain of separation and the desire to show her the world that was real and the heart that was true – this was what drove me. One day I would awake from the dream, gripping the pages of truth.

And I knew that even then it would not be over. It would never end. And I would have to continue the struggle, salvaging scraps of sense, forming little shapes and stories, trying all over again to awaken from my slumber.

I rose from the table as it overturned, clutching a fistful of pages, looking towards the mainland. My friends, the living and the dead, had collapsed in a joyous heap. Out on the bay, I could see the last of the children drifting around the headland. And I saw the distant white speck of the ferry setting out towards the island from the city on the coast.

Clutching my words, I descended the hillside to make the connection.

I reached the water, but the boat was moving too slowly and waiting on the shoreline would have broken my joyful rhythm. So I kicked off my boots and fell splashing into the water. The cool water buoyed me up and held me. My heavy clothes fell away, and I cut through the water, swimming with sure strong strokes, feeling no tiredness.

I had the strength to make it, especially now that I had let the pages go. They floated and drifted about me on the wavetops.

Swimming with a clenched fist was no good, and sodden pages no use to anyone. My words no longer mattered. The only thing was to swim forcefully on, back towards the mainland, to be reunited with my love.

Keith Ridgway

Keith Ridgway is a Dublin writer whose first novel *The Long Falling*, was published in 1998. He is the author of *Standard Time (2001)*, *The Parts* (2003) and *Animals* (2007). His latest book *Hawthorn & Child* was published by Granta Books in July 2012.

Kissing

I was living at that time in a small town on the coast where it might be supposed that secrets are impossible. But the truth of course is that a rich depth of secrets is the only way such towns survive. Without secrets, everyday life would be impossible.

Writing, I spent my days alone, and my evenings in one of the town's several pubs, and sometimes in one of the town's two restaurants. Occasionally a friend would come to visit. We would walk, sometimes swim, get drunk perhaps, and talk. I liked when these visits ended – not because I did not enjoy them, but because I enjoyed them so intensely. As I enjoyed – in a different way – my solitude. These were like different tastes, these two states of being – the sweet and the savoury – and I felt that my appetite for each was moderate and healthy and I thought that there was nothing wrong with me at all.

An old lover visited once, from Paris. The weather was bleak and the wind rushed through the streets with sea-spray and the scent of low-tide rock. I don't think it rained but it was always damp. He walked on the beach and was quiet, much quieter than he had been the last time I'd seen him. He had been in France since leaving university in Dublin, working at various things, piecemeal, avoiding a career, writing some poetry. He'd published some poems in Dublin, but I can't remember anything about them now. We had been boyfriends briefly as teenagers – intense adolescents thinking everything was about our hearts when really it was about our bodies. But we liked each other. We shared a sense of humour. We listened to the same music and went to the same gigs; we read each other's poems; we dressed in a similar way, and we listened to each other's advice about books and about men, as if there were things we knew already, and maybe there were. After school we drifted apart a little, not very far, following different groups of friends, both ending up at UCD, both studying philosophy – though from different angles, as if we'd disagreed. When we were in our early twenties, we fell in love. I think we fell in love. He was less sure than I was. He didn't rule it out, but he thought it was really friendship that was trying too hard. We would argue about whether we were in love or not. He once said, as if this was definitive – 'you've never made me cry'. This was no good measure, I said. Though I knew that it was, and I knew that he was right. We both noticed that I could not say the same to him. But I cry far too easily.

We walked on the beach and he was quiet. I tried to tease out what was on his mind, but he just smiled sadly and insisted that nothing was wrong, that he was just tired, weary of his life a little, that he was happy to see me, to be with me, in this beautiful, melancholy place. But the sand was the colour of UCD concrete and there was not much beauty, and the wind reddened our faces as if we were a little embarrassed. We went for dinner on the first night at the restaurant in the square where the seafood was good and he told me about his work, which seemed very boring, and I told him about my writing, which seemed even more boring, and we asked each other about men and discovered that we had reached a similar state of mind – feeling that we were better single, that we functioned better alone, and that sex was relatively easy and often delightful to find on a one-off or irregular basis with men who we treated as friends, or even not as friends but as physical comforts to us, and us to them, and that such a life was civilised and calm and why did everyone not live like us? The logic of this would have been to sleep with each other that night but we did not.

He took the small second bedroom with its skylight and its view of nothing but a hill. I woke before he did and brought him coffee. He sat up in bed and I was moved by his skin. He was beautiful. He was different of course to the young man I had once thought I loved, but he was beautiful, and it made me nervous.

He stayed four days.

There was in the town, in one of the pubs, a barman I liked. He was handsome, friendly, sarcastic. I had spent several evenings chatting with him about politics, books he was reading, other people. Sometimes I felt that he looked at me, or we looked at each other, in a way that suggested something. But I never knew what that something was. Yearning in a small town is as constant and as dangerous as the sea. But not everybody seemed to like the barman. Some of the regulars were rude to him – dismissive and curt – in contrast to their dealings with the other staff. I liked this. I liked the feeling it gave me of having made a decision, of taking a stand, although the truth was that I had become friendly with him long before I noticed any of that.

I took my old lover to the bar, having mentioned this slightly intriguing barman to him, and they shook hands, which surprised me. I had become a mutual friend. They chatted. They got on. We returned the next night, and we sat up at the counter with him at closing time and he had a drink with us and it was clearer now that the something was a interest, an interest not just in me, but in us – in my old lover and me – and I thought increasingly, with growing confidence, that it was an erotic interest, an interest in erotic possibility, and I was excited by that, and when I asked him to come back to the house with us for a nightcap, we all seemed to pause and exchanged looks – quick silent looks – and all of us seemed to say yes.

But in the end, all we did was kiss. My old lover kissed him first. And then I kissed him. And then my old lover and I kissed. And then everything became something else. Suddenly.

As if we were no longer where we were. As if the town had disappeared and the sea as well, as if the sea had gone away.

The barman soon left, and my old lover and I talked for a long time, well into the day, and kissed, and we held each other's arms and shoulders and we lay against each other and talked and kissed and in the end we both cried, probably from exhaustion, and we fell asleep together. We understood nothing while we talked and nothing while we cried. But while we kissed we seemed to know some bitter, beautiful thing that we could not capture and we could not keep, because you cannot keep on kissing.

He went back to Paris. Last year he called me one night and we spoke about nothing, and he asked me about the town, and whether I would go back, and I said no, I didn't think so, that the work I had done there had turned out badly. He thought that was funny. So did I. We laughed.

'Work is for cowards,' he said.

William Wall

William Wall is the author of five works of fiction including the 2005 Man Booker Prize long-listed *This Is The Country*, and three collections of poetry, the most recent of which is *Ghost Estate* (Salmon Poetry). He has won several prizes for both fiction and poetry, most recently the Virginia Faulkner Award 2012. He lives in Cork, Ireland. www. williamwall. net.

I Follow a Character From One of My Novels

I see Jo Strane in the market. She is buying fish. At first I am shocked by how much older she looks, and then I calculate that about twenty years has elapsed, maybe more. Chronology was always my worst point. I would work away confident that the chronology would fall into place, or could be corrected later, and then my editor would come back with a table of errors proving that none of the people could be as old at such and such a time, or that a certain child would be four or forty by the time such and such an event occurred.

She is thin. Her hair is streaked grey in places and not very full. She looks like she has been using the wrong shampoo for twenty years. She buys a single fillet of plaice and I conclude she lives alone. I am not surprised. I follow her at a discreet distance and watch her buy new potatoes from the man with the big hands and the arthritic knuckles. He tells her the usual, that the potatoes are from Ballycotton and that he has good spinach. As always he looks away when he is talking to her. I have the impression that he is looking directly at me, but I know it's a habit he has developed over the years, a form of politeness perhaps. She goes out onto Prince's Street and turns left. She has that same wary walk. She goes into Porter's and buys a newspaper – I can't see which one. She asks for a bag and while the girl is fishing under the counter for it Jo lifts a magazine off the shelf and slips it into her coat. She pays for the newspaper and leaves.

Later at the bus-stop I see that the magazine is called *Kitchens*.

It used to be *Homes & Gardens*. I can only speculate about the intervening action. Was she arrested for the murder of little Robin? Did she go on to destroy another life? Did she, at some point, either through psychotherapy or force of will, come to a full or partial understanding of what she had done, such an understanding as I had deliberately chosen not to give her? Did she, during that time of anguish, form a concept of me? Or, to paraphrase Aquinas, did she conceive of what I am not, but fail in what I am? Aquinas was writing about God, and I am conscious of falling into the familiar false trope of the writer as omnipotent deity. Nevertheless, even God must be constrained by the forces he devised, otherwise miracles would be commonplaces.

I notice that her breasts have never developed. This was something that escaped me before. I think it fits – arrested development. She probably suffers from amenorrhoea too. Had I noticed this or did she have periods at the time? I think that perhaps I should return to my original notebooks. She wears shoes that are part way between trainers and proper shoes. The light coat is not out of place on a dull, cool June day in Ireland, but underneath she wears something like a party-frock, a confection of green, silky material with sequins in the bodice and a flared A-line skirt. I suspect that she bought it, second-hand, at the Conquer Cancer shop, or Oxfam.

I decide to risk standing in the same bus-shelter. I slip into the far corner and at first pretend to read a poster that advertises the dangers of smoking. Then I turn round and looked directly at her. She glances at me but does not appear to recognise me.

My first reaction is disappointment. Then I think about the impossibility of any contact between creator and created.

It would be like the simultaneous arrival in a particular spot of antimatter and matter. The collision would erase the space in which it occurred. Nothingness would remain. Perhaps she can't see me at all, or whatever lapse in the fabric of things presents her to me is a one-way glass, a non-reflexive function; or perhaps she sees me only in whatever terms she originally conceived of me in, as an indifferent stranger perhaps, someone who didn't really matter to her, or who didn't understand her.

Then I think about Simone Weil's dictum that we must prefer a real hell to an imaginary paradise. Jo Strane has not failed to recognise me but rather at some profound level refused to conceive of my existence. She has chosen to be in her own real hell rather than believe that there exists a creature who could rewrite the whole story, or revise the ending or the beginning – as an American publisher asked me to do – or devise a new second story in which she might be saved from herself. Or one who could have given her a different existence. I recall how, when I was a teenager crippled by Still's Disease, I raged against the God that I then believed in for choosing me to inflict himself on. How quickly I arrived at the Cathar's complaint, that God must also have created and foreseen the existence of evil and was therefore not a loving bystander in the Fall, expulsion and subsequent curse of knowledge and suffering, but the one who conceived and executed the whole sadistic mess. My response, the only rational one in the circumstances, was to become an atheist.

I try to imagine what pain has brought her to this point of seeming calm and I know that the time is not long enough and that I am not equipped. I chose, several years ago, to write a full stop to my part in her life, knowing full well that there are no full stops in reality.

That dot signified my own failure of attention, a refusal to remain engaged, a willingness to sacrifice the contingency of truth in favour of shape and form and a clever ending. I had relinquished her, and over the intervening years experienced at different paces in our different universes (ten or so in mine, twenty or more in hers) she had come to certain conclusions about me, not the least of which was that I wasn't worth believing in.

She takes the Number Eleven and I follow. In the bus she sits very still, never turning her head. She doesn't seem to notice external things, this charming, shabby city where I live, its people with their hearts of gold, silver and lead. I follow her when she gets out. I see her fiddle for her keys. The magazine is now in the bag with the newspaper. Up here, high on the hill, the wind is stronger and the bag blows about uncertainly. Before she can put the key in the lock the door opens and a child of six or seven stands there. She steps through the door and turns with her hand on the latch. At this moment she looks straight at me. I am shocked by her gaze. What does it say? I feel like I'm falling or sliding on a steepening slope. There is nothing to hold on to. Somewhere in the darkness below I will lose everything. Then the door closes. Afterwards there is no sign of movement, no lights coming on – it is now early evening – and no noise.

I may be a little in love with her again. I recall doing something very similar once, many years ago, when I was at college – following a girl to her flat and watching the lights, hoping she wouldn't look out.